Maddox

Maddox

Chris Abrahams

PUNCHER & WATTMANN

For Sherre

First published in 2019
Published by Puncher and Wattmann
PO Box 279
Waratah NSW 2298
http://www.puncherandwattmann.com
puncherandwattmann@bigpond.com

National Library of Australia
Cataloguing-in-Publication entry:
ISBN 978-1-925780-24-6
I. Title
A823.4

Cover design by Miranda Douglas
Text design and typesetting by Christine Bruderlin
Printed by Lightning Source

This project has been assisted by the Australian Government through the Australia Council, its arts funding and advisory body.

PART 1

Fascinated and Uncomfortable

I

I first saw her at the Stella Maris hotel. Earlier that day, I'd had a flare-up with my mother. We'd been at my cousin Lionel's place celebrating his daughter Sky's sixth birthday. It felt different to the normal argy-bargy that takes place in a healthy mother and only offspring relationship; this had about it the smell of shifting paradigm. It was only a whiff of a scent, but it had rattled me.

I'd wanted to have a good look at the balloons. The hired clown had used two Betallatex 260s to make a pink motorcycle—an interesting twist although I felt she'd stuffed up the handlebars. Being unfamiliar with the Betallatex balloons, I was eager to compare their latex density and texture to the Qualitex range, which I knew. I'd waited almost forty minutes for my chance to hold the motorcycle in my hands—forty minutes after Sky had told me that I could have it 'within five minutes'. I knew that the longer Sky and her friends had possession of it, the more chance there was of the thing bursting—they'd already managed to burst the poodle, the giraffe and the aeroplane.

Eventually, sensing that she had no intention of letting me hold it, I'd taken matters into my own hands and removed it from her in the hallway. I might have erred slightly on the aggressive side and I might have startled her but I think the idea that I'd frightened her was a massive exaggeration. There was, I admit, a small scuffle as I pulled the motorbike from her grip.

In a performance deserving a Mo Award, Sky screamed, causing Lionel to rush into the hallway. Many of the adult guests had been outside on Lionel's recently constructed patio (waste of money if you ask me) and Sky's outburst also brought them into the hallway to rubberneck.

Lionel had been fixing for a fight all afternoon. It wasn't that he'd said anything explicitly insulting to me—that's not his way. It was more that everything he'd said had a snide and mocking subtext which he'd managed to convey with just his tone of voice and facial expression. He's a virtuoso at this. And with my life's endeavours sneered at and my buttons well and truly pushed, I'd returned his veiled insults in kind by besmirching *his* profession—that of lawyerdom—using my own tonal and facial weapons of derisive innuendo.

Being roughly the same age, it had been easy over the years to compare Lionel and I concerning various 'important' life performance metrics. That he'd done at kindergarten, primary school, high school, university and career, has been thoroughly and repeatedly pointed out to me by my mother. The pride she's exhibited in his achievements is more in keeping with the pride a mother shows towards a biological son. Furthermore, with the recent passing of Nancy—Lionel's real mother—my mother has become Sky's self-appointed granny. She's even said she's given Lionel power of attorney over her affairs, should the need arise, because 'he's a professional'.

The only smudge in Lionel's otherwise perfectly kept copybook is that his wife Sally, quite rightly, had left him for a man 15 years younger—a regional airline pilot named, I think, Eric. Although I never exchanged more than a few words with Sally during the three years she was my cousin-in-law, it was obvious she could do much better than Lionel, much better. She was a free spirit, a creative woman—a graphic designer in fact—with a zest for life who'd found herself imprisoned in a grim, pedantic and judgemental world with the wrong man. And Sally, if you happen to be reading this, I hope your new life with Eric has lifted you up and through the dark nimbus clouds of your failed marriage with its purported Xanax addiction, kleptomania, self-harm and exhibitionism, and onwards into the blue skies of normal marriage. You deserve it.

Lionel had managed to get sole custody of Sky by expertly calling Sally's mental health into question during the divorce proceedings. The two of them lived in an overpriced house in the wrong part of Mosman.

Lionel probably saw the balloon incident as a good opportunity for him to up the ante and bring his disdain for me out into the open.

I chose to play to the crowd gathered in the hallway, explaining my side of the story and telling of Sky's duplicity and her lack of gratitude towards me—considering I was part of the team that had given her an expensive harmonica (my mother had thought of it, picked it out and paid for it, but I had carried it from the car into the house and had physically given it to her).

'I was waiting for forty minutes to have a hold of the balloon,' I asserted. 'She said I could.'

The mob of adults, consisting entirely of Lionel's friends, was in no mood for my explanation. Save for the sound of tongues clicking and ice clinking in nervously held glasses, my words were met with silence. Sky was sniffling when she broke it with: 'He grabbed the balloon out of my hands and frightened me.'

Lionel sucked in hard through his nostrils. He pinned back his shoulders and fixed me with a look of anger and disgust that signalled a new low in our relations. I too tensed up.

My mother intervened, positioning her body between the two of us—something I thought a bit showy.

Obviously, under the circumstances, mum and I had no option but to leave the party early, before the cake. She was effusively apologetic to her nephew and great niece; I was withdrawn and sullen.

Initially I experienced feelings of pride at having burnt yet another bridge and I took pleasure in the knowledge that I'd pissed Lionel off. But deep down I knew that these positive feelings were chiefly the result of the adrenalin rush caused by the act of transgression itself and, once my excited hormones calmed down, they would shape-shift into well-known feelings of shame and self-loathing.

In the car on the way home, among her usual 'I'm so disappointed in you' statements, my mother was adamant that I should find somewhere else to live. I'd heard this threat many times before but somehow, on that day, it had more gravitas to it. I countered by telling her I'd like nothing better than to move out and gave her my usual 'You've wrecked my life' line, which was kind of true.

We arrived at the apartment and rather than commence, alone in my bedroom, the lengthy period of comfort eating that normally followed our disagreements, I stormed off up the street in order to get drunk at the Stella Maris Hotel.

*

So there I was, perched on a stool at the bar of the Stella on a quiet Sunday night, feeling sorry for myself. It must have been about 9pm. I'd had four schooners, more or less by myself, while casually watching the greyhound races on one of the pub's wall-mounted TV screens, of which there were about ten spread throughout the establishment.

I'd told the tale of the birthday party to Gary, the publican, who was serving behind the bar.

'You were totally within your rights,' he said. 'You did absolutely nothing wrong.'

Gary was there to sell drinks and this probably involved agreeing with mostly everything a customer said. His indignation at what had happened to me that afternoon, however, seemed to be heartfelt.

'It's like Megan,' he said, 'always promising but never delivering. She promised me her mother wouldn't move in with us when her father karked it. Yeah right! She was in the spare room within a month.'

Gary had had a difficult run with his marriage to Megan and had formed the habit of metamorphosing virtually any subject under discussion into that of his own toxic domestic situation. It had become boring and predictable. At the mention of Megan's name, my attention began to drift. I maintained eye contact, nodded appropriately and even managed to glean something about his mother-in-law having left lipstick stains on the bathroom mirror as a result of kissing herself. But I was more focussed on the greyhounds.

I like greyhound races. They're more believable, more analogous to real life than horse races. Whichever dog gets out first invariably wins. There's none of the 'neck and neck down the straight' stuff; none of the 'coming from way back in the field to win by a nose' rubbish; no heroic narrative, no suspense. With the dogs, as in life, whoever gets out first wins, no surprises.

I felt a tap on my shoulder. I swivelled on my stool.

It was Laird. It had been over a week since I'd seen him. It had gone by quickly.

'I called around to your house and your mother told me you'd probably be down here.'

'Laird,' I said. 'I don't have any money on me so I can't buy you a drink.'

His fleece was zipped up to his neck.

'I don't want you to buy me a drink. I can buy one myself.' He turned to the bar. 'Gary, I'll have a Jack Daniels and Coke please.'

'Coming right up.'

With his right hand, Laird pulled from his trouser pocket a bunch of fifty dollar bills. There must have been at least $500. I'd never known him to have so much cash in hand. By the way he held the wad—manipulating it with his fingers while staring me in the eye and grinning—it was obvious he wanted me to ask him how he'd amassed his fortune.

But I wasn't going to play ball. I stared straight back at him and kept my mouth shut. I was counting on Gary to say something. He was behind the bar transfixed by Laird's unpleasant display of cash.

'Where did you get the money?' Gary finally asked, bringing our stare-off to an end.

'I earned it,' said Laird.

I couldn't help but snigger at the affectation of pride.

'I came up with an idea and followed it through. To this.' He waved the bills in my face. I felt wind on my lips but I maintained my stance of not dignifying his boasting with an enquiry.

'An idea eh?' said Gary.

'It doesn't matter.' Laird shrugged, deciding to punish our reactions with silence.

With a squirt of brown liquid from the bar gun, Gary put the finishing touches on Laird's drink. He set it on the bar top and nodded at him to fetch. Laird moved towards the counter.

'That'll be $9.20,' said Gary.

Laird placed his wad of fifties on the bar and motioned for Gary to help himself to the top most bill. Gary took the note and set about getting change from the till. Once Gary had the change in hand, Laird pointed once more at the pile and in obeisance Gary placed the money on the mound of notes. Laird scooped up the cash with his right hand and stuffed it back into his trouser pocket. He picked his glass up off the bar counter, again with his right hand, and returned to his spot.

I resumed watching the TV screen where arcane statistics on betting odds were being displayed. Gary moved to the nut and crisp section behind the bar and busied himself with some manner of maintenance.

I knew Laird wouldn't be able to hold onto the secret of his idea for very long. I heard slurping noises as he probed the ice at the bottom of his glass with the end of his sucked-on straw—something he knew I found irritating.

Eventually, having sucked up the remnants of his drink, he made his statement.

'Waiting rooms.'

I rotated on the stool and looked at him, puzzled.

'*Waiting rooms!*' he said impatiently as if it was obvious what he meant.

He paused for a moment before continuing, an overdone look of disbelief on his face: 'You know, the waiting rooms where you need to get a ticket with a number on it and then you have to go and sit and wait for half an hour until your number's called. Well, I came up with an idea as to how a person can make money out of them.'

I maintained a confused expression.

'You sell the tickets!'

I blinked my eyes rapidly, hoping to express bewilderment; bewilderment not at his genius but at the state of his mental hygiene.

'You take a bunch of them," he continued. "Then wait for a bit. A man comes in and he takes a ticket. His ticket says 961. A flashing sign says that it's ticket number 895's turn.'

Laird had put some effort into memorising this presentation. I pictured him practicing, alone in his bedroom, talking to an imaginary audience.

'In your hand,' he continued, 'you've got ticket number 897. You offer this ticket to the man. It will save him 25 minutes of waiting for his number. You ask for $2. He gives it to you. You give him the ticket. Another man comes in and you do the same thing. It's simple.'

The idea did show some ingenuity. I tried to conceal my acknowledgment of this, helped by my belief that there was no way in the world he could have come up with such a plan by himself. Laird's smug grin as he stood studying my face suggested I hadn't been fully successful in masking my admiration.

I set about finding ways to criticise the scheme. 'Yeah but for how long can you do that in one place? I mean they're going to throw you out pretty quickly.'

'Well I was able to sell about twenty tickets in about ten minutes at the Bondi Junction RTA and I left under my own steam—to Medicare as it happens—where I spent half an hour making $80. You see $2 is the bargain price. You get a QC in an NRMA and he wants to be in and out of there in five minutes. Well that's going to cost him. I made twenty bucks off a scientist down at the Russian Embassy. I only needed to sell five tickets there and I made $70. Went and bought myself a camera.'

He unzipped his fleece and from underneath the garment he

pulled out a large digital camera complete with leather strap and zoom lens. Laird had managed to keep it hidden by wedging it into the cavity of his left armpit. It must have been uncomfortable. The spectacular 'reveal' was obviously the planned climax of his performance.

'What, for $70?' I asked.

'Try $400. Mate, I've been doing this for a couple of weeks. It sure beats the squeegee. Not that you can't make money at that. I know a homeless guy who clears a $150 grand a year with just an empty plastic coffee cup.'

'What the fuck am I doing working here then?' asked Gary, who'd re-joined the conversation. Although he was having sport with Laird, there was an element of genuine inquiry to the question.

'So how much money do you make a week from this then?' I asked.

'I reckon about $6000.'

I knew with Laird you had to divide everything by ten. But still, that made $600 tax-free.

'You get to talk to all kinds of interesting people. I sold a ticket to Stan Macey.'

He'd either gotten the celebrity's name wrong or had simply made one up. I suspected the latter.

'Yeah, well I don't know who he is,' said Gary dismissively.

'Neither do I,' I said, standing up from the stool. I excused myself and walked off in the direction of the toilets.

It was then that I saw her.

She was standing with her back to me, in the process of getting cash out from the ATM that stood against the far-left wall of the pub, next to the gaming room. I had to walk past it in order to get to the Men's toilets. The closer I got, the more I sensed she would adhere closely to my established concept of attractiveness. For the purposes of brevity,

9

I'll use descriptive shorthand and just say that she resembled a certain flaxen-haired pop icon from the seventies whose bohemian stylings and facile mysticism played a significant role in my traversal of the awkward passage from puberty to adolescence.

She was wearing a thick, off-white, woollen poncho draped over stonewashed Levis with knee-high brown leather boots. I caught the glint of several metal bracelets encircling her right wrist. I passed by her just as she was removing her credit card from the machine. Her face remained obscured by her shoulder length hair and the tilt of her head.

When I emerged from the Men's toilets, a minute later she was gone.

*

Back at the bar Laird and Gary were having hot words over the Sydney Olympics. Laird's camera now hung from the strap around his neck so that it banged against his chest as he moved his upper body.

Gary was almost shouting. 'What do you mean it did nothing for Australia? It put us on the map. Sure it was expensive but in terms of trade and tourism it was a great thing to have done.'

'We're still paying for it,' scoffed Laird. 'We had the opportunity to invest in some infrastructure you know, upgrade the public transport for instance. The public transport system in this city is a joke. But what do we do? We have a fucking party!'

'We had the fucking Olympic Games!'

'Yeah, so what? Every city that's ever hosted it is still paying it off.'

'No they're not.'

'Yes they are.'

'That's just bullshit and you know it.'

'What do you mean bullshit? You're bullshit.'

I knew that the sports mad Gary was passionate about the Sydney 2000 Olympics and I'd heard him defend them before, but his reaction to Laird's criticisms seemed way over the top. Perhaps Gary's jealousy at Laird's queue ticket success had stirred in him emotions he was finding difficult to control. On Laird's part, he probably felt insulted by us not showing enough outward respect for his achievement. There had always been a bit of niggle between the two, but it was unusual to see them be so openly abusive.

A group of four people entered the hotel—two men and two women. One of the women looked decidedly older than the other three. I hadn't seen them before at the Stella. They had obviously just come from the Sydney Cricket Ground as they were dressed in the red and white garb of the Sydney Swans football team. Given that their general demeanour was boisterous and sloppy, I surmised they'd already been drinking. They made their way towards the four booths that ran along the far-right wall of the lounge area.

I turned back to see Gary brandishing a schooner in the direction of Laird's face. Even though the rim of the glass was unbroken and there was a metre-wide bar top separating them, Gary's stance was extremely threatening.

Laird raised the camera to his face and began to take photos with the flash.

'Leave my hotel!' shouted Gary, trying to shield his face from Laird's lightning attack.

'It's not your fucking hotel.'

'What do you mean by that?' Gary asked.

I too was curious as to the meaning of Laird's statement. As far as I knew, Gary was the owner and manager of the Stella. Apart from the procession of temporary bar staff—mostly backpackers put on for the busy nights of the week—he was the only person behind the bar.

'It's not your fucking hotel. That's what I mean,' said Laird. He let go of the camera so that it once more dangled at chest height. This empty explanation was very much in keeping with his general style of arguing.

A young man from the group now lodged in one of the booths, had approached the bar. Seeing him close up, I took him to be in his early to mid-thirties.

'Hey come on! Put the glass down,' he said. 'What's the problem here?'

'This guy's insane!' Laird explained, his face showing over-acted bewilderment. 'We were just talking about sport and all of a sudden he lost it.'

'Leave my hotel!' ordered Gary. The edges of his mouth were moist.

'I've got things to do anyway.'

He left.

'I would never have used this,' said Gary, referring to the schooner, which he put down on the bar top.

I nodded and shook my head, an ambiguous gesture I myself didn't understand.

'Four bourbons and coke please,' said the guy from the booth.

Gary turned his back to us and set about filling the order.

'Jesus, things looked a bit tense there,' said the guy from the booth.

'Oh they're old friends.'

'Gavin's my name,' he said.

He held out his hand and I shook it.

'Geoff.'

'Nice to meet you.'

'Just come from the game?' I asked.

'Yeah we got thrashed. Thought we'd come here and drown our sorrows.'

'Hey baby, hurry up with the drinks!' called the older woman from the booth. The harsh frequencies in her voice made her easily audible even though she was some distance away.

Gavin looked at me and shrugged. 'Women!'

Gary returned and positioned four dark drinks on the bar top. 'That'll be $36.80.'

Gavin handed over two 20-dollar bills, picked up the drinks and began his journey back to the booth. At a point midway to the booth he stopped and looked back over his shoulder.

'You want to join us?' he shouted.

Automatically, I stood up from my stool and walked towards him.

*

The booth consisted of a rectangular table flanked on either side by bench seats attached to the respective booth-dividing walls. The older woman, who I took to be in her mid-sixties, had been sitting alone on her bench seat, facing the young couple on the other side of the table. As soon as Gavin sat down next to her, they began to hold hands affectionately.

'This is Geoff,' he announced. 'We've just bonded at the bar.'

There was space enough next to Gavin on the end of the bench seat. I sat down.

The older woman took a sip of her bourbon and coke. 'Hi ya darling. I'm Wendy.' I noticed she was chewing gum.

'And I'm Terry,' said the younger woman. 'And this is Marko.'

Marko leaned across the table with his hand outstretched. I shook it. Both Terry and Marko looked to be roughly the same age as Gavin.

'Sorry about the match,' I said, hoping to break the ice with a football-related remark.

My condolence went unacknowledged. I could hear the nursery rhyme melody from a distant poker machine.

'What brings you to the Stella?' I asked

'They won't let us in at the Lord Casey,' said Wendy.

'Won't let *you* in, you mean,' said Gavin.

Wendy responded with a self-satisfied snort.

'You live around here?' I asked.

Wendy nodded as she swallowed a gulp of bourbon and coke.

'Wendy and I, we live on Ellis Street,' said Gavin, 'and Terry and Marko live in Haberfield.'

I noticed that Gavin's hand was now stroking Wendy's thigh under the table.

'How long have you been in Ellis Street?'

'More or less my whole life,' answered Gavin. 'I was born in Tasmania. We moved here when I was three.'

Wendy began to run her fingers through Gavin's hair.

'Thirty-five years now!' she said. 'It's a long time.'

I nodded.

'Did you all meet through the football?' I wasn't really interested, but I asked anyway.

'Gavin and I are cousins,' interjected Terry. 'I come from Melbourne originally. My dad was a South Melbourne supporter and crossed over to Sydney in the eighties. Marko and me, we moved up here five years ago.'

'What do you do?' I asked her.

Her hand disappeared below the line of the tabletop and re-emerged brandishing a wallet from which she removed a business card. She reached across the table and handed it to me. Written on the card above an email address and phone number were the words: Terry Fountain, Consultant.

'You're a consultant then?'

'Yes.'

'Thanks for this.' I slid the card into my right trouser pocket.

'What do you do Mark?' I asked, turning to Terry's partner.

'Marko,' he corrected.

'Sorry, Marko.'

Marko began to explain what it was he did—something to do with veterinary science—but I was finding it difficult to focus. Gavin and Wendy appeared to be engaged in what looked an awful lot like a kiss. It was a brief engagement and when they broke apart, I noticed that Gavin was now chewing gum.

I gazed at a button in the leather upholstery of the bench seat opposite. Situated at head height between Terry and Marko, the ten cent-sized disk sat snug in a leather crater, an inch or so of puckered skin fanning out from its rim . . .

'She asked you a question,' said Wendy. Her threatening tone jolted me back into the world of words.

'I'm sorry, I've got some water in my ear,' I said.

'She asked what you did for a buck,' said Wendy. I assumed she was referring to Terry.

'I'm actually between jobs at the moment. I used to manage a jazz club but I sold the business a while ago.'

This was in fact true.

'I hate jazz,' hissed Wendy, 'All that screeching!'

Everyone laughed, except me.

'I had a friend,' she continued, 'who played the saxophone—jazz saxophone. It sounded like a cat being strangled. Gawd it was awful! They tried to make you learn sax at high school didn't they Gavvy?'

Gavin nodded with a grimace. 'Told them to fuck off! And they did!'

'On ya Gav!' Terry clapped her hands.

'It's pretty awful stuff,' remarked Marko sagely as he looked at his drink.

There was a collective sigh followed by another pause as the table pondered the dreadfulness of the musical idiom.

'Let's have some crisps,' said Wendy. 'Gav, go and order us some crisps.'

'She who must be obeyed!' Gavin put on a mock pained expression and made a whip cracking sound accompanied by a whip-cracking motion in the air.

Once he was out of earshot, Wendy turned to me.

'He's a good boy. I'm very lucky.'

'Yes,' I said.

It was time to leave the booth. I stood up.

'Look, I'd better get moving. It was really nice to meet you. I hope the Swans do better next week.'

'Come on, have another drink,' Wendy pleaded.

'No really, I've got to get going.'

'Aw come on! Just one more drink won't hurt you.'

Wendy's voice was becoming belligerent.

'No really, I need to talk to someone.'

'Oh for fuck's sake, just one drink!'

I stood up and shook my head. 'No.'

'Fuck off then!' There seemed to be real hatred in her voice.

As I walked away I heard Terry say: 'Auntie Wendy, there was no need for that.'

'He was an arsehole,' (I'm fairly certain) Wendy said in her defence. The remark brought forth a loud guffaw from Marko.

As I approached the bar, I passed Gavin heading back to the booth. He was carrying two large bags of corn chips.

'Women!' he said, rolling his eyes towards the ceiling before continuing on his way to re-join his friends.

*

She was sitting on a stool at one of the high circular lounge tables, drinking an expensive looking cocktail; a yellow plastic straw poked out from a mound of ice cubes and mint leaves and a semi-circular slice of tired orange was clamped onto the side of the glass. It was the woman from the ATM.

I took her to be somewhere in her mid to late twenties. Lying open on its side on the table in front of her was a large canister of Hume's crisps. She kept turning her head towards the entrance as if she was expecting someone. At one point, she looked towards the bar and I was at last able to view her face from straight on.

By what template do we measure beauty? Of course, I'd already made up my mind back at the ATM that this face would be beautiful and so I had a motive to find her beautiful—to confirm my powers of prediction. I was a compromised beholder to be sure, but surely this face was beautiful *in and of itself*, unfiltered by the lens of my unreliable subjectivity. The fact that I wanted and expected it to be beautiful was irrelevant.

I ordered another drink from Gary who duly poured and placed a new schooner on the bar top.

'So anyway, how about that birthday party!' I said, handing over the cash.

'I didn't really want to do anything, but Carter . . . he's gone ahead and organised it,' answered Gary.

Carter Highland, a long time regular, was the self-appointed instigator of pub events at the Stella.

'Organised what?'

'My party—my fiftieth.'

'Oh?' I said. I'd actually been referring to the birthday party I'd been removed from that afternoon.

'Yeah, he wants to do some sort of roast—you know where they get people to crack jokes about . . . '

He was cut off by the woman from the ATM who had left her table and was now approaching the bar.

'Can I get another cylinder of Hume's crisps?' she asked on arrival.

'A what?' asked Gary

'Another packet of Hume's,' said the girl.

'What flavour?'

'Ocean salt.'

Gary nodded and set off to look for the item in the crisps and nuts rack.

'I noticed you already had a can of Hume's.' I said, trying to make small talk. My breath had become shallow and I realized that I was sort of panting when I spoke.

She looked at me, puzzled.

I wanted to say to her how much I liked the 'stadium' shape of the Hume's crisp and, by way of this interesting observation, construct an initial bond—a shared liking of Hume's. I realised though that my opening statement might have sounded like I'd been surreptitiously observing her. I was unlikely to rectify the situation with further comments, so I decided to keep quiet.

After several awkward seconds of eye contact, I turned my head downwards and studied the surface of the liquid in my glass. We stood thus, unconversant.

Gary came back with the crisps. She paid him and returned to her stool.

I glanced over at the booth and saw Wendy kissing a corn chip and then putting it in Gavin's mouth.

'Lot of chips going down tonight!' I said.

Gary nodded.

I lifted my glass of beer to my mouth.

I watched a man enter the hotel. He was over six foot with a wiry build. He wore his long hair in a ponytail and in his left ear was a metallic stud. He walked over to the table at which the poncho-wearing, Hume's-chomping woman was sitting. Upon his reaching the table, she stood up and embraced him affectionately. She was smiling when they broke apart. He sat down on a vacant stool, on the opposite side of the table to her. They looked at each other for several seconds before he lent forward across the table and spoke into her right ear. What he said was obviously amusing because they both burst out laughing. He lent back, removed a crisp from the can and put it in his mouth. As he began to chew, he scrunched his face up in a hammy grimace and, with his eyes shut tight in mock pain, he swallowed the pulp. They both laughed again.

I turned away from the mirror.

Above me, the television no longer showed greyhound racing but golf—beamed from some distant, sun-drenched golf course. A professional golfer dressed in a tam-o-shanter with plus fours and a tartan cardigan swung his club to strike a ball perfectly down a 300-metre, cliff-edged fairway. It was some sort of 'masters' tournament' and I wondered if the small crowd at the course, outdoors and gathered around the sportsmen, had any notion that millions of people all over the world in melancholic, darkened bar rooms were catching glimpses of them; glimpses caught during idle moments of distraction from millions of aimless, drunken conversations.

The pony-tailed friend of the girl stood up and approached the bar.

'I'll have a schooner of New and a cylinder of Hume's ocean salt, thanks boss.'

Gary went about his business.

Considering the facial gesture the man had just made, I was surprised he was ordering more of the crisps.

The man turned to me. 'Jesus, this place is chock-full of vibe!'

'It's not so bad,' I said. 'You should try the Achnacarry Castle on Moore Street, now that's a real dump!' I was trying to be blokey.

'Achnacarry Castle eh? I'll remember that.'

On the other side of the bar, Gary arrived with the comestibles, causing the man to turn his head 90 degrees away from me. I felt I hadn't finished my 'bad pub' routine.

'Or the Captain Stevens, that's even...'

I was talking to the side of his head. At the point at which I would have said 'worse', he looked at me with a pained half-smile on his face, a potent illustration of how he saw the power dynamics in the relationship. I had bored him.

Upon receiving his items, he about-faced and, without so much as a goodbye, returned to the table and the woman.

I watched as he placed the Hume's packet down on the table. He did this with a flourish which caused both of them to burst out laughing. He then said something to the woman and nodded in my direction, causing further amusement.

'Nice guy!' said Gary. 'I liked the way he just turned his back on you when you were trying to start up a conversation. He reminds me of Megan's brother—too cool to have a conversation with the likes of me.'

'It doesn't matter,' I said.

And it didn't really.

From behind the bar, Gary continued to malign his wife's sibling while I looked at the television screen and ruminated over my current life situation. I could feel my mood deteriorating rapidly. I tried to focus on the golf. An out of shape middle-aged man was attempting to chip his ball out of a sand trap. He swung his club and produced an explosion of dry sand out of which popped the ball. It flew straight into the lip of the bunker then rolled back down the slope of the trap, coming to rest at his feet,

'Would you like to join us?'

I looked up. It was the woman.

'All right.'

I left Gary mid-sentence—talking about some restraining order Megan's brother had taken out on him—and accompanied her to the Hume's-laden table.

'This is Roderick,' said the girl.

I shook his hand and sat down.

'I'm Geoff.'

'And I'm Amber.'

'Hello Amber.'

'Hello Geoff,' she said with mock formality.

We both laughed. After a beat, Roderick laughed too.

'Would you like a Hume's?' asked Roderick.

Both he and Amber renewed their laughter.

'Thanks. I like these crisps. I know some people think of them as a poor man's Pringle, but I reckon they've got their own thing.'

I had no idea why I was suddenly defending Hume's crisps. Gary bought the stock in bulk off a friend of Carter Highland's for a third of the price of normal crisps. He then on sold them as a 'boutique' item.

'Their shape reminds me of a football stadium,' I said.

'A football stadium eh,' said Roderick.

I interpreted his reaction as patronising.

'Yes, a football stadium. One of those modern ones.' I picked out a whole crisp from the can. 'You see, here are the grandstands. Many modern stadiums have a similar sort of camber to them don't you think?'

I was play-acting naivety, hoping that the resultant irony might elevate me in Amber's estimation—she looked like someone who enjoyed a laugh. I'd given up on Roderick back at the bar. As far as I was concerned this bozo was a has-been hippie with a crisp addiction. He sure didn't deserve Amber and it was I who would teach him this fact.

I needed to slow down.

'Tell me Geoff, where do you come from?' asked Roderick, putting an end to any discussions about sporting-field-shaped crisps.

'I live in a nice house around the corner.' I was finding it difficult to snap out of the mock guilelessness.

'That must be nice for you. Do you come here often?'

'Whenever I want to experience some great night life.' Nor could I help revisiting the sarcasm of my prior conversation with him back at the bar.

'What brings you two here?' I asked.

'The crisps,' said Roderick, deadpan. Amber let out a loud snigger.

'Look, I'd better be getting back to the bar.' I began to rise.

'No please, stay a bit longer.' It was Amber. I sat down again.

'We're just having some fun, Geoff,' said Roderick.

'Yeah, at my expense.' I don't know how I came to say this out loud, but I did.

'No, not at all,' he said. 'I'm sorry you feel that way.'

To many he would have seemed genuinely remorseful but I sensed a tinge of competent thespianism. What with the stud and the pony-tail, training for the stage was not out of the question with this macho, crisp prick.

First impressions can be wrong though. Back at the bar, I'd taken him to be in his mid to late thirties. Now, having spent some time up close, it was clear he was older, by a decade at least. Amber, on the other hand, retained her youthful late-twenties appearance in this up-close context.

'Let me buy you a drink,' he said.

I was wary of accepting his offer, but I did.

'I'll have a Reschs thanks.'

'Amber, will you do the honours?'

I sensed hostility in Amber's face as she rose to carry out the set task.

'So, what do you do Roderick?' I asked.

'As little as possible! I do a bit of theatre—outdoor stuff mostly—and play a bit of music. Actually, I'm Professor of Body Percussion at the Northern Beaches Institute of Performing Arts. What about yourself?'

'Bit of this, bit of that. I used to run a jazz club down at The Rocks.'

'What was it called?'

'Changes,' I said, trying to sound businessman-like.

'Was that just off Argyle Street, a little bit up the hill?'

'That's the one.'

Roderick was the first person I'd met, not employed by or related to me, who'd actually heard of the place. My initial negativity towards him evaporated.

'I used to busk near there. I walked past it a few times. Never went in though.'

'Yeah, well you weren't the only one.' Self-deprecation is for me an important socialising tool. In this instance, though, I spoke the truth; no one did ever come to the club. Well, not before the machines went in.

Roderick's face suddenly registered a thought. 'Hey didn't it catch fire?'

'Yes.'

'Insurance job?'

'I wasn't insured and even if I had been, I wouldn't have burnt it down to make a claim.'

'Of course not.' He was grinning.

Amber returned with three drinks and another cylinder of crisps. She looked annoyed as she plonked everything down onto the middle of the table before sitting down.

'These are so expensive!' she said, pointing at the container of crisps. 'Can't we use anything else?'

'Geoff here ran that place Changes, you remember, that bar in The Rocks.'

'I don't remember it,' said Amber. If she wasn't offended by Roderick's ignoring of her previous comment on the cost of the crisps, she should have been.

'I canned it a couple of years ago,' I explained.

She shrugged.

*

When asked what it is I do, I automatically refer to myself as having been a jazz club owner. That the club was woefully under attended and short-lived, in no way diminishes its usefulness as a calling card. For this purpose, the only requirement it need fill is that at one point in time it actually existed. This is a stable fact. And it means I'm able to truthfully present myself as the sort of person who can imagine and set up such a thing. I was an entrepreneur, a mover and shaker.

My aim had been to provide Sydney with a great Jazz venue for all to enjoy and for me to prosper by. But Changes never really took off, despite heavy investment in renovation, advertising and bribery—yes bribery. At that time, the costs involved in conforming to the NSW liquor licensing regulations were such that my only option was to run the thing black, using the *payola* method. I wouldn't be the first club owner to trip the life nefarious with the boys in blue. And believe me it's not as glamorous as it sounds; that is unless you find having your head shoved down a toilet by an off-duty detective, annoyed at the late payment of his weekly 'fee', glamourous. Despite all of this, for several months Changes opened its doors to those few Sydneysiders wishing to treat themselves to some world's best practice jazz.

I still don't know what the problem was. It may have been the location of the venue, the talent of the artists, the overall 'vibe' of the place, or the indifference of the general public. Whatever the reason, there's no escaping the fact that Changes was, on most nights, empty.

It was during this period that I experienced something of a spiritual awakening. Due to a combination of anxiety and coincidence, I developed a belief in a causal relationship between Christian prayer and material outcome. It was this state of mind—one that persisted until the end of my involvement with the premises—that influenced my decision to fork out a large sum of money in order to get a big-name international star, who happened to be performing in Sydney, to play a short 'afterhours' set at the club. Being somewhat long in the tooth, the star had decided to up sticks from the pop world and, by way of the Great American Songbook, transition into a new mature demographic.

The manager of the artist stipulated that the performance was to be unpublicized. I ignored him and consequently, the place was packed.

The staff working that evening (I wasn't in attendance) were inexperienced and allowed a dark energy to develop among the over-excited and inebriated throng of fans who'd turned up. Things weren't helped by the extreme brevity of the performance—*Making Whoopy* and half of *One For My Baby*—and the fact that the star refused to remove the gridiron helmet they wore. Both the brevity and the helmet were in response to what was considered to be breach of contract due to my advertising of the gig. It was a fair cop. At any rate, a riot ensued and at some point in the night a fire was started. *Changes* suffered extensive damage.

Against all advice, except that which I was convinced came from Heaven, I decided to trade my way out of difficulty. Although damage to the interior of the club was extensive, the damage to the exterior was minimal. I was able, with the last remaining funds at my disposal, to cobble together a functioning venue that was more or less safe (I never quite got rid of the smoky odour caused by the fire) and install several poker machines. I decided not to continue to pursue a live music policy.

Very quickly, a regular clientele was established, brought in by the new gambling arrangement, and this had the effect of turning things around financially. In a matter of weeks, the club began to make money, good money. Not long after that, an acquaintance made me an offer for the purchase of the lease, which I accepted. The sale of the lease enabled me to pay back all my important 'informal' debts.

What remained outstanding, however, was the bank loan for which my mother had gone guarantor.

*

'Where are you from?' I asked Amber.

'Nimbin. I'm *really* glad to be out of there,' she said.

'Oh? But it's so beautiful up there!' I feigned surprise at her comment in the belief it might earn me valuable points. It wasn't so much my insincerity that made me squirm inside, it was more the fact that my reaction had been so quick and unreflective; I couldn't stop myself displaying behaviour designed to win Amber's approval. With my too hasty sympathetic—'Oh?'—had I shone a floodlight on my developing crush?

'She's not really from Nimbin,' said Roderick.

'Well, I wasn't born there,' said Amber.

'She was only there for three years. She's a Sydney girl, from Clifton Gardens.'

'I don't feel like it though,' said Amber.

'She needed to get away from her old man.'

'Shut up!' said Amber. She was trying to act playful.

I thought it rather early on in proceedings for Roderick to be telling me about Amber's intra-familial relations. I felt both uncomfortable and fascinated.

'Have a chip everyone!' shouted Amber with forced joviality. She proffered the pack first to me, who gladly took a bunch, and then to Roderick who shook his head. She too refrained from taking one.

I'd been taking large gulps of beer since joining my two new friends and, consequently, a level of drunkenness had crept up on me. I was no stranger to this level and have been able, over the years, to develop, through trial and error, a fair amount of self-awareness as to the degree of intoxication allowable in order to remain reasonably autonomous and coherent. I knew I was now pushing the envelope.

'I bet you're a performer.' I faltered over the fricative in the last word. I was beginning to slur my speech.

'I'm studying contemporary movement and body percussion. Roderick's my professor.'

'That's great!'

'Here.'

She bent down from her chair and scrabbled in her shoulder bag on the floor. She returned upright, clutching a business card, which she handed to me. The calligraphy was gold embossed and read: *Amber Lockhart. Movement Artist.* Underneath this, written in plain ink, was an email address.

'Thanks,' I said.

I slid the card into my trouser pocket alongside Terry's. It was my second business card of the evening!

'She's an A-grade student,' said Roderick who was rolling a cigarette from tobacco and papers extracted from a leather pouch. 'I'm going to have a smoke,' he said, rising from his stool.

'Could you roll me one?' asked Amber.

Roderick nodded and sat down again. 'She has a show coming up in ten days' time.'

Once more Amber reached down into her shoulder bag, this time returning with a flyer, which she handed to me. It advertised the *Northern Beaches Institute of Performing Arts End of Term Final Presentations.*

The image on the flyer was of a rocky coastline during a storm. A huge wall of churning white water crashed against a cliff face. The address for the performance was the Sigley Theatre in Mona Vale, quite some distance from where we now sat in Chatswood.

'Please come along,' she pleaded. 'We need an audience.'

Was I misreading something due to alcohol intake? Why on earth would this be happening? Why should she invite me to her performance? Was there a possible 'chemistry' between us? I'd read on the internet that it wasn't unusual for a younger woman to be attracted to a more mature man. Indeed, it was quite common in times of yore— Shakespeare and Jane Austen provide ample proof of this. Besides, I was probably the same age as the buffoon she was already with.

I looked at Roderick. His face bore a hint of ribald amusement mixed with disbelief; the feigned disbelief of the host towards the houseguest on whose lap the family cat, normally standoffish with strangers, has decided to coil up. This facial expression nearly always has the effect of making the guest feel that he or she *does* have some inner quality with which the pet has miraculously found deep affinity. I needed to be wary of drawing false conclusions.

To my credit, I stopped short of interpreting signs of jealousy in Roderick's face.

'I would love to come.' I folded the flyer and put it in my back pocket.

'We're going to have a cigarette,' said Roderick. 'Where's the smoking area?'

'I'll show you.'

All three of us got up. Amber paid special attention to gathering up the four packets of Hume's on the table. She put one under each of her arms and handed one each to Roderick and myself. I led the way towards the glass doors at the rear of the lounge. I pushed open the right-hand door and stood holding it open, allowing Amber and Roderick to pass on through.

*

The beer garden of the Stella Maris is about the size of a tennis court. A section of it is covered by a corrugated metal awning attached to the wall space above the glass access doors through which we'd just passed. Two all-weather pool tables stand several meters apart, protected by this roof. Both of them were in use.

There were about 40 people, mainly smokers, spread out around the outdoor area. Most of them sat in clumps of four or five at the round wooden tables positioned beyond the protection of the awning. It was a large crowd for a Sunday night in winter. Gary's recent investment in the large, mushroom-shaped outdoor gas heaters was paying off.

All the tables had been taken, so we had to stand. I watched as Roderick and Amber lit up. I felt the first drops of rain on my scalp.

'I love beer gardens,' said Amber.

I nodded.

Very quickly the rain intensified.

'Let's get out of the rain,' said Roderick. 'Quick.'

We moved towards the covered area to escape the downpour, as did everyone else. Very soon the space became crammed with people. The influx of patrons under the awning seriously interfered with the two games of pool being played. Undaunted, the players continued, somehow managing to weave their cues between the tightly packed horde.

The sound of the rain falling on the metal roof became so loud that people had to shout to be heard. I was about to continue the conversation with Amber—agreeing with her about how great beer gardens were—when I got pushed, back-first, against the rails of a pool table. I was forced to place my left hand on the fabric of the playing surface in order to steady myself. The shouted insults from the poised shot maker were mostly covered over by the noise of the crowd and rain; the words 'soft cock', however, were quite audible.

As much as I wanted to stay close to Amber, I also felt a strong urge to return to the relative peace of the hotel interior. I felt confident that, with an almost full cylinder of crisps still in my possession, Amber would soon come looking for me.

I returned to the table and waited. I felt sobered up by the exposure to the cold. In comparison to the din outside, I found the noise of the poker machines coming from the gaming room almost pleasant to the ear. There's a carnivalesque quality to the music of the poker machine; a quality that brings to mind festivities stretching back in time to the Middle Ages and beyond; a quality that reasserts time-honoured notions of robust entertainment. And the more successful the gambler, the bigger the aural reward. Somewhere in the gaming room there was a very lucky punter—maybe Carter Highland, the local addict—whose machine was just then erupting in victorious song.

Behind the bar, Gary sat on a stool watching the UFC that had replaced the golf on the pub television system. Two men were on their knees on the canvas. One had the other in a frontal headlock while he brought his right knee hard into the crown of the other man's head.

I waited.

I helped myself to a Hume's from the packet I was in possession of.

Over at the booth, Gavin had fallen asleep with his head resting on Wendy's shoulder. She, in turn, was holding court, telling a comical story to Terry and Marko, who were both laughing. Their table was festooned with the empty glasses from four briskly consumed rounds.

I waited.

The left-hand glass door of the exit to the beer garden swung open and Roderick and Amber re-entered the lounge. They were both smiling. They made straight for the hotel's front entrance doors with Amber in the lead. They left the building.

At a table nearby, I could hear Bronwyn, a pub regular in her early forties, speaking loudly to Kelly, a much younger woman. Bronwyn was a person of strong opinions who, especially after a few drinks, enjoyed establishing her intellectual superiority over all and sundry. She prided herself in telling it like it is but I, along with many other regulars, found her brutal honesty to be at times little more than bullying. I believe she'd had a short career as a visual artist before making the move into part-time telemarketing. She was hectoring Kelly as to why it was that she hadn't read anything. Kelly wasn't offering up much of a defence.

'You're right,' said Kelly, 'I do need to read more.'

The scene resembled that of a frustrated teacher berating a lazy student.

I got up and made my way to the exit. Once outside, I stood looking up at the night sky. The rain had now stopped and I could see, in places, white pinpricks of starlight. With the Hume's packet under my arm and the dance flyer in my back pocket I began the walk home.

II

When viewed from the front gate, our unit—my mother's and (one day) mine—is on the upper level of a block of four, on the right-hand side. My mother purchased it decades ago when she down-sized from the Californian bungalow (which she'd inherited) several streets away. A substantial lawn area lies between the building and the imposing dark and spikey aluminium boundary fence and a cra-zy-paved path leads down the gentle slope of the lawn to a central, internal stairwell containing two dog leg staircases—one going up to the front of the first floor, the other to the back. Our front door opens onto a balcony connected to the front stairwell. My mother once told me that it was the balcony that had clinched the purchase for her, but the only time I can recall her ever using it, apart from entering or exit-ing the flat, was when she stood at its far corner, late one night, and threw an overripe banana at a drunken pedestrian urinating against the front fence.

We live in Lane Cove North, a lower north shore suburb of Sydney the bulk of whose citizens belong firmly to that class of society known as middle. It's a suburb of contentment, with very few inhabitants har-bouring strong aspirations to move up the ladder and migrate further north to the mansion-riddled bushlands of Lindfield or Wahroonga. Testament to this contentment are my mother and I—both of us birthed, reared and aged within hearing distance of the traffic at the intersection of Mowbray Road and the Pacific Highway.

It was tough getting out of bed. The winter sun outside made little difference to the cold temperature inside. The heating had been turned off—whether this was a newly instigated economy drive or a blunt message from my mother concerning my recent behaviour was ambiguous.

The roof of my mouth was coated with the hardened mud of hangover phlegm, which provided an adhesive surface against which my dry tongue could play. Both my temples throbbed more or less in time with my heartbeat.

Trying hard not to move my neck, I began to shuffle as smoothly as possible from my bedroom to the kitchen. It being midday, I was alone in the house.

*

At first, my mother hadn't wanted to guarantee the bank loan for the jazz club. To her it was yet another of my hair-brained schemes—the product of a personality that had never been able to stick with anything and always opted for the easy road. Eventually, however, I'd worn her down with declamations about it being the one true thing I'd ever wanted to do with my life and strong references to the poor start I'd had—something which always played well upon her guilt at having not provided me with a proper father-mother-sibling style upbringing.

These weren't new tactics. I've played the broken family card to solicit funds on numerous other occasions—my venture into soy milk production being one, the purchase of 293 wetsuits for the purpose of re-selling them on to Qantas being another. Both these were ventures in which my mother had invested, lost and gotten on with things. Both too, I daresay, were things I could have been talked out of had there been a strong, non-enabling parent or parental figure on hand.

Shortly after I sold the lease to Changes, my mother came out of retirement. A colleague of my cousin Lionel had invested in 'Class Axe', an axe throwing parlour in the inner West of Sydney—axe throwing having become the latest 'hip' pastime and tool for corporate team-building. By calling in repayment for a large favour, Lionel had managed to get his aunt a full-time position at the parlour serving behind the refreshment counter, carrying out light bookkeeping duties and cleaning.

My mother claims that she had to re-enter the work force in order to keep her head above water financially. But I see it more as an exercise in martyrdom and showy self-punishment aimed at shaming me. The outstanding bank debt accrued as a result of the jazz club was around 80K. With the mortgage on the flat having been dealt with long ago and her generous librarian's superannuation income, she could have easily serviced the loan without recourse to a six-day-a-week, full-time job. I think she actually enjoyed the work—and all the attention.

Because of the job, I have the house to myself between 10:30am and 8:30pm, Monday to Saturday. Sometimes, when one of the other staff members is ill or otherwise indisposed she works a later shift till 11pm, but this is unusual.

As I entered the kitchen I noticed lying next to each other on the Formica table a hand-written note and the harmonica I'd given Sky.

Normally there's a pre-cooked hot breakfast waiting in the microwave if I've left my night note on the table requesting it. If there's no pre-cooked breakfast, there's the second option of a cold breakfast consisting of cereals and muffins. This morning there was neither.

I picked the note up and began to read:

Geoffrey, I've come to the end of my tether. Your behaviour
yesterday at the party was inexcusable. Lionel came around
last night while you were out getting drunk and returned the
harmonica.

I looked at the harmonica. Part of its mouth had been caved in—a
modification that could have only feasibly been carried out using a
boot on an adult foot or some sort of mallet. I picked up the instrument, put it in my mouth, and held it in place with my lips. I began to
breathe in and out to see if the reeds of the instrument could still be
engaged after such rough handling. They could. I read the rest of my
mother's letter accompanied by the repetition of the wheezy perfect
cadence that resulted from each breath.

> I can no longer support you. I work a full-time job in order to
> feed and house you. I get nothing in return. I can't take this shit
> anymore.

Upon reaching the expletive, I stopped breathing. This was serious—
Mum didn't swear. Were we now entering new territory? I was more
than a bit confused—surely she was overreacting. I hadn't treated *her*
like shit, I'd merely gotten a little annoyed at the duplicity of Sky. My recollection was that, apart from me telling my mother that she'd wrecked
my life, the argument had been between myself, Sky and Lionel.

I began once more to breathe through the harmonica, thus bringing the two-chord vamp back to life, and read on.

> You have to find somewhere else to live, Why don't you do
> something with your life? I hereby give you notice to leave this flat
> in a month's time.

With the harmonica still in my mouth, I played on for half a minute, standing upright in the middle of the kitchen, ruminating over the contents of the note.

I felt abandoned.

I didn't like the way things had turned out any more than she did. But that's the way they'd turned out and that's what we had to deal with. It was a bit rich for her to play the blame game. She was my *mother* after all. I hadn't asked to be here on this earth, and if she couldn't hack the unconditional generosity that parenthood required then she shouldn't have embarked upon the 'great journey'.

But now was not the time to go down the road of blaming my mother for her failed marriage and the rudderless boat ride that had been my childhood; a childhood lacking any strong male mentor figure.

No. Now was the time to be constructive, to devise some sort of strategy with which to calm the turbulence.

Besides, where would I go? Or, more to the point, *how* would I go? Since moving back to the family home, I'd been successfully 'adolescentised'; I'd reverted back to an earlier teen-age model of subsistence, the core of which consisted of invisibly fulfilled expectations. As a result, my ability to adapt quickly to dynamic external forces had been seriously impaired. The world was a different place now to what it had been before Changes. Would the meagre allowance bequeathed to me by my dead uncle—whom I loved—cover the extortionate rent I'd be forced to pay? With this new scenario, there was a good chance that the next time Mum would see her evicted son would be on a slab with a tag around his toe. That'd teach her!

I unclenched my mouth muscles and let the harmonica drop to the floor. The clatter brought me back into the world of phenomena and quotidian bodily needs.

I set about making coffee. I pushed a generic brand coffee pod into the slot of the espresso machine Lionel had given mum for her 70th birthday. I heard the buzz of the small motor and watched as a thin jet of hot dark liquid splashed against the bottom of my goblin-themed mug, eventually filling it one third full.

From the fridge, I removed four slices of processed cheese which I plated. I then took a box of Jatz biscuits from the pantry cupboard and, with mug, plate and box in hand, I broke my fast.

A month was a long time.

*

After breakfast, I spent a good deal of time trying to teach myself the main melody from the Vaughan Williams harmonica concerto—a tune that had been the theme for the weather report on the television when I was a child. After several hours, I'd managed to semi-articulate the opening bar.

I was disturbed in my labours by a knock at the front door. I rose from the table and made my way out of the kitchen, down the hallway and into the living room. Through the frosted glass window of the front door, I could discern a familiar human outline.

Normally, Laird dressed himself modestly: unwashed T-shirts, flannel shirts, jeans and desert boots. During the colder months, he favoured the nylon fleece for warmth. Today, he was wearing a charcoal suit over a grey (still unwashed) T-shirt and black designer running shoes. It was an obvious and unsuccessful attempt at looking stylish.

'What's the difference between manslaughter and grievous bodily harm occasioning death?' he asked.

He was out of breath, presumably from running up the stairs.

'I'm not a lawyer,' I said.

'My understanding,' he continued, 'is that grievous bodily harm requires the intent to cause grievous bodily harm whereas manslaughter doesn't. With manslaughter, you may have intended to injure someone, but not grievously—that's the difference. It's the kind of injury the person suffers and whether or not the infliction of that injury was intentional on behalf of the defendant. Like, I can punch someone in the face and kill them, but it would be grievous bodily harm, not man—no hang on, I mean, manslaughter not grievous bodily harm occasioning death—because I wouldn't have intended the punch to have inflicted grievous bodily harm.'

Laird was floundering.

'Isn't it different for different jurisdictions?' I asked.

'Is it?'

'I don't know, I'm asking you.'

In an attempt to salvage his demonstration of knowledge, he settled for a less detailed piece of information: 'They both carry the same maximum jail term.'

He waited for me to respond.

'Yeah. Twenty years,' he said.

We were still in our original positions, with me standing inside the house and Laird outside on the concrete balcony.

'Why are you interested in this?'

'No reason.'

'I like the suit.'

'I bought it yesterday. It's more of a summer suit but I thought: what the hell.'

'Yeah, what the hell.'

'Can I come in?'

39

'I'm actually pretty busy at the moment.'

'Yeah . . . right!'

'I am.'

'What with?'

'A legal problem concerning my mother.'

'I'll only be a few minutes. You might be interested in what I have to say.'

I looked at him.

He looked at me.

He moved forward and I stood aside, allowing him to pass. He walked across the living room towards the hallway.

I followed him.

Having seated himself at the kitchen table, he removed from the inner pocket of his suit jacket a metal object about eight inches long that looked like an oversized boat whistle or an antique gas fitting. Its exterior was highly polished and, half way down its length was wrapped a one-inch wide, dark brown leather band.

'What's that?' I asked

'Just a little device I've been playing with.'

He unscrewed the top section of the object and placed it on the kitchen table.

'How's your mother then? Is she in a spot of bother down at Class Axe?'

Laird's use of the phrase 'spot of bother' jarred.

'No. It's nothing really, just a small hassle here with the body corporate,' I said.

From his left trouser pocket, he fished out a small plastic bottle. I thought he was going to administer eye drops.

'Ah yes, the joys of land ownership!' he said pompously while depositing several drops of the liquid from the bottle into an opening at the top of the thing he held in his hand.

'Yes.' I said

Satisfied with the number of drops, Laird put the bottle back in his trouser pocket, picked up the part he'd put down on the table and screwed it back into the main body of the metal object.

'I'm going to go in there,' he said pointing in the direction of the living room, 'and enjoy myself.'

'Look Laird, what is this?'

'Patience, patience, all will be revealed.'

I knew, but only because he'd explained it to me in the past, that Laird was talking in the voice of Stuart Wagstaff, the glamorous 'ladies' man' from the Benson and Hedges cigarette commercials of the seventies. His impressions of Wagstaff were a regular feature at the Stella, the incompetency of his mimicry unremarked upon due to the obscurity of the reference.

He stood up from the chair and strode confidently out of the kitchen, whistling tunelessly.

I followed him once more.

Having laid his suit coat on the coffee table, Laird collapsed on the sofa, his back propped up by the armrest, his legs stretched out lengthways so that the heels of his shoes dug into the seat cushion at the far end.

'Nice day! Weatherwise that is,' he said.

I stood watching him.

'Do you mind if I smoke?'

I knew then what this was all about.

*

A decade earlier Laird and I had been involved in an attempt to create a non-carcinogenic cigarette with a then Stella regular by the name of Earl Carlin. The premise was sound enough: if we could invent a cigarette that moved away from smoke-based technology to that of dry ice, there would be a huge demand for such a product.

Earl had had the original idea as a child—or so he claimed. While enjoying a family picnic, he noticed the smoke-like vapour coming off a block of dry ice and straightaway discerned a similarity between this and the tobacco smoke coming out of his parents' mouths and nostrils.

While still in his teens, he'd constructed crude smoking devices by placing blocks of frozen carbon dioxide inside lengths of copper tubing. But these pipes proved vastly inferior to the tea and toilet paper cigarettes that were his preferred tools for the inhalation of smoke—a preference that survived right up to his death.

In the late 1980s Earl had briefly studied electrical engineering and it was during this time that he'd met Simon McGuigan, an impressionable fellow student and heavy smoker, who'd agreed to come on board as a partner in 'Cumulus'—the fledgling enterprise tasked with the development of a health cigarette. Over the next 18 years, little progress was made towards the goal of realising this dream.

By the time I got to know Earl, at the Stella Maris, he was a man of 38 years for whom time was running out. Other groups, better organised and funded than Cumulus were developing sophisticated vapour-based products. He was being rapidly overtaken.

Not having come from a fact-prioritising background, however, I took Earl's statements at face value. I believed him when he alluded to the fortune we would likely make on completion of a functioning prototype.

For him the pleasure of smoking was *not* to be found in the inges-
tion of nicotine, but in the bite from the smoke felt at the commence-
ment of drawback.

'It's milk from the breast,' he told us one night. 'But the milk comes
with a sting.' He was adamant that this pain was what the smoker
hoped to purchase, over and over again. Without it, the smoker just
breathed coloured air. His product would be about the *pain*, not about
the pleasure!

Laird and I were impressed by his rhetoric.

Earl's chief legacy, in my opinion, has been the ongoing influence
he casts over Laird. As an impressionable 37-year-old, Laird came to
regard Earl as his mentor even though the latter was no more than six-
months his senior. Earl's general dishonesty and pursuit of easy money
embodied many of the attributes Laird held in high regard.

The team working on the project comprised four individuals:
myself, Laird, Earl and Simon. The cost of the prototype development would be borne by Earl, Laird and I, with McGuigan acting
as 'McGuinea pig' for the experiments carried out in Earl's garage. I
personally provided $1000 in seed funding—a lot of money at the
time.

Even though Earl already had several decades with which to bring
into the world an idea he purported to have had when he was a nine-
year-old, his prototype consisted of several extremely basic items: the
box from a small wooden chess set, a length of garden hose with the
nipple from a baby bottle gaffer-taped onto one end, some sealant
and a plastic ground sheet. Quite clearly, the cost of these items came
nowhere near the amount of money I'd invested.

Earl placed a small block of dry ice in the wooden box. The length
of hose had been threaded through a small hole in the box's lid and

the gap sealed with putty. Earl slid the lid of the box into place. He got McGuigan to stand on the ground sheet with the gaffer-taped rubber nipple in his mouth and breathe.

At first, McGuigan got no vapour due to the barrier of the rubber nipple. It was decided that the nipple be removed. Even with the mist inhaled, unfiltered, into McGuigan's lungs, there was little evidence of any smoke-like substance in the exhalation. Nor was there, more importantly, any real sensation of the 'pain' that was so important to the success of the product—for this we had to take McGuigan's word for it, he having remarked that it was 'not like a real durry'. Although carbon dioxide is relatively harmless, neither Earl, Laird or myself had any interest in having a go on the hose ourselves.

It was at this point that Earl decided to deviate from the script he'd workshopped with us at the Stella Maris.

Placing a 'pill' of swimming pool chlorine in the wooden chess box must have always been part of the plan—Earl's lack of a swimming pool made coincidental possession of such a tablet highly unlikely.

At the time, none of the rest of us knew what the white circular disk he placed in the box was. I initially thought it might have been a 'Little Lucifer Fire Starter'. Once placed inside, Earl jabbed at the block with the sharp end of his biro to break off powdery crumbs—an odd activity I remember thinking.

Laird, to this day, feels certain Earl didn't mean to harm McGuigan. For him, Earl was just testing the water, gradually introducing an irritant in order to mimic the drawback stab. The chlorine pill was just a temporary measure, a proxy used in the prototype; one that stood in for the harmless irritant Earl would no doubt bring to the finished product. It was always his intention to stop just short of causing any permanent damage.

Other people felt differently, myself included. They saw a man who, having conceived a brilliant idea, had stood by and watched as the rest of the world caught up with him; a man still toying around with chess sets and rubber hoses when other manufacturers were bringing out elegant designer E cigarettes.

And when it came to finding a much-needed target at which to direct the frustration, well, poor old Simon McGuigan was as good a target as any. In the grim backlot of Earl's subconscious, it had been decided that it was McGuigan, his long-time partner, who'd held him back and it was now time for McGuigan to pay the price. Earl's fixation with the inhaler's need to experience the 'pain' for reasons of cigarette verisimilitude was, in actuality, just a vapour screen for the punishment of Simon McGuigan for having ruined Earl's life.

And McGuigan sucked hard on that hose, wanting to please; wanting so badly to turn Earl's toxic dream into a reality; wanting to feel the 'pain'.

He sucked twice—two deep, belly-filling parcels of mist. The first inhalation seemed innocuous. McGuigan removed the hose from his mouth, stood for a moment and shook his head, smiling—nothing. The second breath was a different story. The jovial hit me with your best shot demeanour transformed into one of fear. We all knew he had felt the 'pain'.

'That's better,' said Earl.

Then came the coughing, the vomit and the blood. I won't go into too much detail—suffice to say the groundsheet had been the only decent idea Earl had that afternoon.

The testing finished at that point—as did the whole project.

Earl had failed.

McGuigan didn't die, at least not straight away. He lived on, albeit with a permanently ulcerated respiratory tract and chronic pulmonary edema.

During the court case, Earl's lawyer successfully argued that McGuigan's illnesses were caused more by the effects of conventional tobacco smoke than from his brief exposure to pool chemicals. Consequently, Earl got off with an 18-month good behaviour bond.

Laird and I were given warnings with no convictions recorded (to this day my name remains absent from any records pertaining to criminality).

Maybe it was his failure at making a competent health cigarette; maybe it was the inevitable reckoning with his own subconscious and its submerged hatred of Simon McGuigan; maybe it went even deeper. Whatever it was, it proved too big for Earl to handle. He took his own life a year later, in his car, in the same garage where the experiment had taken place, possibly with the same piece of hose.

*

'Yes, Laird, I do mind. You can't smoke in here.'

'Good, because I'm not going to.'

He placed the narrow end of the whistle-like device in his mouth. I heard a click as his right index finger pressed down on a small metal button next to the leather grip. He looked at me with the device in his mouth, and raised his eyebrows—'mischievously' doesn't really do credit to the offensive effect of his facial movement.

Rather than a haunting tone conjuring a distant harbour at night, or a sparkling jig from an Irish virtuoso, the 'whistle' remained silent. Laird removed it from his mouth and from that mouth and both nostrils came a thick pall of smoke. He finished off by clicking his jaw and pushing out a donut-shaped plume that wobbled briefly in the air in front of his face, before vanishing.

'Butterscotch,' he announced.

'I've got to get some work done.' I said. I left the living room and headed for my bedroom.

*

I sat on the bed and stared at the wall. Then at the floor. Then at the half-empty Hume's crisp tube lying where I'd dropped it the previous night.

My thoughts led to Amber and I remembered the flyer in the back pocket of my jeans. I extracted it from the pocket and unfolded it.

The concert was scheduled for the twentieth of June, nine days away.

I was still peeved at the way she and Roderick had left the pub without saying goodbye.

From a drawer in my desk, I pulled out my 'Week to an Opening' diary. As it turned out, I had nothing scheduled for that week. I made an entry for Wednesday, the 20th of June. It felt good to be writing in my diary. I'd arrived at a small oasis of non-aimlessness.

*

Back in the living room, Laird had fallen asleep on the sofa. With heavy tread, I walked into the centre of the room. The vibrations from my stomping caused him to wake suddenly from his power nap.

'Let *me* squash it!' he shouted, panicked. It took him a couple of seconds to understand his dawning consciousness, at which point he said, while rubbing his eyes, 'Fucking hell. Sorry.'

I gave him a moment to come to terms with his newly awake state before I asked: 'What's that thing called?' I motioned towards the apparatus lying on the coffee table.

'It's a Saratoga Cloudmaker E130 Deluxe Mechanical Mod. 'Today's the anniversary of Earl's suicide. I thought I'd honour it with the purchase of this handcrafted, limited edition, vaping tool. Ain't it a little honey? None of this could have come about without Earl's work.'

At first, I was taken aback by this extraordinary manifestation of sentimentality. Had Laird miraculously forged new neural pathways that allowed him to commemorate a friend? But then I realized that the whole thing had been about display. The mod was really just one more signifier of wealth; one more chance to ostentatiously display the success he now enjoyed with his queue ticket racket.

Sometimes I wonder if I'm afraid that Laird might succeed at something—an outcome that strikes me as incredibly unfair—and perhaps I transform this fear into anger and dislike. On this occasion, however, I was certain that Laird's use of a friend's death, for the purposes of showing off, was genuinely offensive.

Yet I was intrigued by the mod and so I let my gaze fall on it for a length of time sufficient, I thought, for Laird to offer me a vape.

'May I have a vape?' I asked eventually.

'Ok.' Laird's tone wasn't confident. I assumed he felt uneasy about sharing a possession with someone else.

I picked the mod up from the coffee table.

'I might just,' I began to unscrew the top part of the device.

'Hey, what are you doing?' Laird was up off the sofa. He grabbed at the mod, but I turned around and managed to keep it out of his reach.

'I just want to give this mouthpiece a quick clean under the tap,' I was holding the mod in my left hand, high above my head.

'Over my dead body!' said Laird, 'It's a precision instrument; I put the coil in myself—1.3 ohms.'

'Hey lighten up!' I said, lowering my arm and handing over the Cloudmaker E130. .

With his prized toy back in his grasp, Laird calmed down, although he continued to shake his head and sigh somewhat woodenly. At that moment, I felt sorry for him, which is about as friendly as it gets in the tranche of feelings I have for Laird.

He sat back down on the sofa, this time keeping his feet on the carpet.

I stood standing.

'Did you feel you needed to wash it because it'd been in my mouth?'

I nodded.

Whether or not Laird had a pressing engagement at the Chinese embassy was of no import. What was important was that very soon after changing his mind about letting me use his mod, he put it back in the box and left.

I was free to get on with my day.

III

Many residents hate the local mall with its small-business destroying mega overarch, its de-humanising global discourse and the massive glass and concrete soullessness of its architectural design. Yet, I'm drawn to the mall. I'm drawn to its *inevitability*. Being so far beyond my own understanding of how these massive structures come into being, its meaning achieves the geological. It is an *urstructure*, a sacred landmass providing a still forming creation myth.

I'm drawn to the mall also by the way it positions me within its ambiguous framework of comfortable contemporary serfdom. I experience the thrill of opposites as I rejoice in my own insignificance while being prized as a customer. I'm dazzled by the surfaces whose reflected radiance warms my ego while obscuring the reality of the situation, which is that I neither understand nor matter.

I've come to treat the mall as a medieval Christian may have treated his or her local village church and thus to it I go almost on a daily basis to have my sense of both place and non-place, my feelings of both belonging and of being excluded, simultaneously reconfirmed.

My first stop is always *Muffin Siesta*, a franchised café situated in the food court area on the first floor. This is not the main food court, which is on the other side of the mall. It's more of a secondary food court housed in a section that branches off at right angles from the grand atrium. Freestanding and positioned in the centre of this section, *Muffin Siesta* has the feeling of a gateway. Being flanked on both sides by other food outlets that run the length of the hall further emphasises its toll-gate quality.

One detects at *Muffin Siesta* a certain *al fresco* quality achieved by way of half a dozen small tables and chairs scattered close by the service hut and placed atop an expanse of green carpet. The hut's ochre-coloured panelling with dark chocolate-coloured detail combines with the moulded glass of the display counter to imbue the enterprise with a powerful blandness that speaks of the dominance of large franchises. The staff, in their slacks, polo shirts and baseball caps, wear the exact same colours as the cabinetry.

I'm a creature of firm habit. As usual, I ordered a flat-white coffee and a blueberry muffin and sat myself at one of the tables. While waiting for my order to arrive, I listened to the mall ambience—a hazy aural drone drenched in the smooth reverb that vastness bestows; a reverb whereby the normally piercing screams of young children are rendered harmonious with the monotones of air conditioners, escalators, generators and the runny melodies of faintly audible MOR pop tunes piped from hidden speakers.

As usual, I was disappointed with the muffin whose cold and greasy, sweat-and-bacon flavour implied a lengthy fridge-life too closely neighboured with savoury products. I showed my disdain for the muffin by leaving half of it, fork-bashed and uneaten, on the plate where I hoped the proprietor would find it and be hurt.

With this ritual completed, I left *Muffin Siesta* and headed for *There and Back*, a sports shoe store situated on the second floor of the mezzanine overlooking the main atrium of the mall.

Greeting me as I entered *There and Back* was a two-metre-high display column on whose surface was painted a gaudy foot contour map. A monitor screen, attached to the structure at average head height, showed data. On the floor in front of the display sat a set of electronic scales, the haptic interface for the information shown on the mounted screen.

The central piece of furniture in the shop was a structure comprised of two opposite-facing, black vinyl sofas whose curved backs followed the outline of a surfboard-shaped bench that separated them. On the bench, which at its widest point had a breadth of about a metre and half, sat a pair of (presumably) very special running shoes.

While the majority of the merchandise was displayed on wall-mounted shelving, some shoes were housed in free-standing Perspex cabinets. On the wall above the shelves, posters of athletic stars endorsing brands of footwear had been hung in the hope of planting ambitions in the impressionable.

There and Back had no other customers except me. This didn't surprise me seeing as it was mid-afternoon on a weekday.

Presently I was approached by a fit looking man dressed in the navy-blue staff uniform of running shorts and polo shirt. Hanging from a lanyard round his neck was a laminated identity card with the name Joel clearly readable.

'Can I help you?' he politely inquired.

'Just looking actually,' I said.

'Ok, let me know when you need some help.'

'Thanks.'

I walked into the store and began to properly browse. The brighter-coloured shoes caught my eye. Displayed on a shelf attached to the right-hand wall was a pair of pink platform sneakers whose cushion layer must have been at least two inches wide. Several metres away on the same shelf was a pair of LED shoes, each shoe having a ring of dimly flashing LED lights attached to the rim of its base. I compared the price of both pairs of shoes; the pink pair was slightly more expensive which I thought strange. I was nonetheless mindful of a positive feeling caused by the acquisition of information. I set out to find the most expensive pair of shoes and then the cheapest. The quest took roughly three minutes to complete, after which I felt the time was right to ask for assistance—on my own terms.

Joel was kneeling on both knees and making micro adjustments to the positioning of a pair of Shimano R315 cycling shoes that lay on the lowest shelf of a Perspex cabinet. The cabinet stood against the left wall of the shop below a large poster depicting a smiling Carl Lewis. He sensed me standing behind him and swivelled on his knees to look up at me.

'Can you help me?' I asked. 'I'm interested in buying some shoes.'

'What were you after?'

'Running shoes.'

He stood up.

'Please, follow me sir.'

I was led to the main Fitprint machine.

'Have you ever had a foot scan done before?'

'No.'

'Well, if you could just step on the platform here, we'll get a computer readout of the shape of your soles.'

'Why?'

'Well, it'll tell us how high your arch is, whether or not you're flat-footed and how much support's needed for your instep among other things. It's really important to get an accurate assessment of the pressure points—each foot is different.'

I removed my shoes, stepped onto the platform and, with my socks still on, got scanned.

'I didn't realise that shoes catered for these sort of differences,' I said dishonestly.

'Yeah.'

'I suppose in the old days getting a shoe to fit high arches would have required going the bespoke route,' I said.

Joel silently studied the resultant image of the topography of my soles.

'You have fairly flat feet. This would suggest that you'd be an overpronator.'

'Is that a good thing?'

'Not really. It means your feet will tend to roll inward when you run, causing stress. From the looks of your print, though, it's not too bad. If it were any worse I'd recommend using orthotics. Definitely, though we're looking at motion-controlled footwear.'

He signalled for me to get off the scanner and pointed to the left-hand side, banana-shaped, black couch.

'If you'll just take a seat, I'll take a measurement with this.'

He was referring to the Brannock Device, the old-fashioned, metallic measuring instrument that he'd picked up from the top of a display cabinet and was now holding in his right hand.

'Don't trust the computer?' I asked.

'It's good for certain things but I find I can get a better size fitting with this.'

I enjoyed having my feet placed on the board of the machine.

And I enjoyed having Joel kneeling before me, slipping my socked feet into the interiors of the many types of running shoes on offer.

Over the course of the next 25 minutes I subjected each of the various brands Joel fetched from all corners of the shop, to methodical testing. The test went as follows: I walked up and down a five metre stretch of carpet, jogged up and down the same stretch and, finally, hopped up the five metres on my right foot and hopped back on my left. During the testing, several customers came, perused and left. Much to Joel's credit he remained focussed on the task at hand.

We tried the Asics 'Gel-Foundation' Stabilizer shoes, the Brooks 'Addiction' shoes, Mizuno 'Wave Alchemy', Saucony 'Grid Hurricane', the Nike 'Zoom Equalon+4' as well as the Nike 'Lunar Eclipse', the Adidas 'Adistar Salvation 2', both the Montrail 'Badrock' and the Montrail 'Masochist'. Each shoe was tested and rejected.

Every test began positively—'I think these are it!' I'd say on completion of the initial walking part of my investigation. Whereupon— for the first few times—Joel would say something like, 'They're a great shoe!'

However, mid-way through the jogging segment of the exam I would start to display doubts, often using a voluble tongue click or a skewed mouth expression to communicate approaching dissatisfaction. By the end of the final segment of the trial, the left-foot-hop, I'd shake my head and, with an apologetic smile on my face, say something along the lines of, 'Yeah, I'm not so sure about these now. Sorry. We're almost there though.'

By the time I turned down the Puma 'Complete Velosis 2' shoe, Joel was clearly losing patience.

'I think we're running out of options,' he said, kneeling on the carpet.

'What about Reebok?'

Joel got to his feet and walked away. He returned with a pair of Reebok 'Zigsonic' shoes.

They failed the test.

'One more?' I asked. 'I really think we're on the verge.'

'I've got stuff I need to get on with,' he said

'What about those five-toed shoes?'

'What about them?' asked Joel.

'What do you think of them?'

'I think they're a wank.' Joel's irritation had resulted in a less than professional conversational style.

'But they really build up the calve muscles,' I said parroting something I'd picked up on the internet.

'And stink to high heaven,' said Joel. 'Everyone I know who uses them says the odour problem is pretty fucking bad.'

'But they make you run in the way we're supposed to.'

'Yeah, well I don't believe it.'

'I read on the web that these sort of shoes,' I made a sweeping gesture taking in much of the store's stock, 'force you to run heel first, which leads to back problems, whereas the five-toed shoe forces you to utilize the ball of the foot and thus helps to lessen chronic back pain. They also help with balance.'

'Yeah well I don't believe it. I think they're just a fashion accessory for weekend joggers. Your serious runner just isn't going to get the protection he needs. It takes one piece of glass and you're out of action.'

'They're built to withstand that sort of thing. I've got a friend who swears by them and he runs 70 kilometres a week—cross country.'

'Well why don't you go and buy a pair then?'

'I don't know.'

We stared at each other.

I was seated on the vinyl couch; he was still kneeling on the carpet, looking up at me. The truthfulness of my confession was compromised by a snigger I was unable to stifle.

The exact thing that struck me as funny was difficult to ascertain. Maybe it was the haggard look on Joel's face; maybe I was enjoying the absurd idea of Laird running 70km a week; or maybe I'd become over-stimulated by the dazzling whites and yellows of the athletic footwear. I will never know. What I did know however was that with that snigger, my time with Joel in *There and Back* had come to an abrupt end.

He got to his feet and walked to the service desk at the back of the shop. He busied himself with some obviously bogus paperwork while I slipped my own shoes back on my feet. When I rose from the couch to leave I turned to face him and half shouted: 'thank you'. I stood for a moment looking at him. He continued shuffling papers around the surface of the desk never once raising his head or acknowledging my friendly utterance.

*

I walked along the smooth and polished surface of the tiled floor towards *Sushi Ghan,* the mall's sushi train restaurant, a journey that required crossing over an exterior street by way of a covered walkway. At the end of the walkway I made a right-hand turn, walked fifty more metres to an escalator and escalated one level. I was now in the main food court of the mall.

Housed inside a conventional shop space, *Sushi Ghan* had a clock-wise rotating conveyer belt that ferried a conventional cargo of mall sushi.

It was well past lunchtime and the place was empty of diners save for a large, sunglasses-wearing man seated with his back to the entrance. He was dressed in white slacks, a blue shirt and Blundstone boots. I helped myself to a can of cola from a glass fronted fridge and sat down next to him, upstream.

Two sushi chefs stood inactive in the central preparation area while a uniformed waitress lolled behind a payment counter in the right-hand corner of the premises.

The expanses of empty beltway between the various moving plates signalled a narrowing of an already narrow choice. I opened my account with a six-piece salmon and avocado maki set (blue plate, second cheapest) followed by two pieces of prawn and mayonnaise sushi (red plate, second most expensive). Between mouthfuls of food, I used gulps of cola to help flush the seafood through my oesophagus.

I gathered a salmon and avocado set from the train (red plate) and swigged on my can.

In the distance an eight-metre-high video screen, cabled to the ceiling, hung down next to the escalators. The screen showed a penguin standing alone on a snow-covered shorefront gazing over its shoulder at a distant flock of other penguins. I empathised with the image's signification—the dawning of the awareness that individualism and loneliness go hand in hand and that both become the overarching constituents of adult life, with individualism gradually morphing into isolation, and loneliness into despair.

I chose another salmon and avocado maki set from the belt. The dish, having already passed me by, had technically entered the grab area of my neighbour. I lunged at the dish and in the process my left elbow brushed against a small soy sauce bottle, causing it to topple over. It rolled on its side, in a curved path, before falling off the edge of the bench on to the floor, without breaking.

'Hey look out!' said the neighbour.

'I'm sorry.'

I placed the maki set that I held in my hand on the counter in front of me. It looked like a miniature flying saucer.

'Just keep to your fucking area of reach,' he added.

'Ok.'

His baritone voice gave to the demand an air of authority and although the voice's tone registered in me an inkling of prior knowledge, it wasn't until I looked him flush in the face that this vague sense of *deja entendu* transformed into sharp recognition. The small chunk of flesh missing from his right earlobe made it certain.

It was Jock Williams.

*

I will try and keep the following 'back story' as brief as possible . . .

Several years earlier, Laird and I had met Jock Williams at a bar in Kings Cross called *The Beard*. Prior to our arrival at the bar, I'd purchased a blow-up doll, and Laird had persuaded me to accompany him for a nightcap, ostensibly to celebrate the impending loss of my enclosed-air virginity. It is not a memory that fills me with pride.

At *The Beard*, Williams struck up a conversation with us saying he was a horse breeder from rural New South Wales down for the Spring Carnival at Randwick. Back then he wore an eye-patch, which is part of the reason I hadn't straightaway recognised him at the sushi restaurant.

The upshot of our brief relationship—begun and ended on that night—was that, under the guise of procuring for us a flesh-based sex worker at a brothel, he managed to gain access to my credit card account, by surreptitiously memorising my PIN and, consequently, cleaned me out.

This, of course, presented problems when it came time to settle the account at the brothel—a settling that had been rushed forward due to Laird having attempted to kiss the sex worker on the mouth, causing her to call for support from the two large, male managerial staff members at the brothel. Laird's wrist was broken in the ensuing rough handling.

With the in-house ATM telling me I'd reached my daily limit for withdrawals, I pleaded with the staff that we be driven to the airport where an early opening Travelex bureau might provide cash relief to pay the bill; a bill that, due to various penalty loadings occasioned by Laird's behaviour, had been very much increased.

Once at the airport, it was discovered that, thanks to Williams, my account had been cleaned out *entirely*. At this point it appeared likely that both Laird and I would finish our night out somewhere among the sand dunes of Botany Bay—as lifeless as Ms Oxygen, who I'd been forced to carry about with me, inflated, for the purposes of humiliation.

At the final moment, however, Laird, who had, up until that point, maintained he had no cash or credit card on his person, suddenly remembered that he, in fact, was carrying his mother's MasterCard. I'm certain to this day that had he not personally been in line for a potentially life-ending beating—indeed, had it only been *my* neck on the chopping board—he would have kept quiet about the card.

After all these years, I feel angrier at Laird for the way he conducted himself on that evening than at Williams, even though it was Williams who'd stolen my money in the first place.

*

'I remember you,' I said, turning on my stool so as to face him flush in the profile. His powerful jaws worked impressively upon a large chunk of sushi in his mouth.

'You're mistaken,' he replied, the contents of his mouth interfering with the crispness of his consonant pronunciation. He proceeded to swallow and restock his mouth—seemingly at the same time.

It was him alright.

'You're Jock Williams,' I said.

He sat chewing and stared into the riced glug of used soy sauce that stood stagnant in a small circular dish in front of him—Narcissus gazing at his own reflection. He swallowed once more and I detected the stifled beginnings of a smile breaking on his face.

He turned to look at me.

'My name is Harry. Harry Bailey.'

'Do you remember a night about five years ago at *The Beard*?' I asked.

'Never heard of it.'

'I was there with a friend and a blow-up doll. We met in the food area downstairs and then you took us to a brothel and you used my credit card to steal $3500 from the account.'

'I have no idea what you're talking about, mate.'

'Look what's passed is passed. I don't want the money now—I don't need it.'

'You need help buddy.'

'Jock, come on!'

'My name's not Jock.'

'Come on, I know you're lying. You said you were a horse breeder.'

'You've got the wrong guy. I'm a workplace consultant. I help companies maximise their potential through implementing better business strategies.' He described his current vocation with a swagger that conveyed he knew I knew he was lying, but that he held all the cards and there was nothing I could do about it.

'I've got to get to a meeting,' he said rising from his stool.

'Well I'm glad to see you're on the up and up.'

He bent down to pick up a black leather briefcase and I noticed that his hand was shaking. It was him alright.

'Off to rip someone else off,' I mused churlishly.

'You should see a psychiatrist,' he said.

'Oh I do, Jock, I do. Don't you worry about that!' By focussing too heavily on the use of a mocking tone of voice as a weapon, I'd failed to realize that the information conveyed in my last parry tended rather to support his insult.

'Get a life,' he said, stretching his shoulder muscles and pumping out his chest. It was an impressive chest as was his stack of empty sushi plates, arranged in two towers, each twelve inches in height.

And with that he moved to the counter. I watched him settle his bill with the traditionally dressed waitress before walking away, a little too briskly.

IV

A steady rain fell as I got out of the taxi, forcing me to jog the several metres to the steps leading up to the Stella Maris's entrance. Slightly out of breath, I pushed open the door and made my way inside.

Gary was standing behind the bar, polishing a glass with a towel. He stared out into the middle distance. Attached to the ceiling above the bar counter was a string of multi-coloured bunting.

'Hey, happy birthday!' I said, realising the significance of the decorations.

'Thanks.'

His acknowledgement of my birthday wishes sounded like the sarcastic reply to an insult. I didn't want to push things so, eschewing further conversation, I ordered a beer, thinking it better that he remain active—fetching drinks and the like—rather than pondering the meaningless of a life that was now almost over.

With beer in hand, I strolled away from the bar. I stood and watched as Carter Highland, ex-financial planner and Gary's old school mate, wheeled out extra seating to cater for the crowd he was expecting for the roast. The portable stage, normally positioned against the wall adjacent to the bar, had been moved to a position near the gaming room. This was another sign that a large turnout was anticipated.

'Whose idea was this?'

It was Bronwyn, the intimidating, ex-abstract expressionist painter and pub regular. She held in her right hand a half empty glass of merlot.

Being early in the night meant she'd be more predictable, less prone to unprovoked insult and more tolerant of those lacking her cognitive abilities. Nevertheless, I felt myself tense up at having to converse with her.

'Carter's.'

'That'd be right.' She took a gulp of wine. 'And why are we roasting Gary?'

'It's his fiftieth birthday.'

'I understand that, but why do we have to have a roast?'

'Yeah, I don't know. Why don't you ask Carter?' I said pointing at the man who was busy running an electrical cable from the back of an audio mixing desk to the vacant wall socket next to the ATM.

At this suggestion, Bronwyn snorted and moved away. She hadn't come to the pub to celebrate a birthday or to engage in a roast. She'd come to the pub because *that's what she did*. For all of us, with the possible exception of Carter, pre-planned events and celebrations were things of the real world outside and were met, by and large, with disinterest.

*

The front door swung open, causing a subtle increase in the noise from the outside traffic. A clump of half a dozen people entered. Among them was Laird. He was dressed in the same suit he'd worn when he'd visited me on the day of Earl's anniversary. In the glare of the fluorescent lighting I noticed that his suit had a silvery sparkle to it.

He walked over to me with a grin on his face.

'Good evening,' he said, over-formally.

I nodded.

Considering it had been a mere six days since his Olympic-themed argument with Gary, it might seem weird for Laird to show his face so soon. In actuality, Laird had attended the pub several times in the preceding days without incident. At the Stella Maris, arguments— even physical ones caused by long-standing gripes—tended to blow over quickly, often during the course of one evening. Such was the case here. His and Gary's recent altercation was now a thing of the past. Laird would continue to infuriate Gary and there would be other confrontations but he would still go on frequenting the pub and Gary would still go on selling him alcohol.

'How's the ticket scam going?' I asked. I searched his face for any evidence of offense caused by my use of such a derogatory word to describe his newfound vocation.

He pulled from his inner breast pocket a wallet thickly stuffed with cash.

'Ok.' He said, nonchalantly extracting a fifty-dollar bill. 'I might get myself a beverage. Hey!' He shouted across the room at Gary, 'I'll have a Bourbon and Mother.' This was a drink of Laird's own design that utilized the Mother Energy Drink. It hadn't really caught on.

Gary stood unmoved with his arms folded, deep in thought. Laird had intended his 'distance ordering' to be brash, but Gary's lack of reaction rendered it comical. Laird clicked his tongue in annoyance and walked over to the bar.

I moved to a table close by—coincidentally the same table at which I'd conversed with Roderick and Amber.

*

'Should be an interesting night,' mused Laird as he sat down next to me.

Gavin, Wendy, Marko and Terry entered through the front doors. Gavin and Wendy were holding hands and laughing. They made their way to the booth they'd occupied on the night I'd met Amber—was this to be their regular booth, I wondered. They sat down in the same configuration as before except for Gavin who remained standing. I assumed he was being given drink orders. As he turned to begin his march to the bar, Wendy leant over and pinched him on the backside.

Over the course of the next fifteen minutes, a steady stream of people entered through the doors of the pub. I remained at the table, on the receiving end of Laird's irritating boasting. The boasts ranged over many subjects, including, weirdly, polo. With the recent change in his financial circumstances he'd inquired with a local polo club as to how he might join up. I had a vague recollection of him having mentioned something about a relative who'd played polo in the '70s, so the idea hadn't just come out of thin air. No doubt the perceived elitism of the sport, coupled with the opportunity for animal cruelty, appealed to his bloated sense of self-worth.

'You can rent the horses from the club. One day I might buy, but for the time being I'm happy to rent—saves a whole lot of hassle.'

'Can you ride?' I asked him.

'Yeah, well I'll have to brush up on it a bit. There's a horse ranch out near Penrith. It's something I've always wanted to do; that and stand...'

'...up on a surfboard. I know.' My interruption left him stunned. It was probably cruel of me, but I was sick of listening to him express this dream.

I looked around the room. Carter, standing alone on the stage with a cordless microphone, was conducting a rudimentary sound check over the pub's karaoke sound system: 'Check one two, check one two,' he repeated, affecting a 'beefy' Aussie accent in a snobbish and outdated ridicule of pub rock roadies, much to the amusement of no one.

I estimated the crowd size to be around 60 or so people. I dimly remembered Gary's 40th birthday being somewhat under attended. I was impressed. Gary was more popular than I'd thought.

Absent, I noticed, was Megan, Gary's wife. This didn't surprise me. It had been years since she'd set foot in the pub.

Carter rang the Bell, the traditional means of drawing the attention of the Stella Maris crowd. It was used on such occasions as the Wednesday night meat-tray raffle as well as the various trivia and karaoke contests that had become a largely ignored feature of the pub. It was also used to sound 'Last Drinks' accompanied by a brief strobing of the overhead lights. Legend had it that Gary had stolen it from his primary school on the Lower North Shore, where he'd been 'bell boy' for a term.

The sounding of the Bell having sufficiently quietened the crowd, Carter brought the microphone to his mouth and began his address.

'Welcome ladies and Gentlemen to this auspicious event! Tonight is the night of the year—the night of the century in fact!'

'Get on with it!' yelled Wendy from her booth, causing guffaws from her three compatriots and subdued ironic cheers from other isolated pockets of the room.

'Patience, patience my fellow revellers!' postured Carter theatrically, 'the night is but young and we have all before us!'

'Well I don't want you before me!' yelled Wendy, very audibly. The sharp formants of her voice were more than a match for the electronic amplification provided by the public address system Carter was using.

Various members of the audience shushed Wendy. Carter looked pissed off and, trying to ignore the tiresome interjections, he continued.

'Tonight is a very special night ... '

'I want to have a special night tonight! Maybe not here though!' rasped Wendy, successfully distracting attention away from Carter.

Although Terry, Gavin and Marko roared with supportive laughter at this interruption, I could sense the room was quickly getting tired of Wendy's behaviour. A male from the other side of the room shouted, 'Shut up and let him talk!'

'Tonight is a very special night,' repeated Carter, 'it's Gary's anniversary, marking his half century.'

There were cheers and these cheers momentarily drowned out another instalment of Wendy's heckling. Gary, from behind the bar, waved a red bar towel in a circular motion above his head and smiled somewhat unconvincingly.

The yells of support died down. Like a wave receding from the ocean shore leaving behind flotsam stuck in the sand, the dying down left uncovered the sole voice of Wendy who continued her harangue: 'Shout us all a free fucking drink I say!' Not even her immediate family found this amusing and it was met with stony silence by the rest of the audience.

'Ok everyone! As planned, I'm very proud to be the MC for tonight's festivities. He paused for applause that didn't come. 'Ladies and Gentlemen' he continued, 'without further ado, we're going to have ourselves a roast!'

The eruption of applause this time didn't quite drown out Wendy who managed to screech out a toilet-themed quip that no one understood. Once the ruckus had subsided, she attempted to repeat the *bon mots*—no doubt hoping for a more positive reception second time round. However, with barely three words spoken, Terry interrupted her mid-sentence.

'Come on Wendy, give it a rest.'

'Go fuck yourself!' exclaimed Wendy and, try as they might, the majority of those gathered in the room couldn't restrain themselves from laughing.

'All right,' continued Carter, 'tonight there are going to be three speeches by three pre-chosen...'

'I wouldn't fucking choose you!' shouted Wendy.

'Um...' in focusing on trying not to focus on Wendy, Carter was clearly struggling to string his sentences together, 'by um, three pre-chosen friends of Gary's. Each speech will last three minutes. The speakers will hear a buzzing sound.' On cue, a comical flatulent sound effect came over the PA.

'Oh! Pardon me!' shouted Wendy in a mock ladylike tone of voice.

'This will mean that the speaker has thirty seconds to wind things up.'

'You're winding me up!' bellowed Wendy.

'After these three speeches,' Carter went on, 'there will be the oppor-tunity for anyone to get up and talk for no longer than one minute.'

'My ex-husband couldn't last more than a minute!' rasped Wendy whose belligerence and determination were starting to win her some fans. I too was finding her stubbornness at refusing to keep quiet absurdly amusing.

At first, three minutes seemed to me to be a paltry length of time for someone to get up and deliver a speech—particularly one com-memorating fifty years of a person's life. But the more I thought about it, the more I could see Carter's reasoning. To put it in as nice a way as possible, the Stella Maris was not exactly the Algonquin Hotel. I could see that the evening could—and probably would—descend into beer-fuelled anarchy. The idea of keeping things short was a sound one.

'OK let's get things underway on this roast! First up we have Tracey. Tracey is a lifelong friend of Gary's who once went camping with him in the eighties!'

The crowd erupted with whooping and cat calling and almost drowned out Wendy, who shouted, 'I didn't know he was gay!' twice, just in case people missed it the first time. I now realise she was making play with the word 'camping' but at the time her wordplay went over my and everyone else's head.

A short woman dressed in jeans and a navy-blue tracksuit top made her way through the mob to the stage. She was holding in her right hand a wine glass full of red wine. Carter handed her the microphone which she took with her left hand.

The woman was clearly very drunk and her address to the audience, what little address there was of it, was punctuated with wind pops caused by over pronounced fricatives, and clunks caused by the intermittent engagement of the microphone with various parts of her face. So slurred was her speech, it was difficult to make out anything except for the words 'I'm a Christian,' which she repeated often.

I estimated her roast to have lasted about two minutes before she came to a stop. She took a pull from her drink and just stood there staring into the distance. The room was silent—even Wendy, who should by rights have seized on this opportunity to show off more of her sparkling wit, was strangely at a loss for words.

The flatulent sounding warning noise was triggered early.

'I'm a Christian,' Tracey reaffirmed and remained standing. She dropped the microphone on the floor of the stage, sending a thud through the PA.

A male friend stepped up on to the stage, put an arm around her shoulders and guided her off.

Carter picked up the microphone and tapped it in order to test it. Satisfied it was still working, he held it to his mouth.

'Well, thank you Tracey!' he beamed.

There was some desultory applause.

'Have another drink!' yelled Wendy.

'What did you say?' It was Tracey, who'd sprung back to life since exiting the stage. She seemed pissed off.

'Have another drink,' repeated Wendy.

The crowd became animated at the verbal fracas developing between Wendy and Tracey.

'Come here and say that!' shouted Tracey.

'Oh Jesus, all I said was 'have another drink', for god's sake.'

'I'm a Christian.'

'You fucking told us that before luv!'

Terry, Marko and Gavin were visibly enjoying this banter. 'You tell her Wendy!' Terry said.

A commotion erupted in the scrum of people surrounding Tracey as she tried to wrestle herself free from her male friend's embrace in order to carry on the argument at a closer proximity to Wendy's booth.

'Aw, calm down darling!' reacted Wendy, 'I was only having a bit of fun.'

Other restraining arms joined those of Tracey's friend and she was firmly conveyed to the confines of the gaming room behind the stage.

'Ok then!' announced Carter resuming his duty as MC, 'Let's keep this moving along. Next up we have Mandy.

'Has someone got some Mandies?' shrieked Wendy—causing small levels of mirth amongst both those finding her unrelenting interjections funny in themselves, and those who were old enough to remember the popular seventies sedative, Mandrax.

'Now Mandy,' continued Carter, 'lives in Queensland and has come all the way down here to be with us tonight. Let's give it up for Mandy!'

There was applause and a small bespectacled woman stepped into the spotlight. She wore a black evening dress and around her neck was a string of pearls.

'I like your pearl necklace!' shouted Wendy.

Mandy had brought with her a pre-composed speech, written out by hand on several pages of loose A4 paper that she held in her right hand. With her free hand, she brought the microphone to her mouth and began her roast. I noticed that the hand holding the pages was shaking.

'I'd like to say a few words about my dear friend Gary. I've known Gary for a long time—a long, long time. While composing this speech, I got to thinking about how well someone can know somebody else.'

'Get on with it!' barked Wendy

Mandy cleared her throat. 'Well, I can say I know Gary about as well as I know anyone in this world. He's been like a brother to me.'

'Keep it clean!' taunted Wendy, eliciting a negative response from a good number of the crowd, who shushed her again while she busied herself laughing at her own joke.

'He's been like a brother to me; a brother who's stuck with me through thick and thin. Through the hard times—'

'Steady on!' rasped Wendy—I noticed Gavin now shaking his head violently at Wendy, trying to get her to rein herself in.

'Through the hard times' continued Mandy, her voice more forceful due to the interruption, 'and the easy times; the good and the bad. And do you know what?'

'What?' It was Wendy once more.

'Gary's never let me down. Not once has he ever said, 'sorry Mandy, I haven't got time.' Never once has he said, 'I won't be able to help out this time, I'm just too busy.' Never has he told me . . . '

'We get the fucking point sis!' This was funny and Wendy was rewarded with sincere sniggering. Even Laird, who up until then had sat grim-faced, cracked a grin.

'Never has he told me,' Mandy went on, 'find somebody else to help you.' He has always given his all to his friends and I count myself lucky to be one of those friends. Another side to Gary that I'm sure you've all witnessed, is his great sense of humour. To put it simply: the guy cracks me up.'

'What's up your crack?' yelled Wendy, undoing most of the good work of the previous interruption.

In order to begin reading the next page of the address, Mandy was forced to place the microphone in her right armpit while she shuffled the pages she held. The manoeuvre caused the mic to feed back. People frantically covered their ears trying to protect themselves from the high-pitched squeal. Carter jumped on stage and pulled the mic from her armpit.

He handed the mic back to Mandy shaking his head.

She found her spot on the next page and continued reading.

'I remember spending a weekend with friends up near Avoca. A group of us had all pitched in and we'd rented a beach house—it's a great part of the world by the way, and I recommend to you all that you spend some time on the Central Coast if you haven't already done so. Anyway, there we were at the house, after coming back from the local pub, having spent most of the day hanging out down at the beach. It was about midnight and we all went to bed'

'Ou la la!' interjected Wendy with a racy inflexion to her voice.

'Separate beds!' said Mandy, in a mock chiding tone, continuing the joke and receiving a few good-natured laughs from several members of the audience. 'Anyway, there I was trying to get to sleep and I heard this strange scratching noise coming from somewhere. I got out of my bunk and tiptoed to the lounge room. There it was again—scratch, scratch.

'Now earlier, at dinner at the pub, Gary had told me about a grizzly murder that he said had happened at the very house we were staying in. It was sometime in the sixties, he told me, and involved a hippy doctor who'd done away with his wife and three children.'

'Bullshit!' yelled Wendy, who was angrily shushed.

'Now, I'm a very superstitious person so this type of thing really scares me and so I'm walking around this house hearing all these strange noises, not knowing where they're coming from.'

'It's fucking Gary dressed up as a ghost!' shouted Wendy, causing angry and disappointed groans to emanate from parts of the room.

Although clearly angered by having her story ruined, Mandy continued with the fairly obvious anecdote. I admired her for it.

'Anyway, I hear this banging coming from a built-in cupboard—oh, I forgot to mention that Gary had told me earlier that the doctor had murdered his family with a hammer. Anyway, this banging sounded really like a hammer.'

'It's Gary,' groaned Wendy in an incompetent imitation of the 'Here's Johnny' quote from the film *The Shining*. 'Ooh, I'm *so* frightened!'

I heard Carter, who was standing behind her, on stage, say, off-mic, 'Ok.' He then motioned with his hands for Mandy to give him the microphone. Taking hold of the device, he stepped forward and cleared his throat.

'Look, whatever your name is,' he addressed Wendy directly, 'if you don't want to stay, why don't you leave? You're ruining it for everyone.'

At these words, a tumultuous collective cheer erupted in the room. While the ruckus was still decaying, the flatulent noise came over the PA system once more and this caused further laughter.

Carter turned around to Mandy and offered her the microphone. Mandy was done. With a resigned smile on her face, she shook her head and then, eschewing the use of the mic, shouted: 'Happy Birthday Gary! I hope you have another fifty years!'

To this there was another resounding cheer.

I thought it a prudent decision, on Mandy's part, to conclude her speech. Although Wendy's spoiling tactics had been both bullying and disrespectful, I felt that most people in the room were relieved that Mandy's well-meaning but bland roast had been brought to an end.

I looked over to Wendy's booth during the celebration, and noticed the two Stella security personnel, Steve and Megan, conversing forcefully with Team Wendy. They were being given 'notice'.

'Ok, ok,' Carter began to quell the boisterous attendees. 'Can we have a bit of quiet? The next person who's going to speak is Laird. Is Laird here?'

I was confused. Laird, like me, had never shown the slightest interest in participating in any of the pub's events. He pulled from his suit pocket a crumpled sheet of notepaper and, having risen to his feet, strode confidently towards the stage, bumping shoulders with several patrons along the way. Normally he conducted himself furtively, preferring to work his misanthropy from the sidelines; here he was now, basking in the spotlight!

He grabbed the mic out of Carter's hands. Athough he was smiling, his expression in no way conveyed to me that what he was about to say would be funny.

'Ok, lady,' he began, pointing at Wendy, 'one more word out of you and you and your friends are gonna be out on the footpath.' There was a hint of an American accent to his speech.

'Fuck off!' returned Wendy.

'I mean it.'

'So do I!' There was sniggering at Wendy's brilliant comeback. Laird probably thought about continuing the dialogue with her, but decided to forge on with his prepared speech

'Ok. Now then, Gary, where are you? I can't see you.'

'He's over there!' Someone shouted, pointing towards the far-right wall of the pub.

Sure enough, Gary was there, seated on a stool, looking miserable. Laird waved at him. Gary remained sitting with his hands folded in his lap, staring.

'Firstly, congratulations Gary, for all the fucking oxygen you've breathed in, and all the waste material you've produced.' By any measure this was a 'strong' opening. The room fell silent. 'It was strange hearing about that ghost story you told your old girlfriend.'

'I wasn't his girlfriend,' said Mandy from somewhere in the crowd.

'Shut up whoever you are,' said Laird. His blunt retort elicited whoops from certain members of the crowd—those who sensed that something vaguely resembling a roast was now underway.

'Yes Gary,' continued Laird, 'it was strange that you of all people should be going around telling tales of murder.'

Laird paused, allowing his words to take effect, which they did. I and, no doubt, many other people in the room began to wonder where Laird was taking this. Things seemed to be escalating beyond the boundaries of good-natured insult comedy.

'Strange that!' Laird clicked his tongue and tilted his head jauntily. He was clearly enjoying the attention of the crowd. 'Just wondering if you could tell us all how many children you've got *now* Gary. How many, that is, on the last count?'

Carter now realised where this was going and began to shake his head ostentatiously. Under his breath, he muttered: 'oh man!'

Most of Gary's friends would have known what Laird was alluding to. Fifteen years earlier, Megan, Gary's wife, had, while intoxicated, accidently caused the drowning death of their three-month old daughter while bathing her. I cannot here do justice, with words, to the enormity of the tragedy that befell Gary and his family—to do so would risk a massive diversion away from the task at hand; that being to shed more light on why I dislike Laird. Readers will have to make do with this rather stark, abbreviated version of events.

Carter attempted to grab the microphone from Laird's hands, however Laird managed to hold him at bay and keep his voice broadcast over the public-address system.

'Or perhaps you could tell us all how many kids you started with. Eh Gary? How many was that?'

I looked over at Gary who was cradling his head in his hands.

'Get off!' shouted Mandy.

'Bring it on!' a female voice shouted. It was Bronwyn. This didn't surprise me.

Carter managed to get Laird in a sort of bear hug, from behind. Laird, bent forward and managed to keep the microphone close to his mouth.

He began to sing.

'I'm gonna have myself a good old bath
And wash my blues away
Rub a dub dub gonna let my old tub
Wash my baby away . . .

There were a few people in the crowd who began to sing along to the Bunk Thompson classic. I hoped they were ignorant of the awful subtext the context of the roast had lent to it.

The singalong was cut short by Carter who was finally able to successfully wrest the microphone from Laird's hands, thus bringing to an end the speech.

'It's a fucking roast isn't it?' Laird shouted as he was shoved backwards, courtesy of a firm shoulder bump from Carter.

I was curious to see what effect all this was having on Gary. I watched as he rose from the chair and walked slowly to the bar.

I swung my attention back towards the stage where Laird was conducting a spirited conversation with several members of the audience, explaining to them that it was a 'fucking roast' and 'just a bit of fun'.

Laird had placed himself in a dangerous situation. Many people in the room were very angry, and for good reason. He must have predicted this. Or was he so deluded that he thought his speech had comic value? I was more intrigued by the grotesquery of Laird's solipsism than worried by the possibility that he might be seriously injured.

In all the confusion, no one noticed that Gary, now behind the bar, held in his hands the medium-sized, red fire extinguisher he'd been forced to purchase as part of a recent safety upgrade foisted upon him by the state government.

It was Bronwyn who tried to alert everyone that Gary was wielding a fire extinguisher.

'He's going to spray us!' she shouted.

Gary stood behind the bar, more or less in the centre, and swung the extinguisher hard at the closest of the two beer 'cobras'—the multi-fanged beer dispensers that stood mounted a metre apart on the bar top. He swung sideways and with the base of the extinguisher landed a blow to the centre of the shaft that bent it sideways. He pulled back and swung again, hitting the same spot, this time snapping the dispenser off at its base and rendering the plastic pull levers irrelevant. The ensuing fountain of beer that spurted freely from the now unstopped beer lines was both spectacular and, I assumed, expensive. Gary moved towards the second tap, looking very focused.

Carter was shouting over the PA. His pleas for calm were at odds with his demeanour.

Laird was now nowhere to be seen. He had left the building.

People began to gather around the bar and to hold out their empty schooner glasses, hoping to catch some of the fountaining beer that was on offer. I too joined the undignified scramble for free airborne lager.

Gary successfully bashed out the second cobra, however this time there was no resultant geyser of booze. I noticed that somewhere between the bashing of the first and second cobras, the stern and focussed expression on Gary's face had been replaced by a smiling and happy one. What had seemed at first to be a gesture of anger was now one of joyful celebration.

Gary had bashed his way into the party spirit!

The 'smashing of the beer taps' is now an established highlight in the oral history of the Stella Maris and many people have their own opinions about the meaning behind Gary's act of vandalism. On one level, it seems clear that Gary never wanted to have a fiftieth birthday roast—he was bullied into it by Carter, a man who seized on any opportunity to organise a celebration in order to plug the void in his own sad life. Gary's violent reaction can be seen then as an outlet for his anger; anger at Carter's insensitivity; and anger at the use, by Laird, of Gary's tragedy to stage a cowardly attack on him.

But there was another way to look at it—through the eyes of Gary, the *father*. Could not the smashing of the cobras signify the first public bar acknowledgment of the momentous happening that had so influenced his married life? Maybe Laird's overly vicious roast had somehow acted as a point of access to a final stage of the grieving process. Maybe the joyful look on Gary's face, as he set about destroying his own property, was brought about by feelings of relief; he'd finally turned the corner.

The act of smashing alcohol-conveying vessels holds strong kinship with other, well-accepted ceremonies such as those seen on postrace victory podia or at the launching of newly built boats. I believe that, with this act of pub vandalism, Gary was launching a new era in his life, in a profound and healthy way.

It was Wendy who first began to sing. Her abrasive voice lent to the innocent lyrics a sarcastic and unsettling nuance.

Happy Birthday to you
Happy Birthday to you
Happy Birthday dear Gary
Happy Birthday to you

It took only two lines of the song being sung before other people joined in. Very soon the whole crowd (except for me and probably Bronwyn) was singing. Carter chose to use the microphone and as a result, his amplified voice was the most prominent in the microtonal din of the happy, singing mob.

V

A long and expensive taxi ride bore me north eastwards, from the lower North Shore to the Northern Beaches, along the stretch of forest road known as the Wakehurst Parkway and then onwards through numerous ocean-side suburbs before depositing me outside the main entrance to the 'Northern Beaches Institute of Performing Arts'. It had been day when I'd left Lane Cove North; by journey's end it was night.

I'd come to attend the End of Term Final Presentations.

A large sign stood next to the entranceway, welcoming visitors and giving a brief history of the site. The NBIPA complex had taken over the grounds of a psychiatric hospital that had been decommissioned in the seventies due to a shift in medical culture from the use of institutional residential care to a more community-based approach.

Subsequent to the brief episode that was his marriage to my mother, my father had lived for several years in Mona Vale and so it was natural that my thoughts turned to him during the journey. In truth, I don't remember a great deal about my Dad; my chief memory was of a large, bearded person wearing a woman's one-piece bathing costume and pouring milk over his head. I would have been about two at the time.

After Mona Vale he left for South Australia to pursue an opal mining career in the remote community of Mintabie. At least that's the story my mother tells. I sometimes suspect this to be a fabrication, a myth whose function has been to place him in the rugged Australian outback and thus outside the realm of my suburban middle-class imagination. To a large extent this has worked.

My mother has always played her cards close to her chest whenever the subject of my dad comes up, and what little information she offers has never strayed far from her core belief that he was a failure of a man and that their marriage was nasty, brutish and short. The topic is normally brought to conclusion with the blunt suggestion that I should 'just forget about him'. I've more or less followed her advice. But sometimes I can't help but think about that afternoon with the milk and the fact that this is the only major visual memory I have of the man responsible for bringing me into the world.

I made my way across a carpark and then down a stone pathway that led to a glass-fronted, single-storied building that bore the name Sigley Theatre. In front of the theatre was a small queue of people waiting to gain entrance.

The door charge was $15 full price and $10 concession. The woman at the box-office refused to believe I was a mature age dance student who'd forgotten his student card. I paid the $15.

In the foyer, on a long table pushed against the front tinted glass wall, were various trays of cheap biscuits and bagged teas. There was also an elderly metal urn standing next to stacked columns of thin plastic cups and a catering-sized tub of instant coffee. I helped myself to a coffee even though the advertised price was an exorbitant $3 per cup. I took advantage of the honour system by depositing a one dollar coin into the coin jar.

The crowd that had gathered for the evening's performance was comprised mostly of family and friends—very close ones I assumed. In truth, I wasn't counting on much. My default expectation when it comes to the quality of entertainment at these sorts of events is one of pessimism.

The doors leading from the foyer to the performance space were still closed, due, we were told, to a last minute technical hitch.

I couldn't help but overhear an older man, who I presumed to be the father of one of the aspiring artists, talking to another man of similar age about the state of his son's future prospects. His colleague was nodding in robust agreement.

'Let's just hope he makes an arse of himself and gets this thing out of his system. It's Joan's fault we're in this. I said I'd allow him three years of a course and if nothing happened, then he'd at least have had a shot. I think that's fair.'

'Very fair,' said the other man who, with his right hand in his trouser pocket, jiggled some metal objects therein.

'Fucking expensive though.'

'Tell me about it.'

I was pretending to study a poster depicting the correct method of aiding a choking victim and so my back was turned away from the two interlocutors. The poster was housed in a glass frame and, owing to the reflection, I was able to get decent quality mirrored vision of the two men without them noticing.

'But it was Joan who encouraged him,' the first man continued. 'She insisted he have piano lessons. I wanted Ron Berry—you know Ron?'

'I know Ron.'

'Yeah, well I wanted Ron to listen to him play and give his opinion about whether it was worth spending any more money on it. But she said, no, Ron only knows about classical, he wouldn't know about jazz.' This last bit was pronounced with a mocking, prissy lisp. 'I wish I'd been firm about it.'

'Oh well what's done is done. I'm worried about Amber.' Again the man's right hand shook the objects in his trousers. At the mention of her name I began to be aware of a slight tightness in my throat. The man who had just spoken could be none other than Amber's father.

It was clear that Amber took after her mother in the looks department. 'Mr Amber' was bald and short. He looked like an ex-rug-by-union hooker. He was wearing a big-collared, cream-coloured suit, unbuttoned to reveal a black and green Hawaiian shirt whose fabric featured a repeating pattern depicting the flower and stem of some tropical plant. The shirt hung down, untucked, below Mr Amber's waistline so that one of the flowers affixed to a curved stem was positioned at the same coordinates of bodily latitude and longitude as his penis. He did himself no favours by scrimmaging with his hand amongst the stuff in the interior of his pants' pocket, an action that caused the printed flower to rise and fall.

The other man—the man worried about his son's jazz piano aspirations—wore a brown bomber jacket over a horizontally-striped blue and white polo shirt and jeans. White socks and brown sandals completed the ensemble.

'She's still going around with that prick Roderick—in fact he's teaching her! When she introduced him to us, about six months after they'd started whatever it is they've started, she omitted telling us that he was her teacher. I thought that sort of thing was illegal.'

'Only in high-school I'm afraid!'

'She'll grow out of it, I hope,' said Mr Amber, sounding hopeless.

'So do I.'

I noticed that Mr Amber was in no way furtive in his speech. It was as if he wanted everyone in his vicinity to hear his views about the current state of his daughter's life-style.

'At least we got her back from Nimbin.'

'Christ yes!'

'Hi Steven! Is Gordon boasting about our Amber again?' It was a woman's voice. She had come up from behind the khaki-clad man so that he now turned suddenly, and nervously, to face her.

She moved into the frame of vision afforded by the reflective glass frame of the choking poster and, in profile, I made out a clear similarity with Amber.

'Hello Marian,' said Mr non-Amber. 'Nice to see you.'

'Nice to see you too Steven.'

'Eavesdropping were you darling?' said Mr Amber, who presumably was also Gordon.

'I didn't have to. I could hear you over at the coffee urn. Please try and show some sensitivity.'

Gordon took a deep breath, causing the shoulders of his suit coat to rise, and looked at the carpet. The jiggling of the contents in his pocket increased with Marian's arrival.

'Gordon, this is very important to Amber. I told you not to come if you were going to be like this.' It was Marian now who was speaking loud so that every word was intelligible to anyone interested.

Clearly Gordon was stuck between hating the lifestyle that Amber had chosen and not wanting to be seen as unsupportive. He was there because he felt he had to be—probably like most of the parents gathered in the foyer.

The volume and clear enunciation of Marian's remarks were embarrassing him. I could see in the glass that he was trying to use his facial muscles—by way of exaggerated smiling—to convey to her that now was not the time to have an argument. I sensed, even though no eyes were overtly looking at the three parents, that the half-dozen or so other people standing about were intently listening to every word, just as I was. Gordon's only outlet for the release of the pressure building inside him was the rattling of his pocketed belongings that caused the floral genitalia on his shirt to leap upwards and outwards from his groin.

Marian, sensing that she had her husband trapped between his rage and public restraint, drove home her advantage.

'You always do this. Can't you for once think of someone else.'

'Yes Marian,' whispered Gordon filling the utterance with as much passive venom as he could under the circumstances.

Steven lent his earnest telepathic support to his brother in arms.

'Hi Mum! Hi Dad!' It was Amber. She was wearing her costume which consisted of a huge and grubby blonde wig—in the style of Marie Antoinette—and a ruined silk ball gown adorned with blood coloured stains and holes where chunks of fabric had been cut out. Trimmings of grubby lace completed the garment. Her face was coloured white except for small patches of skin where blotches of purples and reds inaccurately depicted various sizes of boil. On her feet she wore grimy pink ballet slippers. A plastic meat cleaver was stuck blade-first at a point just below the nape of her neck. As she waited for a response to her greeting she fanned herself nervously with a battered hand fan.

It was strange she would show herself made-up in the foyer of the auditorium just before her performance. Maybe this was the contemporary way of doing things; a clever ploy to remove the barriers between audience and performer.

I couldn't help but find her costume a little ostentatious and clichéd. I felt embarrassed for her—a feeling not all that unpleasant.

'Hello darling,' said Marian, 'you look great!'

'Yes,' stated Gordon evenly.

'I just came out to say hello. I think I'm second on so I can't stay talking for long.'

'When will the doors open?' asked Gordon. 'My legs are getting stiff from all this standing around.'

'They're just doing the final focus for the lights.'

Amber turned and saw my reflection in the pane of glass. We made eye contact. Her face exhibited no discernible signs of recognition. I turned around and waved my right hand. Her blank expression shifted to one of confusion as I began to walk towards her.

'Oh hello! You made it,' she said. It was clear she had no idea who I was.

'Hi!' I said trying to smile.

The three older people looked at me. At first the various expressions on their faces followed clear gender lines; the men showed embarrassment at the prospect of the recent argument having been overheard by a stranger who knew Amber. Marian, naturally protective of her daughter, and possibly bearing a sub-conscious grudge against all men of my age, looked more malevolent. Nevertheless, they all forced a smile at my greeting.

'Gordon Lockhart.' Gordon's hand shot out to make tactile connection. I could tell he was relieved that the unpleasant situation with his wife had been interrupted, but this was a minor influence on what was otherwise a hostile vibe.

'Geoff. Geoff Maddox,' I replied, grasping his hand in a suitably manly fashion. 'Glad to meet you!' My voice, having not been called upon to speak in the last 16 hours was a high-pitched rasp. I was reminded of an evening once at the Stella involving a canister of helium gas that Laird had stolen from a party supply shop.

'Hi I'm Marian, Gordon's wife,' said Marian. 'Do you have off-spring on the stage today as well?'

'No.'

'Oh so you're a teacher then.'

'No. Actually I'm not.'

I had to think fast. 'I'm very interested in the arts . . . ' I swallowed hard, 'especially student productions, because they're our future.' This was a poor effort and it met with the silence it deserved.

'How do you know Amber?' asked Gordon after the short but uncomfortable period of time had elapsed.

'Oh, we met the other night at the Stella Maris Hotel,' I said. Although it was Gordon's question, my reply was directed at Amber.

'I really should be getting back-stage,' said Amber.

We all wished her luck. Steven even offered a 'break a leg!' to which Amber humorously replied 'I hope not!'

We stood among the milling guests, waiting quietly for the doors to the theatre to open while Gordon's right hand rummaged among the objects in his pocket. After thirty seconds, I decided to go and get another instant coffee.

*

I chose to sit on my own near the back-right corner of the auditorium. The population of the hall varied greatly in size from act to act—with parents and friends exiting the room straight away upon the completion of their particular artist's segment. This was the case with Gordon and Marian.

Amber's performance 'utilised parody in a send up of seventies horror film culture to examine notions of gender and class'—at least that's what it said in the program deposited on the seats. Whispered vocals, plucked acoustic guitars, a hand-played drum and what sounded like a toy piano provided ghostly background music as Amber bashed a doll, head-first, against the side of a school desk. It lasted for about ten minutes and was the best act I saw that night.

I found it difficult to focus though. I was stung by the obvious lack of an impression I'd made on Amber. What the fuck was I doing here? Had I really travelled all the way to Mona Vale to make contact with a woman twenty years my junior who couldn't remember having met me? Why should she remember? Why should anyone?

There were two more acts after Amber's—one involving some fairly ordinary break-dancing, the other a *Swan Lake* style ballet duet between a man and a woman set to a John Howard speech.

By the time the interval arrived, I'd had enough. I decided to make a beeline through the foyer, out the front doors and across the car park to the main road and the steady stream of taxis that would be making their way south towards the city.

My hopes that the dimly lit car park would facilitate an unseen escape were soon dashed when I saw Roderick packing the boot of a Hyundai Getz with what looked to be photographic equipment. Amber was standing next to him, still in costume. He looked up and made eye contact with me.

'Hey! It's you! Thanks for coming!' beamed Roderick. He meant it—the 'you' part at least. It was clear he'd remembered me from the Stella.

'Not at all. It was great! I really enjoyed it. I'm Geoff, by the way.'

'Yeah, I know,' said Roderick. 'Geoff, the chip guy.' The offense I would normally have taken at the pejorative moniker, was attenuated by his having recognized me. Still, it stung.

Amber took a deep moist breath through her nose. She either

had a cold or had been crying. I suspected the latter and the dark tracks left by mascara stained tears on her cheeks confirmed my suspicion.

'Well I'm glad someone did,' she mused stoically.

'Had a bit of a family blow-up,' explained Roderick.

'Oh? No . . . I thought it was fantastic. Very funny!' I said.

'There, you see,' said Roderick, his right hand motioning to me, palm upwards, 'here's some *real* feedback!'

'I guess my family didn't think much of my stage debut,' explained Amber, looking me hard in the eyes, searching for evidence of disingenuousness in my praise. I stood my ground and stared back. I wondered if she'd managed to recall who I was yet.

'It was really good,' I said, with as much conviction as I could muster.

'What are you doing now?' asked Roderick.

'I was just going to get a cab home.'

'Why don't you come with us? We're going back to Newtown.'

'Yes, come with us!' enthused Amber.

*

Dark foliage encaved the sinuous forest road. I sat in the back as Roderick drove the vehicle along the twisting bitumen of the Wakehurst Parkway back towards the city. The air inside the car was thick with the smoke from the cigarette Amber and Roderick were sharing.

No one was talking.

I decided to change that.

'Apparently this was built by the Americans.' I had to shout to be heard from the back seat.

'What was?' asked Amber, twisting around in her seat so as to look at me over her shoulder.

'This road.'

I often use trivia to impress and I thought this anecdote would do the trick.

'This road?' asked Amber, in a tone that implied it was a revelation to her that roads needed to be built.

'Yes, during World War Two,' I continued. 'The Americans built it in about six weeks, apparently.'

'That's not right,' interjected Roderick, one hand on the steering wheel, the other holding the cigarette he intermittently presented to his mouth. 'The building didn't start till 1946. It was named after John de Vere Loder, the Baron Wakehurst, who was Governor of NSW in the thirties.'

I was begrudgingly impressed by his knowledge of the Parkway.

I watched as Roderick handed the cigarette over to Amber.

We drove on for a bit.

'Have you ever seen the ghost of Wakehurst Parkway?' I asked, a mock sinister tone to my voice that embarrassed me. I knew I was trying too hard, for a purpose I wasn't entirely cognisant of.

'Ghost?' said Amber, a note of girlish excitement to her delivery. A mist of tobacco smoke accompanied the word.

'A small girl,' I said, eager to continue the fun. 'Apparently, a young girl stands by the side of the road in her night gown holding a lamp, luring motorists to ... '

The guitar introduction to Neil Young's 'Cortez the Killer' cut short my supernatural tale. Roderick had switched the CD player on, loud.

'This is my favourite guitar solo!' yelled Amber as she turned back to face the windscreen. She put her feet up against the glove box, pushed herself back into the chair, and began to sing along, seriously out of tune.

*

The front entrance to the small terrace house was protected by two doors. The first was a military grade security door made of thick black steel, covered with fly screen. The second, a normal wooden door, was the one that had originally been built for the house. I watched as Roderick opened them both and then stood aside, allowing Amber to pass.

'Do come in,' he said, in a bad upper-class British accent. He bowed his head and waved me through with a flourish of his hands. I could hear Amber milling around in the kitchen at the far end of the house.

'I've just got to get a few things out of the boot of the car,' he said, before going back out to the street.

I entered, feeling nervous.

A three-metre-long hallway ran down the right-hand side of the house. On the left, a metre or so from the entrance, was a door to a small front room. This was closed. The hallway continued past this door before opening onto a living room. A steep wooden staircase, running along the left-hand wall of the room, led up to a second floor. Several metres in front of the foot of the stairs, two narrow French doors opened onto a courtyard.

Butted up against the right wall was a large wooden table that bore the scars of having been used as a workbench. On the table was an impressive scattering of loose papers, numerous empty Humes tubes, several ash trays—in various states of fulfilment—and a smallish flat screen television set. Three unmatching wooden dining chairs stood haphazardly around the TV. On the carpet beneath one of the chairs was a small blue feather. Opposite the table, in an alcove formed by the intersection of two walls and the underside of the staircase, was a grubby blue sofa bed.

I would have called the colour of the carpet gravy.

Sometime in the past a permanent opening had been bashed out of the back wall of the living room in order to allow door-free access to the kitchen; it was here where the house narrowed, giving it an over-all 'd' shape and allowing for the courtyard outside to exist with reasonable width. The positioning of this entrance meant that I had to walk around the wooden table in the living room in order to get to the kitchen.

Against the right-hand wall of the kitchen stood a small, square Formica table; several ashtrays and scraps of official looking papers were scattered on its surface. Two wooden school chairs made up the dining set.

Standing with its back to the wall that separated the kitchen from the living room was an off-white electrical stove, its chipped and dis-coloured enamel testament to many decades of rough handling. As I crossed over the threshold from the living room, Amber was busy placing an old kettle on the one ring of the stovetop that appeared sound, the other three having collapsed inward.

'Would you like some Chamomile tea?' she asked.

'That'd be great, thanks.'

The kitchen floor was six inches lower than the sitting room and as I turned back towards the front of the house, I noticed that the absence of a skirting board under the step enabled a view back into the darkness of the foundations.

'Nice house.'

I sat down on one of the chairs and felt it 'give' a little under the strain.

'Thanks.'

'How long have you been here?'

'I moved in about six months ago.'

'I wonder how old these places are,' I said.

'This was built in the early 1800s—I'm pretty sure that's what my father said. He knows about that sort of thing. He owns it actually.'

'Is it heritage listed?'

'I don't know.'

Satisfied that the stove was heating the kettle, Amber turned to face me. She stood with her back resting against the front of the stove.

'Yes, it was a great night tonight,' I said. 'The quality of the performances was very high.'

'Thanks Geoff. It means a lot to me.' She cast her eyes down to the floor, took a a deep breath, then raised them and looked me straight in the eye. 'My father doesn't agree with you.'

'Oh?'

'He doesn't really support me in my dancing.'

'Oh?'

'He's got this thing about Roderick.'

'Oh?'

'You talking about your old man?' It was Roderick. He'd finished unpacking the car and was now striding across the living room.

'I guess so.'

'He's a fuckwit is Amber's dad,' announced Roderick cheerfully, this time in a faux cockney accent, as he stepped down into the kitchen.

'Rod, that's my father you're talking about!' said Amber in what I took to be mock umbrage.

'Well he is!'

They both laughed and I tried to join in even though I was unable to comprehend the bulk of the subtext.

'Anyway,' said Roderick, after the laughter had subsided. 'What have you, sir, been up to?' It occurred to me that Roderick's high spirits might be chemically induced.

'Oh, this and that.'

Roderick sat down on the vacant chair and began to talk about Amber's performance. A lot of what he said I took to be 'critical theory', chiefly because he used the term frequently in explaining her 'practice'. Critical theory was something I'd heard Bronwyn bang on about at the Stella, so it rang a bell and slightly lessened my feelings of intimidation.

Presently, Amber came over and placed my cup of herbal tea on the table.

'Thanks,' I said.

She returned to stand once more with her back against the stove.

'Do your parents often come to your performances?' I asked her.

'Hey, let's not talk about them anymore tonight,' said Roderick.

Whatever it was that Gordon Lockhart had said to his daughter after the performance must have been nasty.

After several awkward exchanges with me about unusually high winter temperatures, Roderick steered the conversation towards the incompetence of the middle-management at the NBIPA. But his voice faded into the background as my thoughts became more and more fixated on Amber's familial situation. My physical attraction to her was now being joined by something more powerful, more emotional. The idea of her abandonment by her own family was intoxicating and I became awestruck by her fearlessness and independence.

With this combination of physical attraction and awe, I passed a tipping point. I was falling in love.

I needed to bring my attention back to the conversation. Roderick had changed tack and was now talking about Patrice Lumumba, the first post-independence leader of the Democratic Republic of Congo who was executed in the early sixties. He was becoming quite passionate in his description of the corruption surrounding the event, but all I could think of was Amber and her lonely sacrifice for self-expression. Fragmented thoughts of a future whereby I provided the proper means by which Amber could fulfil her dreams on the big stages of Australia were crowding my mind.

'Well what do you think?' he said.

I deduced he was referring to some instance of egregious human rights abuse.

'It's complicated,' I extemporised, hoping to tread water until the subject of the question became less ambiguous.

'It's *complicated*? Of course it's fucking complicated! And it'll get more complicated unless people do something about it! Jesus!'

'Honey!' Amber admonished.

I'd been shaken out of my dream state by his outburst. It didn't surprise me that Roderick was politically passionate, but the level of his anger seemed unreasonable. Was he overtired? Were the drugs wearing off? Was he projecting onto me the anger caused by the negativity of Amber's family?

Or was there the possibility that ol' Rodders was jealous of me? Was he freaking out because he'd become aware that Amber had taken my fancy?

'Nobody fucking cares!' said Roderick.

I decided to keep quiet and let the thing blow over.

'Sometimes you can be very arrogant Rod.' Amber was taking my side and I was liking it.

Roderick rose to his feet.

'I'm going to bed.'

Nobody said a word. Roderick left the kitchen and walked into the living room. I heard his footsteps as he trod the steps of the staircase on his way to the first floor where I assumed the bedroom was. Amber moved towards the now vacant chair and sat down. We remained silent, listening to the sounds of Roderick's final preparations for sleep taking place above us.

After a suitable time had elapsed I spoke.

'You shouldn't take your parents' comments too much to heart. You've got the talent to rise above them.'

I was troubled by the tone of voice I'd felt compelled to adopt. It was one of cloying sympathy, a mushy compassion that was far from the rugged cynicism I felt should be displayed in the company of a women I desired.

'That's so sweet of you Geoff,' said Amber whose words were as liquid gold flowing through my spine. 'I've tried to turn my life around with dance. A year ago I was up in Nimbin—I don't want to go into that—but now, I feel I'm actually *doing* something for once.'

Her eyes sparkled, a glint caused by the nexus of emotion and the reflected light from the fluorescent bulb fixed to the ceiling. I noticed too that her voice had begun to break. I became aware of a subtle shifting of the nerves in the vicinity of my lap.

'My father just doesn't respect what I've achieved. Roderick's going to give me a high distinction for my performance tonight.' I felt a constriction somewhere in my stomach at the mention of these words. 'Which means I'll be able to do honours next semester.'

'Wow that's great!'

'But dad, he just laughs at it.'

Her breathing had become heavier. She was on the verge of tears.

Now was my big chance! I rose from the chair. I stood up and gestured with my arms for her to do the same. That she shook her head should have made it obvious that the manoeuvre ought to have been aborted instantly. Instead I chose to ram home my perceived advantage and use the ambiguity that compassion affords to establish a beachhead from where I could better conduct my campaign.

Maybe, with hindsight, I'm being way too hard on myself. Sometimes I think I was genuinely affected by Amber's predicament and thus I shouldn't cast myself in the role of the insensitive and sleazy chancer implied by the above paragraph. Also, it had been many years since I'd enjoyed the companionship of a woman and maybe my gauge wasn't properly calibrated. Still, I should have waited until firmer ground had been reached before commencing my march across the marshlands of romance!

It's all academic now.

Having stood up, I chose to ignore her shaking head and bent down so as to attempt the encirclement of her upper body with my comforting arms.

I was hoping to be able to perform a full, life-affirming hug with my forearms rubbing together somewhere midway between her hind shoulders. This simple hope met with almost immediate failure as she pushed me back violently, using her hands with their palms hard against my chest.

I heard the growl of the chair legs on the kitchen floor as they scraped backwards, obeying simple Newtonian physics. I too was propelled backwards, towards the worn chipboard of the kitchen bench.

She rose up out of her chair. Her sad face morphed swiftly to bewilderment and on into anger.

I took several steps towards her, my hands adopting a beseeching attitude.

'Don't!' She thrust her right hand out before her as a reinforcement of the word.

'I'm sorry! I didn't mean to.'

'Go! Now! Get the fuck out of my house you fucking moron!'

I obeyed, slinking shamefaced out through the living room to the street, all the while apologising profusely.

I heard the front door of the house slam behind me and headed for the main road, hoping to snag a north-bound taxi.

While walking, I began to predict the flood of self-loathing that would inevitably swamp me. It then occurred to me that the prediction *itself* might be the first wave of this loathing. Focussing on this observation was distracting and thus palliative; I realised that by so doing, I was stopping the prediction of self-loathing from becoming self-loathing. To my surprise this secondary observation had a similar effect, providing me with a further buffer before the onslaught of serious, inward-directed criticism arrived.

But not for long. By the time I managed to hail a taxi, I was a whimpering mess.

For the entire journey, the taxi's radio was on and tuned to a late night talk-back show. The driver had set the volume of the radio so low there were only isolated pockets of intelligibility caused by the raising of the shock jock's voice to utter words like 'idiots' or 'clowns'. I sat in the back, snivelling. I kept repeating, mantra like, the short sentence:

I want to die. I spoke it under my breath in order that it be masked by the sound of the car's motor. *I want to die. I want to die . . .*

*

The driver pulled up in front of our building. I thrust my arm between the two front bucket seats, my hand clutching a 50-dollar bill. The driver took the money.

'Keep the change,' I said.

'Thanks.'

I began to work the doorhandle.

'Hey mate,' said the driver, looking back at me through the gap between the seat and the driver's side window. 'It's going to be alright, you'll see.'

This only made matters worse. Here was a cabbie selflessly providing me with much needed emotional support—how this contrasted with my slimy come-on in Amber's kitchen!

'Thank you,' I said and got out of the cab.

*

I stood on the balcony for a moment, looking at the front door of the flat. I unlocked it, pushed it open and moved inside. It felt strange to be returning home at this hour of the night so sure of foot. Normally I would have been in a state of moderate to severe intoxication.

I lay on my back on the sofa breathing hard and contemplating the various forms that my suicide could take. After a while I became aware that I was finding soothing diversion in the perusal of the options. I fired up the computer in my bedroom and began to research the topic on the internet. One link led to another and I ended up looking at videos of cats playing with scorpions.

Sometime before dawn, I crawled into bed. I lay in the foetal position with my head covered by blankets and allowed the vessel of unconsciousness to ferry me far away from my hideous night.

PART 2

A Simple Binary Relationship

I

Although the catastrophe with Amber was the most emotionally
tumultuous event of my recent adult life, it was by no means the
only show in town. When I awoke on that Thursday afternoon, my
mind was occupied with thoughts of my mother. Had I truly crossed
a line by standing my ground over the balloon incident—a line that
separated my familiar old life from a frightening new one devoid of
maternal support?

Adding to this anxiety, I'd had a curious dream wherein I was
standing outdoors on some sort of path, in what I understood to be
Centennial Park. For reasons unknown, I'd been handling a *Bic* biro
which I'd accidently dropped on the ground. When I bent over to pick
it up, I noticed, out of the corner of my eye, another biro lying nearby.
The dream concluded with me pocketing both the original dropped
pen and this newly found one. Basically, I had gained a pen. What did
this symbolise?

'Could mean anything,' said Laird.

We were seated at one of the tables in *Muffin Siesta*'s exclusive
dining area. The time was 2.30pm. It was Friday. One and a half days
now separated me from the Northern Beaches Institute evening.

Laird had been working the NRMA branch on the third floor of
the mall. I'd just come from a lengthy discussion with Julie at *Drench'd*
concerning the pros and cons of silicon egg poachers.

'The path could mean a woman's vagina,' said Laird.

I should have known this would be his default interpretation for the presence of any object in any dreamscape.

'Uptown Girl' by Billy Joel was vaguely audible, blown about the interior of the mall by invisible speakers.

'I wouldn't worry about it,' advised Laird. 'I myself haven't had a dream for five years.'

'You've probably had them but just can't remember them.'

'I'm pretty sure I'd know if I had,' he said.

'You know who I saw down here the other day?' I said.

Laird shook his head.

'Jock Williams.'

'Yeah?'

'He tried to make out he wasn't Jock Williams. But I knew it was him.'

'That's someone I *definitely* don't want to see again!'

The sentence—particularly the way he'd said the word 'definitely'—jarred. It wasn't an adverb I'd heard him use much; it sounded polite, throwaway, as if he didn't really care. I'd expected a more expletive laden response.

'Uptown Girl' had reached the instrumental section. It occurred to me that the song was so massive a hit that it lacked the ability to transport the listener back to the period of time in which it had been a contemporary cultural product. It had been a hit, it had remained a hit and it would always be a hit—it was impervious to nostalgia.

However, no sooner had I reached that conclusion than I began to think about my own life and what it had been like back in 1983, which kind of contradicted my first assertion. I was still at high school; not yet able to fully appreciate that there was no such thing as an even playing field; yet to come to the realisation that I might never find a woman with whom I could build a life. This last 'yet' brought me back to the disastrous embrace of Amber. Were there forces at play I was unaware of—forces that had required me to push her out of my life? Because surely that's what I'd done. Maybe deep down I didn't want to . . .

'Hey!'

It was Laird and he was clicking his thumb and forefinger in the air in front of my face. He was annoyed by my absence from the conversation and lack of overt appreciation for whatever thought jewels he was offering up.

'I reckon,' he continued, 'that the better looking someone is, the worse they can smell.'

Classy stuff. Thankfully my inattention had shielded me from the finer points of his reasoning. I'd been lucky to have switched off. I should also point out that he was dressed in cream-coloured slacks and some sort of cricket jumper. His scrawny and unpleasant face had combined with his attire to affect a cross between Barry Manilow and Charles Manson.

'Anyway, I've got to go to the city,' he said rising to his feet. 'I'm due at the British High Commission in twenty minutes.'

'Happy hunting!' I said, my pleasure at his imminent departure put to work in the guise of friendly good wishes.

'Thanks.'

*

I stood on the ground floor at the foot of the escalator. The mall was busy. Shoppers shuffled to and fro across the huge shiny floor space.

My thoughts returned to Amber and the botched pass—or was it a botched pass? Maybe I *did* have only altruistic reasons for my actions. I see-sawed between two visions of myself: on the one hand, I was the opportunist sensing an advantage to be gained through another's emotional vulnerability; on the other I was a friend whose outstretched hand of support had been misinterpreted by someone with scant knowledge of the true 'me'.

I was suddenly gripped with the desire to write, to put down on paper the reasons for why I had acted as I had. I needed to explain, as much for myself as to Amber, that my behaviour had been motivated by altruism. Yes, I would write Amber a letter. Even if it met with cold hatred, it would make me feel better about myself and provide much needed closure.

A feeling of relief flooded through me—beautiful, uplifting relief. I felt my face break into a smile. I even began to whistle along to 'Uptown Girl'.

But, rather than bask in this relief, I knew I needed to focus my attention elsewhere, lest I overthought things and, by way of mood swing, talked myself out of writing the letter. This was easy. I shifted my thoughts to the home front—namely the cold war with my mother.

Due to a combination of her work hours at Class Axe and my current lifestyle, we hadn't spoken since Sky's birthday party. Buoyed by this lack of communication, I'd had time to come around to the opinion that her threat of eviction was an empty one. For her to make good on it would require a fundamental change in her basic character. My mother blames herself for my lack of direction and the only way she can assuage her guilt over the 'botch up' (her words) that was my maturation is to sacrifice and provide. This is the only logical framework within which her existence can operate.

It hasn't always been so, but with the passing of the years, things have worsened and what used to be a natural—if at times inappropriate—maternal generosity has grown into something resembling self-abasement. Her martyrdom carries with it a parasympathetic anger towards the very thing (me) whose 'stunting' she is striving to atone for. As a result, also present in the mix is a desire to punish me, chiefly through shaming me. There's a toxic circularity at work here whereby the more she punishes herself, the more she experiences loathing towards me. This loathing causes feelings of guilt in her which, in turn, power the need to sacrifice and provide for me by punishing herself, and so on.

Nonetheless a small part of me remained troubled by my mother's strong reaction to the balloon gaffe. Even though I now felt it highly unlikely I would find myself out on the streets, I thought it prudent to get some absolute certainty in the matter. What better way to facilitate burying the hatchet than by way of a sincere apology backed up with a store-bought gift? A gift for the gift giver!

*

I arrived at the *Le Chien Qui Dort*—a pop-up cosmetics shop on the lower ground floor of the mall.

The shop consisted of a trestle table covered in glamorous black fabric and a two-meter-high backdrop, also covered in black. The woman behind the table eyed me suspiciously. She clearly remembered the last time I'd visited the stall—several weeks earlier—when we'd enjoyed a conversation concerning Tartrazine in lipstick.

'I'd like to buy some of this moisturiser for my mother, as a present.' I pointed towards a tube of *Le Chien Qui Dort Moisturizer* lying on the table. It had clearly been used to provide samples for potential buyers.

'Of course, sir.'

'Yes. I'll take a small tube with me now. Do you wrap?'

'We don't physically sell the product here.'

'Oh?'

'You order and pay for it here, but we don't keep any stock on the premises. This is a zero-stock, pop up store.'

This innovative retail method threw me. I stood ruminating for several seconds.

'How about this tube? Can I purchase this?' I pointed to the sample tube lying on the counter. Although the mid-section of the tube bore noticeable indentations from the thumbs and forefingers of previous shoppers, with a bit of patient kneading I stood a good chance of getting it to look like a new tube that had been scuffed around a bit in transit back to the flat. I estimated it to be two-thirds full.

The woman looked a little confused. Eventually she nodded.

'How much?' I asked

'$29.99.'

This was the retail price for a new tube.

I handed over my credit card and wrote my address on the order form

'What will you use for the samples then?' I asked as she handed me the receipt.

'I'll use this new tube.' She bent down and rummaged in what I took to be a box underneath the table. She emerged holding a new tube of moisturizer which she placed on the table.

'Why can't I buy this one?' I asked.

'Because it's new.'

I won't give a blow by blow account of the discussion that now took place. It was a discussion that survived numerous interruptions by other customers and several walkaways and returns by me. Suffice to say, the store manager wouldn't budge from her initial position. I did however persuade her to give me the screw top from the new tube to use on my second hand one, which was a victory of sorts.

I walked through the main entrance of the Mall and out on to the footpath. A cold wind hit my face and I experienced a sudden and strong change of heart. I dropped the tube in the nearest public rubbish bin. That'll fucking teach 'em, I thought. I wasn't going to give my mother a shop-worn piece of merchandise. She would have to make do with an apology. Without the aid of the lubricant, would I be able to slide back into her good books? My punning provoked a laugh, inside.

II

The tone had to be just right for my letter to Amber. Most importantly, it couldn't sound mawkish or cloying. I knew well, from experience, the danger inherent in the use of syrupy rhetoric, having caused several women to 'switch off' due to it. Indeed, the term 'sick puppy' has more than once been deployed to describe my demeanour when I've resorted to a beseechment-based method in the pursuance of romantic fulfilment—not that the situation here was necessarily romantic.

Nor did I want the letter to be devoid of sentiment, lest I come across as a person who didn't really give a fuck. The fact that I'd bothered to write in the first place would be viewed as *prima facie* evidence that I *did* give a fuck and an attempt on my part to play this down in writing would be viewed with suspicion.

I deduced from her emotional outburst in her house that it was hugely important for her to be taken seriously as an artist. Indeed, her father was jeopardising his relationship with his daughter by failing to support her in this. Her social world, I surmised, was split in two: on the one hand were those who didn't accept her as a talented performer; on the other hand were those who did—the former making the latter more attractive to her than might otherwise have been the case. It was a simple binary relationship that provided me with a tool to work with in order to regain her trust. I decided to aggressively praise her in her achievements as a dancer.

And so my letter began with gushing praise for the quality of her art:

Amber,
Just thought I'd write and say how much I enjoyed your performance last night at the concert. I was very much blown away—both by the ideas and concepts you're dealing with and also the quality of the execution with which you carried them out. Having been a performer myself, I know how difficult it can be to believe in oneself. I think you really owe it to the rest of us to continue to develop your craft (not that it could really get much better!) Well done.

That was the easy part. Now came the hard part, the 'business end' of the letter; the actual apology.

I also just want to say that I'm sorry if there was a misunderstanding with regards to the end of the night at your place. Please forgive me if I encroached upon your privacy—this certainly wasn't my intention! But . . .

here I felt the need for some noble words:

. . . if it so happens that things will be too awkward for us to be friends in the future because of it, there's not a lot I can say. Please believe in yourself and your talent!
Say hi to Roderick.
Geoff

Rest assured readers this was not a one-draft, off-the-cuff jotting. What is printed above was the result of a sustained undertaking of writing and re-writing. I agonised over it, typing version after version of the missive, pushing words around, deleting whole paragraphs and fine-tuning the sentences so that they'd have the desired effect.

One hitch I encountered was to do with the decision to finish the letter off with, 'Say hi to Roderick.' A lot of the rewrites alternated between the inclusion and exclusion of this request. On one hand I thought it displayed a fraternal affection. It said: 'I know you are already in a relationship, but you know what? I don't care! My affection is not about *that*! It's more of a spiritual thing.' On the other hand, this 'fraternalism' could unnecessarily close off an avenue that may, under possible future circumstances, become open. In and out it went as I struggled to find stasis with a firm decision. Eventually I flipped a coin! (I think I'd have put it in anyway regardless of the outcome of the toss.)

It was important that the actual letter be handwritten. I used the Eversharp Skyline fountain pen that had belonged to my mother's father. I was named after him and as a consequence, the initials 'G.M.' (my initials) were already engraved on the side—a rare instance where my mother's lack of imagination had paid off.

It took me a few goes to render a mistake-free copy of the letter in copybook cursive but when it was finished I thought it looked magnificent.

I folded the sheet of paper carefully and slid it into the envelope.

I looked at the blank envelope in my hands.

I didn't have her mailing address.

I knew where she lived of course, but I didn't know the name of the street or the house number. Sure, I could walk the letter over and place it in the letterbox myself but, should I be observed, it would display an over-eagerness very damaging to my cause. The last thing I needed was to come across as being too full on and scare her off. No, it was much better to play it cool.

I tore the envelope down the middle, placed the two resultant pieces together and tore again. I then tore the four pieces I'd made and threw the confetti into the air. As the dismal rain fell around me I shouted *'fuuuuck!'* loud enough to be heard by other inhabitants in the apartment block.

Readers may find it unbelievable that I should spend so much time constructing a handwritten letter and forget I didn't have an address to which to post it. You'll just have to trust me. It was a case of getting too carried away and losing focus; of being too busy looking after the creative part of an undertaking and not paying enough attention to the nuts and bolts.

They say necessity is the mother of invention, well, in this instance it proved to be the mother of recollection. I suddenly remembered the business card Amber had handed me at the Stella. It said something about her being a movement something-or-other; maybe it had her contact details as well.

The pair of jeans I'd worn that night lay with other items of clothing in a pile on the floor between the bed and the window. Fortunately, my mother hadn't yet removed them for washing. I began rifling through the pockets and found it straight away, bent slightly, alongside Terry's card in the right hand pocket. I placed it flat on the surface of the desk.

Amber Lockhart.
Movement Artist.
Contact: ambermovement@mailczar.com

'Come on!' I shouted, pumping my right fist like a pro tennis player. I now had an address that Amber herself had given me.

*

An email may not have been the work of art I'd hoped for, but it was a lot better than nothing. I copied my word document and pasted it into an email. I entered her address in the 'To' field and wrote 'hi' in the 'Subject' field. For several moments, my cursor arrow hovered over the send panel. I took a deep breath and pressed down on the mouse.

Instantly, I was gripped with panic. What had I done? What had possessed me to take this course of action? Had I now made a complete fool of myself?

No, I told myself, it's not so bad. So what if she doesn't want to see me again! It really doesn't matter. Nothing really matters. By repeating, out loud those three words—'nothing really matters'—I was able to regain equilibrium and it wasn't long before I came around to thinking that writing to Amber was, actually, a very good thing to have done.

III

The sound of a lock being turned by a key, then the opening and closing of the front door. My mother had returned from work.

I'd been basking in the afterglow of a job well done—my email—and had fallen into a light sleep at my desk, my face resting on my crossed arms. Now awake, I got up to greet her in the living room, entering it just as she closed the door behind her.

'Hi Mum!' I said. 'How was your day?'

Her well-worn woollen coat was wet around the collar and shoulders, as was her hair.

'Did you forget your umbrella?' I asked in a caring tone. I stood in the opening to the small hallway that serviced the bedrooms and bathroom.

She looked at me, neither angry nor sad.

She walked towards me. I stepped aside, allowing her access to the hallway. She moved directly to her bedroom in the back corner of the flat and closed the bedroom door firmly behind her.

I remained standing, studying the advanced pilling in the shag pile of the living room carpet.

I watched as she fried two pieces of chicken schnitzel in a skillet pan on the front left burner of the stove. Three quarters of an hour had passed since her arrival home and my mother still hadn't uttered a word. She plated the two pieces of schnitzel then placed the plates on the kitchen table. With a grunt and a nod of her head in the direction of a plate she beckoned me to partake.

I set about eating my schnitzel. We ate in silence, she slowly, me quickly. It took me minutes to consume my meal. I was surprised at my hunger.

'Did you have a nice day at work?' I asked. Once more my tone was kindly. She nodded. I heard the sustained blast of an angry car horn coming from the main road.

'Look Mum, I know you're still mad with me over the incident at Sky's birthday. Can we put it behind us? I'm sorry.'

She swallowed the piece of meat she'd been working on and put her knife and fork down on the plate. She spoke slowly and evenly.

'You're a disappointment to me.'

This wasn't the first time she'd said these words and, actually, it represented something of a thawing in the current frostiness of our relations. That she was at last conversing I took as a sign that things might soon be back to their pre-balloon state.

'I know,' I replied. 'I know.'

'You're a 48-year-old man.'

'Ever since the jazz club,' I said. 'Ever since then—I just haven't been able to get on with things. It took a lot out of me, Mum. I'm still trying to come to terms with it. I'm sorry. I'm so sorry!'

I was dangerously close to exhausting the potency of the jazz club in its use as leverage in the disputes that occurred between me and my mother.

As far as she knew, I'd been the victim of the brute indifference of an unsophisticated city. Her son had been the naïve but generous entrepreneur whose dream of enriching his civic sphere had met with confidence-destroying failure. As a result, 'allowances' needed to be made on my behalf. That was how I'd presented it to her.

I'd chosen not to tell her that, thanks to me installing poker machines, I had a reasonable exit strategy. Far from ending up crushed by failure, I'd retired from the game on my own terms with my finances, dignity and well-being more or less intact; freed from the drudgery of actually having to manage a club—a task, I realized early on, requiring levels of idealism and commitment I didn't have.

Furthermore, the club taught me something profound, something that had taken me a while to realize. I actually wasn't interested in jazz itself. Jazz had filled a hole in my life. It had been an excuse; a camouflage; a false flag. It was the older brother I never had. Sure, I'd bought a lot of records, but how many of them had I actually listened to the whole way through?

I'd run Changes for six months. By the end of that time, I was well ready to get out. It had been a journey in five acts: the inauguration of the project; the struggle of the early days; the major setback; the recovery from the setback; and finally, the retirement and the passing on of the 'baton'. This was a strong narrative, with all the plot points occurring on their rightful pages. It was good to get out when I did, and it was good to have done the thing in the first place.

My belief in the goodness of the human soul took a bit of a beating though—not that I've ever placed it in that high a regard. It's well known that the ungrateful are over-represented in the field of music and my experience at Changes shone no new light on this. I fed them, I watered them, I put a roof over their heads and I gave them the takings from the door. But rather than give thanks to me for providing them with a creative outlet, they chose instead to find fault and took every opportunity to let me know that they thought my venue was not up to scratch. They seemed oblivious to the fact that the club's perceived infrastructural inadequacies were due primarily to lack of funds, due to lack of audience, due to—surprise, surprise—them, the musos!

All the outstanding informal debts I'd incurred in keeping the club open had been settled. However, my mother's debt to the bank had been a bridge too far. Of course, I'd have liked to have gotten enough money from the sale of the lease to repay her loan—what son wouldn't? But that's not how it turned out. She lost money. I felt bad. We move on.

*

'The jazz club!' she said with breathy distaste.

'Yeah, it was a mistake,' I said.

'I hate jazz,' said my mother, looking at me hard.

She had never before professed such a profound dislike of the jazz idiom. I couldn't recall an occasion where she'd expressed anything more than a mild disinterest in jazz. I surmised that, for her, jazz had pretty much come to stand for everything she hated about her own life. In her mind, jazz had broken her son and destroyed any dream she may have had of a comfortable retirement.

'You know what, Mum,' I said, 'so do I. I hate it too. I hate jazz!'

With the words came a feeling of exhilaration. For most of my adult life I'd had to stand by and listen as every man and his dog denounced the jazz idiom. How often had I just stood there nodding sheepishly while some arsehole bloviated about their dislike of jazz? Of course, I'd try to not let it get to me—in many ways it strengthened my support for the idiom. But you get tired of making allowances all the time; get tired of trying to forgive people on the grounds of ignorance. Gradually you slip into an 'us versus them' mentality and learn to just expect disappointment.

But things had just changed. Here I was giving voice to the very words that had once wounded me. By looking jazz straight in the eye

120

and telling it exactly what I thought of it, a weight had been lifted from my shoulders. I felt empowered.

I strode jubilantly to my bedroom where my jazz records were housed in an old-fashioned plastic milk crate. I picked out the Shane Snaith Quintet album *Boiling Point,* tucked it under my arm and marched back out to the kitchen.

'I hate it,' I stated again as I entered the room.

'So do I,' answered my mother.

'This is what I think of it,' I said, removing the vinyl from its sleeve.

'I fucking hate it,' intoned my mother, now rocking slightly in her chair as if possessed by a higher spirit. Her vocabulary had definitely broadened since starting work at *Class Axe.*

I bent the record hoping to snap it in two. It proved far more resilient than I'd expected and formed itself into a wonky cylinder instead.

I went to the pantry where on a shelf an old toolbox stood among kitchen appliances. Extracting a large pair of pliers, I returned to the task of damaging the album. The pliers had a wide enough span to hold the cylinder in its 'jaw'. Using both my hands to bear down on the handles of the tool, I forced the rolled-up album into a flattened shape, not dissimilar to a large black, squashed taco. Even though the record was ruined, it hadn't been smashed into a myriad of bits as I'd hoped. I'd wanted a 'wow factor' commensurate with the epiphanic moment my mother and I were sharing, but it wasn't to be. I had to make do with hurling the bent disk onto the kitchen floor and then stamping on it. With each stamp I enunciated a syllable of 'I fuck-ing-hate-jazz.'

I gestured to my mother to join me, an invitation that at first she was reluctant to accept. Eventually though she rose from her chair and delivered a number of strong stamps to the record.

Still it did not break!

Out of breath, we slumped back onto our kitchen chairs. Had this been a scene in a movie, my mother and I would have looked to each other, realized how ludicrous our behaviour had been, and then broken into uncontrolled laughter—our enmity quashed by the absurdity.

In reality, we sat in the kitchen, not saying anything, just staring into the middle distance.

Eventually I plucked up the courage to speak: 'So, can I still live here?'

My mother, still breathing hard from the workout, looked me in the face. She seemed older than she was. She spoke the words slowly. 'One more chance.'

I stood up to hug her. She sat unresponsive in her chair as I bent over her. I managed to encircle her upper body with my arms. Had my hug with Amber gone as I had hoped, this embrace would have stood as a dark parody of it. Alas, it felt more like an echo of the former, albeit a less violent replay. When it was done, or should I say 'cut short' by the brushing away movements of my mother's tired arms, she said, 'leave me alone now.'

IV

'So Megan reckons that counselling is the only way forward—and what Megan says is always right!'

Gary stood behind the bar, drying a glass with a bar towel.

It being early in the afternoon, the Stella Maris was practically empty. I had endured a night of restless, intermittent sleep. Now that a détente, of sorts, had been reached with my mother, the worry over possible eviction had been redirected into worry over the reception of my letter to Amber. When sleep did come, the climaxes of short and jagged Amber-themed dreamscapes had jolted me awake and forced me out of bed to pace up and down upon the hippopotamus-themed carpet of my bedroom. I reckoned that, all up, I'd had no more than an hour of sleep.

I'd decided, after breakfast, to seek distraction from the letter with the company of others at the Stella.

'I agree; I don't trust counsellors either,' I said, displaying the support Gary was obviously fishing for.

'I mean,' he continued, 'we'll get to the place and she'll start banging on about my drinking and I'll bang on about her nagging and then, of course, we'll wind up banging on about her mother. Basically, the whole thing'll just be an excuse to have a fight—and to pay for the privilege!'

'Sounds great!' I said while trying to remove a small circle of hair floating in the foam of my almost full schooner of beer.

'It's my last chance, she says.'

'You believe it?'

'Don't know.'

'Don't' know.' It was Laird. He'd crept up and his mimicking of Gary's last comment came as a shock to both of us.

Before Gary or I could say anything, Laird continued: 'Look Gary, I just want to say I'm really sorry if my speech the other night was a bit strong. I guess I may have over-egged it a bit.'

Laird whipped out a polished timber box, about the size of a shoe-box, and placed it on the bar top.

Gary stared at the object as he absentmindedly continued to dry the glass.

'Go on, open it!' urged Laird. 'It's a gift, a birthday gift—a little late but what the fuck.'

Gary remained unmoved. Several seconds passed before Laird, impatient, seized the initiative. He opened the box with a hectoring sigh.

The hinges allowed for the lid to stand open at an angle of only slightly more than 90 degrees. From where I sat, its contents were hidden from view. Gary, however, on seeing the contents, had frozen, the hand towel in mid-wipe. His expression was one of fear.

'Well, what do you think?' asked Laird. There was a nasty chuckle in his voice. He was enjoying Gary's discomfort.

Gary swallowed hard, at a loss for words.

I rose from my stool and moved towards the box, not knowing what I'd see, while at the same time being well aware of Laird's capacity for deluxe edition arseholery.

The first thing I noticed was the green felt that lined the interior of the timber cabinet. Positioned inside was some sort of jug, flanked by two mounds of cloth. Each mound had an insignia on it. I recognised the Australian coat of arms. It was some kind of sporting item. The 'mounds' were actually caps, one Australian and one English. The jug was a miniature replica ashes urn.

'It's a mini baggy green Ashes urn replica set,' said Laird, who was trying, unsuccessfully, to maintain a semblance of pride against the mounting onslaught of hurt feelings due to the lack of jubilant reaction to his gift.

I sat back down on my stool.

Gary was slow to respond. Laird, deciding that Gary should be the next to speak, waited.

Eventually the towel in Gary's hand resumed its glass rubbing.

'I can't accept this.'

'What do you mean?' asked Laird.

'I mean I can't accept this. It's . . . it's inappropriate. It's an inappropriate gift.'

Laird turned to me. Judging from his wide-eyed mugging, it was clear he expected to find an ally who would share in his flabbergast. I maintained a neutral stance. The gift was inappropriate, there was no doubt about that. It was yet another display of wealth designed to impress and belittle. It must have cost him at least $500, unless he'd stolen it—a thought that did flash through my mind. Gary was quite right to be reticent about accepting it.

A small part of me felt sorry for Laird—something I very rarely experience. Although the flamboyance of the gesture was repellent, it was after all a token of generosity. I fought hard to not empathise with Laird whose late birthday present had been spurned.

Finding no visible support from me, Laird turned back to Gary.

'You don't want it?' he asked.

125

Gary shook his head, a note of hesitancy to the action.

'That's a 'no' then?'

Gary nodded his head slowly—his confusion growing more discernible.

'Ok,' Laird said. 'Suit yourself.'

He closed the lid, picked up the box and walked away in the direction of the exit.

As Laird pushed open the left-hand exit door, Gary cleared his throat and shouted: 'Hey Laird, look . . . I'm sorry. Come back!'

The door swung shut and Laird was gone.

'Oh fuck,' whispered Gary, attempting to convey, unconvincingly, that he didn't want me to hear it. 'I feel really bad about that.'

Rather than sit around and listen to Gary beat himself up about not accepting Laird's gift, I decided to follow the latter's example. I stood up, drained my schooner and bade farewell with a jaunty military-style salute. Laird's gift fail had invigorated me. Things were looking up. I no longer had to move out and Amber would by now have read my letter.

I decided to head over to Newtown. A blast of inner-west 'funkiness' would be just the thing to accompany my buoyant mood. I might do some browsing in a second-hand bookshop or savour a flat white in a trendy café on King Street—the world was full of possibilities. The early afternoon sun felt warm on my forehead as I stepped out of the hotel onto the footpath. It was a sparkling winter Tuesday in Sydney. I hailed a cab.

V

When I was a young man, *Smarties Café* had been a butcher shop. I felt that its new owner could have made more of its history in the naming process—*Smarties* to my mind was a piss poor outcome. The cafe stood on King Street, the commercial high street of Newtown, a magnet for the young and hip. I managed to get a table by the front window and I began my Newtown afternoon with a flat white coffee which I drank while gazing upon the bustling bohemian streetscape.

I had two more flat whites before leaving *Smarties* for *Chapters* bookshop, where I browsed for a while in the photography section before heading back to *Smarties* for another flat white. I then visited *Celluloid Discount DVDs* to look at some box sets then coffeed again at *Smarties*. It was fun to rediscover this exciting and rapidly changing inner-city suburb.

*

The row of mangy bushes—topiary gone feral—that lined the perimeter of the neighbourhood centre opposite Amber's house provided adequate cover. I knelt down and peered through a small break in the foliage. It had been easy to enter the neighbourhood centre—the gate was open—and I figured I wasn't trespassing, as it was a neighbourhood centre, thus open to all tax payers and offspring thereof. In any case I wasn't planning on being there for long.

Both the wooden front door and the security door of the house were closed. There was no one home.

It was during my fourth coffee in *Smarties* when the urge to see Amber again, even if only from a distance, consumed me. It would be enough just to watch her enter the house. If she didn't come back— well, that would be all right too. Just looking at the house for a little while would be sufficient.

By the time I'd gotten there, it was getting on for 4.30pm. I promised myself I would only stay till sundown. I would wait half an hour, and then catch a taxi home.

I knelt among the bushes, watching.

Through the fabric of my jeans, I felt moisture from the soil where my kneecaps had made indentations; the garden must have recently been watered. Cars came and went down the narrow laneway that separated the neighbourhood centre from the house opposite. I heard a car stop further up the street on the right and listened to the sound of car doors slamming and people getting out—a family coming home for the evening.

Time went by quicker than expected; I ended up staying till five-thirty. Neither Amber nor Roderick had returned to the house. I felt both satisfied and sorry for myself.

I walked back to King Street through the labyrinthine back laneways of northern Newtown, my knees cold from the rub of damp jeans.

I had another flat white at *Smarties* then treated myself to a bain-marie feast at *Gandhar's Curry Hut.*

I'd eaten the Indian food too quickly and as I once more waited, kneeling in the bushes, I felt and tasted the bite of reflux in the back of my throat. It was sometime around 9pm.

Both front doors were still shut; Amber and Roderick were either still out, or had been and gone while I was away stuffing my face.

I waited in the bushes.

Forty minutes passed.

A car pulled up, two doors down on the left of the house. A man and a woman got out—young, urban, professional. Instinctively, I ducked down and in the process my left forearm caught the sharp end of a protruding twig. It dug into the fabric of my pullover and tore my skin, not deeply, but enough that I let out a grunt of pain—half-stifled, but nonetheless quite audible.

'Did you hear that?' the woman asked.

'What?' said the man.

'I thought I heard a noise over there.'

As quietly as I could I slid flat to the ground—stomach first. This also caused the bushes to stir unnaturally.

'There,' said the woman, 'did you hear that?'

I felt vulnerable.

'Probably just a possum,' said the man.

'You don't want to look?'

'Not really.'

'You coward,' said the woman playfully.

They both laughed.

I waited, holding my breath until I heard the door of their house click shut. Slowly I got to my feet. The front of my pullover was now covered in dirt and when I pulled the left sleeve up past my elbow, I saw a two-inch-long scratch mark on my forearm. I pressed my index finger down on the wound, held it to my nose and smelt blood.

*

Being the last customer at *Smarties* was a melancholy honour. It was 11.30pm. The young man and woman staffing the cafe stood patiently, their backs against the glass display counter and their arms folded, while I sipped at my nightcap flat white. Outside on the street, Newtown pedestrians made their ways either homewards to sleep, or onwards towards the tomorrow-ruining, late-night pubs on King Street.

*

12.30am, and there was still no sign of them. I was back kneeling in the bushes of the neighbourhood centre. The sound of a distant ambulance siren dipped in and out of audibility, its volume dependent on the whims of the not insignificant breeze that had started up. I'd had a number of beers at *The Signal Crossing*, the back bar of a pub near the train station. As a result, I was relaxed and hopeful; a perfect mood for chilling out and watching the house.

I sensed something moving behind me and turned to see a marmalade cat strolling across the neighbourhood centre lawn towards me. In the dim light, I could see that under the animal's chin, attached to a black collar, was a white rectangular-shaped piece of plastic which looked overly large and uncomfortable and brought to mind a priest's clerical collar. The cat stopped and sat down several metres away, no doubt sizing me up from a safe distance. It seemed to be frowning and I noticed that its mouth was slightly open and quivering, as if it was about to burst into tears. It then got to its feet and resumed its advance. Having gotten to within a foot or so of me, it stopped again. It leaned forward, lowered its mouth and deposited on the ground the body of a small dead lizard. The cat then rolled onto its side, presenting me with its stomach, which I assumed it wanted me to stroke in return for the gift of its kill. I obliged, having to reach over the reptilian corpse to do so. It began to purr loudly; so loudly that it could be heard metres away on the street, potentially attracting attention.

With both hands, I took hold of its front and back paws and rolled it onto its other side so that it faced away from me. I then placed my hands underneath it, lifted it onto its feet and gave it a firm push. It let out a purr/growl, confused by my action. Rather than move off into the night, it came towards me once more and began to rub its face— first one side then the other side—against my right thigh as it brushed forwards and back against me. Its loud purr continued unabated.

The front door of a nearby house opened. I heard footsteps getting louder. I got to my feet and peered through the perimeter bushes, crouching down in the hope of remaining hidden. When the man came into view ten or so meters away, I noticed a flashlight in one hand, its batteries so weak that, rather than shining, it glowed like a jumbo cigarette. In the other hand was a smart phone, its screen emitting the dull grey light of on-ness.

'Thomasina,' the man called. 'Thomasina, I know you're there. Come inside!' It was as if he were calling to a naughty child. Clearly the marmalade cat was his and the white rectangle on her collar was a tracking device which he was monitoring on his cell phone.

'Poor cat,' I remember thinking.

Seeing as Thomasina wasn't going to leave me alone and her collar was going to lead the man directly to me, I decided to announce my presence and explain that I was urinating in the bushes—something I was actually thinking of doing once the coast was clear. I straightened my posture.

On seeing my head and shoulders pop up above the line of the bushes, the man halted. I noticed he was wearing a dressing gown.

'Well, well,' he said, 'what have we here then?' I estimated him to be a decade older than me.

'Hi,' I said.

'What are you doing in the neighbourhood centre?'

I detected an upper-class English accent.

'Just taking a slash.'

Emboldened, no doubt, by the effective bush barrier between him and me, he went on the offensive.

'You realise don't you that it's against the law, pissing in public like this. This isn't a public toilet.'

'I'm sorry.'

'You're trespassing.'

'Well, actually it's a neighbourhood centre. It belongs to the public.' My tone was pompous, automatically mimicking that of the cat owner.

He shone his torch directly in my face. The dim light had no effect on my ability to observe his appearance—nasty.

'Well, actually, it's owned by St Amand's.' he said.

'Oh?'

'Yes. I'm their solicitor. I suggest you leave at once before I call the police.'

The edges of his dressing gown were touching the ground. On my forehead, I felt tiny spits of cold rain.

I turned quickly and made for the exit gate, not pausing till I had reached King Street.

*

The bartender, who everyone was calling Bella, placed my triple cognac on the bar top in front of me. I'd needed a warming drink and consequently I'd found myself at *Klonimus,* a slender wine bar at the top end of King Street.

12.30am on a Tuesday night wasn't a peak time, but the place bordered on being crowded—this was Newtown after all. Having paid for the triple cognac, I made my way towards the back of the bar where it narrowed to a corridor wide enough to accommodate only two-person tables, of which there were three positioned in succession, their sides butting up against the interior wall.

I spotted a spare seat on the table nearest the back, manoeuvred my way through a knot of drinkers and deposited myself on the wooden stool.

Opposite me sat a heavyset man I took to be in his mid-sixties. He was bald on top with long unkempt silver hairs hanging from the periphery of his scalp, some of which had formed themselves into dreadlocks. He had a full-face beard that hung half a foot down from his chin and wore thick and battered tortoiseshell spectacles. His jeans and vest were complemented by a grubby plaid jacket, with leather elbow patches which had, at various points, become unstitched from the main garment. He had planted his right foot in the aisle space next to the table and I noticed he wasn't wearing socks inside of his lurid Nike trainers.

On the table before him were two schooners—one full of beer, one empty—as well as a foolscap writing pad on which he jotted down complex equations. It was his intense focus on the pad that enabled me to make such a thorough observation of his appearance and apparel undetected.

'Ok if I sit here?' I asked.

He looked up and nodded.

'Be my guest.'

I set about drinking my cognac. He returned to his equations.

Presently, he put down his pen and, having picked up the schooners—one in each hand—he proceeded to pour the contents of the one he held in his right hand into the empty one he held in his left. He then poured the contents of the now full left-hand glass back into the empty right-hand one. He drank from the schooner in his right hand.

He placed both glasses back on the table and went back to scribbling down mathematical symbols on his pad. Among the dense jumble of numbers, Greek letters and other assorted symbols and function signs, I noticed the words 'Love' and 'Sorrow'. Calculations had been written over the top of other, former calculations. At some points the page had four or more layers of calculations.

He rested his pen and repeated the action with his two glasses of beer, before returning to his theoretical labour.

On the third occasion of the pouring of his beer, I plucked up the courage to ask him what he was doing.

'It's the bubbles,' he said jovially. 'I can't handle the bubbles. I need to remove them, so I pour them out.' He demonstrated once more, as if my question had no basis in prior observation.

'What's wrong with the bubbles?' I asked.

'The gas, it gets in my joints. Gives me arthritis.'

'What are you working on?' I asked, pointing at the foolscap pad.

'Nothing.'

He returned to working on nothing.

I sat and watched him, his labour punctuated evenly by the beer de-gassing ritual.

Sensing that we had reached the limits of our conversation, I began to construct, in my mind, possible narratives to explain how it was that this man had ended up here, at *Klonimus*. In one scenario, he was a professor who'd been the subject of a career-ending complaint from a young student he'd fallen in love with. In another, he was a scientist turned whistle-blower working in a corrupt government department—a man who'd been pushed over the edge by a court case during which his already fragile mental health had been called into question. In still another, he was a one-time brilliant maths student who'd studied too hard and had suffered a crippling nervous breakdown that had condemned him to a vagabond life of alcoholism and junk maths. It occurred to me that in ten years' time, I too could be living such a life—minus the maths of course. The thought was a catalyst to finish my cognac and move on.

*

If I stood on tiptoes, I could see over the wooden fence. I was at the back of the house, in the laneway. Rather than just stand and peer over the fence, I thought it prudent to move around a bit. I began a routine of walking to the second cross street, turning around, returning to the back fence and having a quick peer, before walking off again. To the casual observer, it would look like I was merely taking in the night air. The repetition was soothing but after a while it occurred to me that I was exhibiting the behaviour of a caged animal.

Confident that both Thomasina and her owner would be safely indoors for the night, I returned to kneeling in the bushes of the neighbourhood centre for one final bout of watching the front of the house before heading off home. The inclement weather earlier in the night had cleared and above me was a sky full of bright stars. I couldn't help but think about the vastness of the universe and what an incredible coincidence it was that I should happen to share the same planet as Amber—let alone the fact that we were the same species and that I'd actually met and communicated with her. What were the chances of that happening? Maybe the guy back at *Klonimus* could work that out.

After a while, it became too fatiguing to keep kneeling, so I sat on the damp earth with my legs stretched out in front of me. The wind had died down and in the ensuing stillness I listened to the sound of several crickets stridulating near me. There were three of them, each one emitting short, evenly-spaced bursts of square-shaped sound waves. The resultant counterpoint formed a mesmerising cannon of overlapping rhythms. I lay on my back, on the lawn, looking at the stars and listening.

> *Poor wandering one*
> *Though thou hast surely strayed*
> *Take heart of grace, thy steps retrace*
> *Poor wandering one . . .*

The piano was out of tune and incompetently played. I estimated there to be about twenty voices singing—mostly older women. Above me, a blue, cloudless sky signified morning. The neighbourhood centre was having a breakfast singalong. I had fallen asleep under the bushes.

I stood up and reached around with my right hand, feeling the dankness of the back of my cardigan. How could I have nodded off? I must have been asleep for hours. My back was numb with cold. On the ground nearby, swarming ants covered the body of the lizard given to me by Thomasina.

I studied Amber's house for any sign of arrival or departure. There was none.

Back up on King Street, the noise of the traffic in the sharpness of the morning air sounded harsh. I figured it must have been about 8am.

VI

All the seats in the Medicare Centre were taken. A lot of people were having to stand. It was 4pm and busy. There was even a queue to get a ticket for the queue and I had to wait in line behind four people before I could gain access to the dispensing machine. 'B 987' was the ticket I eventually took. The highest number showing on any of the half dozen counter screens was 'B 790'.

Half an hour earlier, while seated at *Muffin Siesta*, I'd caught sight of Laird lurking around the mezzanine floor of the mall. I assumed he was working one of the queue-ticketed establishments. At first, I'd baulked at the idea of dignifying his vocation by spying on him. I ordered another coffee and stayed put. But then curiosity got the better of me and took me first to the HCF centre where he wasn't and then to the Medicare Centre where he was.

Each service counter had its own electronic number display attached to the wall directly above it and each new display of a number was accompanied by a 'ding', barely audible above the drone made from the coalesced noises of humans and machines.

Laird, with an ipad on his lap, was seated in the row of chairs closest to the service counters. He was looking hard at the tablet's screen. Approaching from the side, I was able to make out what he was studying. It came as no great surprise that he wasn't reading *The London Review of Books*. He was playing virtual snooker. I crouched down in front of him in the space between the chairs and the service counters. Totally immersed in his game, he remained unaware of my presence.

I placed the palm of my right hand, fingers outspread, flat on the screen of the iPad; a spider on a place mat.

'What the fuck!'

It was as if he'd been woken from a dream with a bucket of water, or worse.

I couldn't help but laugh out loud.

When he registered who it was, a look of cold hatred passed over his countenance before it was replaced by neutral unpleasantness.

'Hey Laird,' I said. 'How's it going?'

He remained silent; a stubborn child. I stayed crouched in front of him. 'What's wrong?' I asked.

He closed the flap of his iPad cover and looked at me, hurt.

'What numbers have you got there?' I said, unable to mask the derisive tone of my voice.

He knew I was referring to his tickets and, although he was aware that I was making fun of his newfound career, he was proud of his success. The latter outweighed the former and I sensed a swift improvement in his mood.

'Quite a few actually.'

I stood up from the crouch.

'850 to 920,' he said. 'I'm going to wait till it gets to 820 before I start working.'

'You've got it all worked out.'

Laird checked himself before not responding.

Three seats to our right, a woman's number was called and she left her seat. I quickly sat down in the now vacant chair.

Laird chose not to re-engage with his snooker game. He sat

watching the number screens while he drummed his fingers on the closed cover of the iPad.

*

A 'ding' chimed and 'B 820' flashed above counter four. Laird stood up and made his way back towards the ticket dispenser. I got up and followed him.

He hovered around the dispenser sizing people up—the impatient; those who looked like they had work to get back to or meals to prepare—I assumed that these were the sorts of criteria he used when choosing his prey. I noticed him staring at a well-dressed middle-aged man who was waiting in line to get a queue ticket. In a reversal of the norms of predation, rather than seek out the weak and elderly, Laird was after the strong and vibrant.

Laird let the man take the ticket, but instead of going straight up to him, he stayed put, waiting for the significance of the ticket number to sink in. As if cued, the man sighed. He perused the crowded Medicare Centre, shook his head, and moved away from the machine to take up a standing position near the entrance.

Still Laird kept his cool, not moving.

The man looked at his watch.

Still nothing from Laird.

The man glanced at his watch again; this was the signal Laird had been waiting for. He moved briskly and confidently towards the man. I followed, eager to hear the conversation.

'Hey mate,' called Laird on approach.

Laird's smile wasn't convincing and his forced swagger didn't improve things.

'Want to move up in the queue? I've got an 850 ticket.'

The man looked sternly at Laird's face before scanning the remainder of his body, down then up. Clearly, he didn't like what he saw.

'No thanks.'

'No worries.'

Laird moved away to take up his previous spot near the ticket dispenser. I followed.

A lycra-clad cyclist took a ticket from the machine.

This time Laird walked straight up to her, choosing not to wait for any 'signals'.

The cyclist thought about the offer but clearly smelt a rat and so declined. I got the impression it was 50/50 and that once again Laird's appearance was the deal-breaker. He didn't seem overly disappointed.

Several minutes passed and Laird waited while a number of people he deemed to be non-starters took queue tickets.

Then a mother with a bored toddler took a ticket from the dispenser. Laird's interest picked up.

Close to the machine, a chivalrous customer stood up, and offered his seat to the young mother—a gift she accepted with minimal gratitude. Having sat down, she ordered the child to sit on the floor at her feet, expecting it to stay there.

She wasn't shy about broadcasting her son's name. 'Nile!' she barked numerous times before reverting to threats of corporal punishment. 'Sit still or you'll get a smack.'

Nile of course wouldn't sit still.

Laird seized the moment.

'Excuse me, would you like a ticket?'

By this time, the latest number flashing was 'B 835'

'I already have a ticket,' she said, distracted by the sight of her son sucking on a nearby chair leg, much to the discomfort of the young, male skateboarder who occupied the seat.

'I have ticket number B 850.'

'What?' she asked, annoyed at having to listen to Laird's proposition. 'Nile,' she yapped. 'Come here!—excuse me.'

She stood up, went over to the chair and freed its leg from Nile's mouth. He didn't want to be picked up or brought back to his mother's chair, and vented his feelings through a series of piercing screams followed by more sustained bawling.

'What did you say?' the woman asked Laird, having returned to her seat. She was trying to maintain a firm grip with both hands on Nile's shoulders as he squirmed on the carpet.

'I said I have ticket number B 850.'

The woman looked at her ticket.

'Are you trying to sell me a queue ticket?'

'Yes.'

I could see her looking around the room; doing the maths.

'How much?' she asked.

'$10.'

'Forget it.'

'How about $7.50?' asked Laird.

'How about $5?'

'Done.'

Laird handed over the ticket and the woman paid him with coins.

The cyclist, who must have been following Laird's progress with the mum, walked over.

'Did you just sell that woman a queue ticket?'

Laird nodded.

'How much are you selling them for then?'

'$7.50.'

'What number are you selling?'

'B 851.'

'Ok.'

She paid with a five dollar note and coins. Laird shoved the money in his shirt pocket.

He looked at me, smug.

A priest seated nearby waved his hand. Laird attended to his needs, oily with grin. His fawning was grotesque, but, I had to admit, effective.

The middle-aged man in the expensive suit, who Laird had first approached, had changed his mind. He signalled to Laird who duly trotted over, clearly enjoying his work.

The colour of the note the man handed over was yellow; he didn't get change.

For five or so minutes Laird milled about working the room, stuffing his breast pocket with money. He may not have sold all his tickets, but he sold most of them.

VII

Hey Amber,

How are things? Just wondering if you got my last letter. Things here have been pretty good lately although I seem to have caught a cold, which is a bit of a drag. I've been reading an interesting book on the Pina Bausch Dance Company. Do you know them? They're German and they do some really fascinating work. I can send you the book if you're interested.

Hope you're well,

Geoff

It had been several days since I'd sent the previous letter and had heard nothing back. I decided to give it one last shot. If I didn't hear from her, so be it, I'd let the whole thing drop.

For three consecutive nights, I'd ventured back to Newtown. It served as a welcome break from the routine of the Stella Maris. I enjoyed the groovy vibe of the area and had even begun to consider it as a future option should I ever decide to leave the lower North Shore.

Each night I ended up walking past Amber's house and, as with the very first night, encountered no signs of life. I figured they must be out of town.

One of the benefits that accrued from my evenings spent in Newtown was that I now had Amber's postal address. This meant I could at last use my grandfather's *Eversharp Skyline* pen to express myself by way of a proper, handwritten letter. And I was very pleased with the result. I folded the letter carefully and slid it into an envelope bearing Amber's address. I was about to affix a postage stamp when I changed my mind. Why not save on the postage and pop this new letter into Amber's letter box myself? After all, the likelihood of there being anyone at home was negligible. It was also another opportunity to indulge my growing infatuation with the Inner West.

*

The security door stood open and bordering the edges of the window blind in the front room was bright light. Someone was home. I took up my usual position in the foliage opposite the house.

I could see Roderick's Getz parked on the same side of the street as the house, three doors down.

Dim light was also visible through the frosted glass of the front door which meant there was activity in the back part of the house.

The letterbox stood atop a pole speared into the small patch of dirt to the left of the little path that led up to the front door. I walked out of the neighbourhood centre and stood for a moment on the footpath.

I shuffled quickly across the street.

A hinged flap covered the mouth of the letterbox and needed to be lifted so that items could be placed inside. In my nervousness I was all thumbs and as I tried to lift up the flap, I fumbled it. It fell shut, causing an audible clank—loud enough for a nearby cricket to stop its chirp. I moved quickly back out onto the footpath, the letter still in my hand and walked, fast, to the next cross street.

I waited for the door to open.

It didn't.

I made my way back to the letterbox.

This time I was successful in placing the letter inside without fumbling the flap.

Suddenly the sound of Roderick's voice erupted from inside: 'This is fucking crap!'

I gauged that he was in the kitchen, a safe distance away. I stood my ground listening hard.

'Calm down baby,' I heard Amber say. 'It'll be ok.'

'This stuff doesn't fucking work.'

'Give it time. Ryan said Acepromazine would do the job and he should know.'

'Ryan's a fucking clown,' bellowed Roderick.

'It's ok, baby.'

I heard footsteps inside coming down the hall towards the front door—loud and fast. It was too late for me to make a dash for it; Roderick would see me before I made it to the corner. I had to take my chances there, in the small front yard. I moved sideways to the left of the path and took up a crouching position in the corner of the property, obscured (I hoped) by the night shadows cast by the neighbour's fence.

The front door opened and Roderick stepped out. He shut the door hard behind him. Without looking sideways, he walked straight out to the street and continued onwards at a brisk pace in the direction of King Street.

I waited till I could no longer hear his footsteps and then waited some more, making sure that Amber wasn't going to follow him outside. I stood up from my crouch, tiptoed back to the footpath and set off in a direction perpendicular to the one Roderick had chosen. I half-walked/jogged, travelling parallel to King street with the intention of joining up with it a kilometre or so south of the house.

It had been a close call.

But, rather than replay in my mind the events surrounding my lucky escape or muse over what the consequences might have been had I been discovered, all I could think about was her voice; more specifically the tone of her voice when she'd called him 'baby'. It was very different to her tone when she'd called me a 'fucking moron'.

VIII

Karaoke night at the Stella Maris happens on the first Sunday of each month. Most people choose to ignore it by congregating outside in the beer garden while it runs its course inside. I assume the Karaoke allows for Gary to tick a licence regulation box or obtain some sort of sponsorship, otherwise there'd be no logic to its survival. Even Carter Highland absented himself from it.

Karaoke, I'm told, can be a lot of fun, given the right bunch of people. It wasn't at the Stella. Often it finished after one or two songs. Sometimes it ended nastily, with a small but determined group of regulars heckling whoever was in the process of having a go. Gary ran a pretty loose boat when it came to policing audience behaviour and turned a blind eye to most of the heckling. To his credit, though, he drew the line at objects being thrown at singers. Proof of this was the month-long ban dished out to Doc, an older regular, for emptying a three-quarters full schooner of Reschs over the head of a school teacher who was singing the theme from *The Poseidon Adventure*. The woman wasn't injured, thank god, but she did threaten legal action. Doc claimed he'd merely done what 'the great John Lennon himself had done' fifty-five years earlier at a wedding in Liverpool.

I sat at a table in the beer garden, sipping aggressively from a schooner. It was the night after my brush with Amber's tone of voice. Inside, a karaoke rendition of 'This Old House' echoed around the walls of the more or less empty lounge. At some point, I noticed that the male singer had fallen off the song, leaving the computerised backing track to gallop on riderless.

Both outdoor pool tables were in use and drunken miscues and laughter were evidence of the poor-quality pool being played.

Wendy and Gavin entered the beer garden through the glass doors that connected it with the lounge. Both were draped in the red and white regalia of the Sydney Swans, who must have played a home game that afternoon. Wendy was sporting a mischievous grin, which led me to think that the curtailment of the karaoke singer's performance may have had something to do with her having caused swift, show-stopping offense. They sat down at a table nearby. We made eye contact and I raised my glass half-heartedly. Wendy returned my glass raise and beckoned me, with her free hand, to join her and Gavin at their table.

Being on my own and not engaged in any obvious activity, no excuse to not join them sprang readily to mind. I obeyed Wendy's demand and went over, schooner in hand. The truth of the matter was that I felt intimidated by Wendy and, seeing as she was becoming a regular at the pub, I deemed it prudent to try to get into her good books.

'How you doing beautiful?' asked Wendy.

'Good,' I said, sitting down. 'And you?'

'Great!' they both answered.

'Looks like you've been to the footy, yeah?'

'That's right,' said Wendy.

'You win?' I asked.

'Slaughtered 'em!' answered Wendy.

'What've you been up to?' asked Gavin.

'Oh, just the usual,' I said.

'You look like you've lost some weight?' said Wendy.

'Been pining over a woman?' She dug into me, playfully, with her elbow.

'Knock it off, Wendy,' said Gavin, sensing my discomfort.

'Just ignore her,' he said, turning to me.

A woman playing on the table nearest us hit the cue ball too hard, causing it to leap the confines of the table and land with a clack on the concrete floor. The ball rolled towards us and stopped inches away from Wendy's feet. A young man came over to retrieve it. On the right side of his neck was a tattoo, drawn in stick figures, of a man hanging from a gallows. He bent over to pick the ball up, but as he reached down with his right hand, Wendy kicked it away. The man stood upright looking very pissed off—a look that Wendy mimicked sarcastically, before bursting into laughter.

'Sorry about that mate, couldn't help myself,' she said, through the dregs of her cackle.

It was a tense moment—I'd seen vicious fights erupt over less—however the young man chose not to escalate the situation and went to pick the ball up from its new position, muttering expletives under his breath.

'Wimp,' said Wendy, looking at me.

'Yes,' I said.

Wendy and Gavin set about recounting to me the highlights of the football game they'd watched that afternoon.

Wendy's behaviour with the cue ball had quelled the enthusiasm of the pool players and the table soon became vacant.

'How's about a game of pool?' she asked.

'There's only three of us,' I said, in a vain attempt to dodge what I had every reason to think would be unpleasant.

'I'll play both of you,' said Wendy. She unwound the Swans' scarf from around her neck and placed it on the table.

'Great,' I said, I felt more comfortable having Gavin there.

'You know, I might sit this one out,' said Gavin. 'Does anyone want something from the bar?'

'Get some chips,' said Wendy. She stood and took off her red fleece to reveal a sleeveless Swans' T-shirt. I noticed the outline of a five-cornered star tattooed on her upper right arm. We moved to the pool table and tossed a coin to see who would break. I lost and Wendy opted to break. She hit the cue ball powerfully, scattering the balls evenly around the table. I watched as the five ball rolled slowly towards the top left-hand pocket and fell in.

'I'm on solids.'

I nodded.

The cue ball was up near the baulk cushion, behind the twelve ball and the eight ball, and thus blocked from a direct shot on any other solid balls. Wendy aimed the cue ball at the right cushion at a point below the right middle pocket. She had the ball come off the right cushion, then off the top cushion before potting the four ball into the left side pocket. The cue ball came to rest in perfect position to pot the three ball into the top left pocket, something she completed easily, screwing the cue ball back almost half the length of the table to set up an easy pot on the seven ball into the right side pocket. She made it using screw back to deftly disturb a clump of balls containing the one and the two so that they both were pottable into the top left and bottom left pockets respectively—tasks she accomplished with ease. However, after potting the two ball, her shot on the six ball into the top right pocket was blocked by the thirteen ball. I watched as she paused to apply chalk to the tip of her cue after which she held it level with her eye line. She studied it for a moment, squinting.

'These cues are fucked,' she said.

I nodded.

She bent back down to the table for her shot.

She raised the back of the cue so that it was almost perpendicular to the table surface. She aimed the cue tip high on the right-hand side of the cue ball and struck it hard, causing it to pass the thirteen ball several inches to the left, before swerving vigorously to the right to hit the six ball and pot it firmly. The cue ball was now a foot equidistant from the top cushion and the right cushion. The eight ball was sitting a few inches away from the left side pocket, providing Wendy with a simple straight pot to win the game. Rather than knock it in directly, Wendy aimed the cue ball at a point midway between the left side pocket and the bottom left pocket. She hit the ball firmly. It came off the left cushion, then the baulk cushion, then the right cushion just below the side pocket, then the top cushion and headed directly towards the eight ball. The cue ball kissed it, causing it to roll towards the side pocket. It stopped on the cusp.

'Scheisse!' said Wendy, grinning.

At last I was to have a turn at the table.

I took aim at the twelve ball, hoping to pot it into the top left pocket. It was a relatively easy shot, requiring only a slight angle on the ball.

'You know what you've got to do if I pot all my balls before you pot any don't you?' asked Wendy.

'No. What?'

'You've got to pull your daks down.'

I smiled and took aim.

'And your undies too,' she added.

I felt the uncomfortable reverberations through the wood of the cue as I miscued and missed the twelve ball altogether. The cue ball came off the top cushion and stopped almost exactly where it had been for Wendy's last shot.

Rather than repeat the four-cushion trick shot, she shot the cue ball directly at the eight ball, knocking it in.

'Take 'em off,' said Wendy.

'Excuse me?'

'Your strides. Drop 'em.'

Gavin returned with several bags of chips.

'I bet she won, right?' he said cheerfully.

'I pantsed him,' announced Wendy proudly.

'Look,' I said, 'I really don't think . . . '

'It doesn't matter what you think,' said Wendy. 'I beat you seven nil, so take your fucking trousers off.'

The four players on the other table had stopped their game in order to watch.

'You'd better do as the lady says,' said one of them, grinning.

'I'm going inside,' I said. 'Thanks for the game.'

I turned and walked towards the entrance to the lounge. I should have run. Wendy moved quickly and managed to step in front of me, blocking ingress.

'Take—your—fuck—ing—trou—sers—off!' She spoke evenly and coldly, gapping each of her syllables with menace. Her previous manner, derived from the entertainment expected at seeing someone humiliated, had now been replaced with anger at having her command disobeyed.

Several of the players on the other table let out ironic whoops. I also heard sounds of clapping coming from other patrons scattered around the beer garden.

I looked at Gavin who was sitting down chewing on a mouth full of crisps. He shrugged.

His shrug annoyed me.

'Get out of my way! I'm not taking my trousers off,' I said,

'You'd better do as I fucking say, smartarse,'

'Get out of my way, you fucking moron.'

The opening piano chords of 'You Light Up My Life' sounded in the lounge. I remember feeling surprised that the karaoke had lasted this long.

'Hey!' Gavin shouted through his mouthful of crisps. He seemed genuinely startled that someone had stood up to Wendy.

'Did you call me a fucking moron?' Wendy asked.

A female karaoke participant began to sing the words of the Debbie Boone classic with the sort of passion that would have had a packed room cheering at most hotels.

'Look, I didn't mean . . . '

Wendy tilted her head back as if she was about to sneeze. I heard a hoicking noise as she summoned disparate phlegmatic material to coalesce in her mouth, and then, leaning forward towards me, she spat—not at me, thank god—but on the ground between us. So voluminous was the parcel of fluid that, even with the sound of the karaoke coming from the lounge, I heard the splash as it landed.

I didn't look down at the deposit but kept my gaze fixed on Wendy's face.

'I'm watching you,' she said. 'I'm watching you, with my third fucking eye.'

She smiled—a smile full of malevolence and condescension. 'You poor fucken' idiot,' she said. 'You don't know what you've done.'

I stepped around her and walked on into the lounge. Gripped with the need to wash, I moved directly to the toilets. I stood at the wash basin, filled my cupped hands with tap water and pushed my face down into them. The water felt cold as I massaged my skin.

Far from refreshed, I made my way out into the main room. The karaoke performer was by now well into the second half of the song. The sight of the talentless singer 'having a go' was a much-needed tonic and, although embarrassed by her awkward histrionics as she belted out the last few lines of the song, I welcomed this timely glimpse of good-natured humanity. Directly in front of the small stage stood three people, two of whom were friends or relatives of the singer. The third was Gary, waiting impatiently beside one of the mounted speakers.

The final chord of the backing music sounded and decayed. The two audience members clapped encouragingly, the performer bowed ironically—blushing nonetheless—and Gary sprang into action.

'Ok, that's it,' he said. 'I need to pack this shit away.'

*

I continued to drink at the hotel that night. I wasn't going to give Wendy the satisfaction of knowing she'd caused me to modify my social life. Even so, I had no desire to venture anywhere near the pool tables and my trips to the toilet, which involved walking past the glass doors that opened onto the beer garden, were conducted very matter-of-factly. Fortunately, I was spared any further interaction with Wendy or Gavin. I deduced later that their departure must have coincided with one of my toilet breaks, something I couldn't have known at the time.

I was spooked. In my mind's eye, I replayed over and over, in slow motion, the action of her spit—the moment when, with her loose jowl wobbling, she set her face to work, summoned up the fluid and with a backward tilt of the head launched the gob. I may have been suffering from mild Post Traumatic Stress Disorder and I regretted not having looked at the phlegm deposit on the ground as it might have provided some sort of closure.

As it was, I could only self-medicate with beer among the small group of regulars comprising Bronwyn, Doc and several others who were gathered around the bar.

At 9pm Laird arrived. He walked through the entrance doors with his arm around the waist of a woman—something I'd never before witnessed. She looked to be in her early thirties and was dressed in an orange leather mini skirt combined with an off-white woollen cardigan which she wore over a black, rock band T-shirt. Black, fish-net stockings and knee-length, caramel-coloured, high-heeled boots completed the outfit.

After walking several metres in from the entrance, the woman slipped forcefully out of Laird's grip and fended off his arm as he tried to re-drape it around her. They proceeded independently towards us at the bar.

'This is Gwen,' said Laird.

Gwen, who stood a couple of meters back from her partner, reacted to the introduction with a shrug.

'What'll you have Gwen?' Laird asked, an overdone jauntiness to his voice.

'Ginger ale,' answered Gwen.

'Bourbon and Coke and a ginger ale, thanks Gary. '

'What do you do Gwen?' asked Gary as he prepared the drinks.

To the untrained ear, Gary's words were inclusive and welcoming—an innocent enquiry designed to break the ice with a new arrival. However, to the trained ear, his tone carried something darker and more complex. It was subtle, but I detected elements of disapproval, jealousy, confusion, even shame. Lending support to my observation, was the angle at which he held his chin and a slight clenching of his jaw muscles that had caused a vein in his left temple to subtly bulge.

'I'm an actor,' she said.

'Here ya go,' said Gary, handing the two drinks to Laird. The broad smile on his face vibrated at the edges of his mouth from the effort to sustain it.

'Are you in something at the moment?' shouted Gary.

'Several,' answered Gwen.

'I've always wanted to know how people did that.' This statement came from Bronwyn. 'How do actors keep all those lines in their heads?' There was a breezy inquisitiveness to her manner which was out of character.

'You just take it as it comes; try not to get ahead of yourself,' said Gwen, seeming to thaw as a result of Bronwyn's questioning.

'I'll drink to that,' said Bronwyn, raising her half-empty wine glass above her head.

'Here, here,' some of us muttered.

'What are the names of some of the things you're in?' shouted Gary.

'Keep your shirt on Gary! Let the girl drink her ginger ale in peace,' said Bronwyn.

Although the altruism of Bronwyn's sisterly request was undermined by her mockery of Gwen's choice of beverage, we nevertheless laughed at Gary, her intended target, who duly halted his line of questioning.

'So, where did you two meet?' I asked Gwen. I'd gotten up from my stool and moved to where she and Laird now stood on the fringes of the small gathering.

'At the Opera bar,' said Laird, eager to answer on Gwen's behalf. Gwen nodded.

'It's great there!' I said, trying to be friendly, while mentally scanning Bennelong Point for ticketed waiting rooms.

'Great view!' said Laird.

'Spectacular,' I said.

I looked at Gwen, causing her to nod in agreement, begrudgingly.

'I notice,' I continued, 'that they got Utzon's son back in to fix up the boardwalk area.'

'Yes,' said Laird, 'it was a shame they didn't follow Utzon's original plan.'

'Yes,' I said, once more looking at Gwen and causing her to nod. 'Apparently, Utzon had plans for a carpark and everything.'

'Yes,' said Laird. 'Originally the Opera theatre was to be the Concert Hall, and vice versa.'

'Excuse me,' said Gwen. 'Where are the toilets?'

'Over by the poker machine room,' shouted Gary from behind the bar, pointing in that direction. I was impressed by his hearing.

Gwen left.

Laird and I stood unconversant.

While we'd been chatting, Bronwyn had begun to read aloud from a notebook, much to the amusement of Doc and several of the other men seated around her. I couldn't help but let my attention drift over to her.

'*Bronwyn was really hurtful to me today,*' she read, putting on a whiny tone of voice presumably in imitation of the author. '*She said my T-shirt design looked like I'd thrown up on it.'* Well I swear to God it did!' Bronwyn slapped her thigh in raucous merriment.

'There's another one . . . where is it?' She leafed through the book, searching for a page. 'Here it is—*May 19:'* Once more Bronwyn put on a wimpy voice. *'Nobody seems to find my jokes funny. Today at dinner I told my joke about the Ananda Marga lady that I know is funny, and no one laughed.'*

'Oh my god that's so pathetic!' shrieked Bronwyn amidst the laughter of her audience.

Laird was also laughing now.

'Wait, wait—this is the best one!' Once more she flicked through the pages of the book in order to find an entry and, having found it, she cleared her throat in preparation for another malicious imperson-ation. *'Bronwyn is so great. I wish I could be more like her. If only my parents had encouraged me to paint.'*

'Aw, gee, it's heartbreaking!' said Bronwyn.

Bronwyn had somehow gotten hold of her friend Kelly's diary. The fact that Bronwyn was over forty and should have grown out of this sort of behaviour three decades earlier, was sad. I'd often seen her revert to a childishness that was anathema to her intellectual arrogance. Sometimes, this immaturity took the form of a tantrum. At other times, it was represented by an underdeveloped 'zany' sense of humour that expressed itself in unfunny wordplay and poorly per-formed mimicry. And then there were moments such as this one; inappropriate, vulgar and cruel.

'That's probably enough,' said Bronwyn, well pleased with the reception the mockery of her friend's naïve writings had elicited.

'C'mon, let's hear some more,' Doc said. He was supported by sev-eral others in the group, myself included.

'Ok,' said Bronwyn. 'Let's see ...' her fingers worked the pages of the book. 'Here we are, *May 30: the worst one is a middle-aged guy called Laird. He makes my skin crawl. I make sure I'm always with someone else when I have to talk to him.*'

The group erupted in laughter. Laughing loudest of all was Gary. The hurt expression on Laird's face acted as an accelerant for the mirth, and it took almost 30 seconds for calm to be restored.

'*And there are others,*' continued Bronwyn. '*There's this repulsive guy Gary who's the barman ...*'

'Ok,' interrupted Gary, jolted into seriousness by the mention of his own name. 'I think we've heard enough. Put the thing away Bronwyn.'

Bronwyn let the book rest on her knees.

'You can't just stop there,' protested Laird. Other people agreed and voiced their desire to hear what Kelly had written about Gary.

'It doesn't feel right to be reading someone's personal stuff out loud like this,' said Gary.

'Get over it!' wheezed Doc.

Bronwyn brought the book back to a reading position.

Gary, unable to control the situation, retreated to the far end of the bar.

'*He keeps offering me free drinks,*' read Bronwyn, adopting once more the whiny twang. '*He thinks he's really cool, but he looks more like a sicko priest.*'

'Way to go Gary!' yelled Laird, toasting the air with his drink.

'Well, she said you were the worst, mate,' said Gary, returning the toast with the empty schooner glass he was polishing.

I detected, among the crowd, a developing uneasiness. Now that individuals were being named, the appetite for continuing was waning. I too was no longer finding it as amusing as I had done at the start.

'*And then there's Doc,*' Bronwyn read, '*he's like the grandfather from hell.*'

Doc's face, until then beaming with pleasure, now looked nervous and worried.

Both Gary and Laird were laughing.

'Go Doc!' shouted Laird.

'*He smells bad,*' continued Bronwyn, '*and B . . .*' Here Bronwyn almost certainly aborted the utterance of her own name. '*And I've heard,*' she continued, '*he has a nitrous oxide bulb addiction, which is really gross.*'

'That's bullshit!' said Doc, rising from his stool. 'I am not an addict.'

'Get over it!' shouted Laird, mimicking Doc's own words.

'Shall I go on?' asked Bronwyn. 'There's more.'

There were now three people in the room who'd been discussed and this constituted a sizeable minority that very much wished to see other people described like they'd been.

Bronwyn continued to read. I was the next cab off the rank and copped the adjective 'sleazy', which was a bit rich considering we hadn't spoken more than a dozen words to each other.

A pattern emerged: each time a person was diarised, that person left the group of nervous listeners who wanted the ordeal to end, and joined the ranks of the insulted, now wishing for the fun to continue so that another person would experience the same humiliation. Also, the ability of Kelly's criticisms to cause offence diminished as the reading wore on so that by the end of it a negative description in Kelly's diary became almost a source of pride. After all, to be mentioned in the journal meant you were a bona fide regular at the Stella Maris.

With all the distraction caused by the book reading, Gwen's departure went unobserved. It was several minutes after Bronwyn closed the diary for the last time that Laird realised she'd never come back from the toilet.

IX

I could feel the polyester on the skin of the soles of my feet, both of which had successfully touched down on the carpeted floor of my bedroom. It was early afternoon.

Migraine and phlegm combined to make concentration on any task difficult. I felt relieved that I had no pressing major decisions to make. I yawned—a yawn that included my whole upper body in its execution—and waddled out to the kitchen where my breakfast muffin stood plated on the Formica table. I made quick work of the small cake, washing it down as I ate with gulps of lukewarm tap water from a glass I refilled at the sink.

Winter rain pelted the kitchen window.

I thought about heading over to Newtown to have a coffee and a browse. It then struck me: I'd been conscious for over ten minutes and hadn't once thought of Amber. From this scant evidence, I deduced that the whole Amber thing was fast subsiding. Puff . . . gone! For a few short days, she'd provided a middle-aged man with a bogus teleology; a distraction from the hopeless and repetitive vortex in which he'd found himself trapped.

I searched for another muffin among the slim pickings of the fridge, eventually finding one in the back right-hand corner. Then I remembered Wendy and her gob.

*

I was back in my bedroom on the computer, Googling the term 'third eye'. A few sentences on Wikipedia later and I had a fairly good idea what she was on about. What I'd originally understood as pertaining to Wendy watching over me using her anus—a threat very much in keeping with her Rabelaisian sensibility—actually meant something more metaphysical. Was she some kind of witch? I snorted at the thought and bit into the muffin. Straight away I tasted antibiotics. Examining the muffin closer, I noticed that what I'd taken to be fresh crust was, in fact, grey, furry mould.

X

'Yeah, it's not so much that real shit happens—it's more that the person who gets cursed ends up mentally obsessed by it,' said Laird. 'What's the name of that group?'

We were at *Muffin Siesta*. It was two days after my encounter with Wendy.

'What group?' I asked.

'That rock group.'

'Placebo?'

'Yeah, placebo, it's like a placebo. What ol' Wendy is hoping to do is fuck with your mind and let your body do all the work. You'll probably starve to death or get cancer. I suggest you get your affairs in order.'

It was hard to tell if Laird was joking.

I looked around at the bustling throng of Saturday afternoon shoppers.

The sight of a man in the distance brought our esoteric discussion to an end. The man was Jock Williams and he was standing over at *Pearl River*, the Chinese bain-marie stall in the hall.

'There he is!' I said, getting to my feet.

'Who?'

'Jock Williams.'

Laird too got up from his seat. We both moved towards the stall.

Williams stood grim-faced at the display counter of the eatery, pointing out his food choices by prodding the glass forcefully with the index finger of his right hand. As on our last meeting, he was wearing dark glasses which further added to the arrogance of his gestures. On the other side of the counter, a bored male employee followed Williams' instructions, ladling the various constituents of a meal from the designated bain-marie tubs onto a plate. So engrossed was Williams in his lunch design that he failed to notice us approach and take up positions on either side of him; myself on the right, Laird on the left.

'How's the *Zocola* going?' asked Laird, referring to the one-time brothel that Williams had spruiked for (since demolished for luxury apartments). It was at the *Zocola* that Laird and I had almost been killed and my credit card account had been fraudulently emptied. As it was, Laird's right wrist was broken violently by one of the staff—an injury that had affected his love life for some time.

The question caught Williams by surprise and he quickly turned to Laird.

'Forked any ATMs lately?' I added, causing Williams to turn abruptly to the right. Williams had used the ATM in the front office of the *Zocola* to empty my credit card account. Technically, he hadn't forked it (a crude method whereby cash is extracted from an ATM by means of a piece of cutlery); he'd merely memorized my card numbers and emptied it that way.

It occurred to me that, in assailing Williams now, Laird and I were working together—a very rare thing that made me uncomfortable.

'I don't know what you're talking about,' said Williams, removing his wallet from his coat's inner breast pocket. He moved towards the till at the end of the counter, forcing Laird out of the way in the process.

We watched him pay and accept his plate of food from the employee at the cash register. He made his way to a vacant table several metres away. We followed him.

'Do you mind if we join you?' asked Laird with mock politeness. I wondered whether Laird would be displaying such bravado had I not been there.

'Do you mind if I call security?' asked Williams as he sat down at the table.

There were only two chairs at the table and Laird quickly maxed out the seating capacity. There were no other unused chairs in the vicinity, so I had to stand while Laird and Williams sat. Consequently, I felt like a minder for Laird; a hired tough protecting his boss.

'Long time, no see Williams,' said Laird in a display of street wise rhetoric that was both clichéd and unconvincing.

'My name's not Williams,' said Williams.

'Nice try,' I said.

'Unfortunately, Williams,' said Laird, 'the ear lobe is a dead give-away.' He fondled his right ear to illustrate the point.

Williams stayed the movement of his fork-holding hand midway through its mouthward journey. He placed the fork back down on his plate of food, and wiped his mouth with the back of his hand.

'What do you want?'

'An explanation,' said Laird.

Instead of responding to Laird, Williams looked up at me. 'You were the guy with the blow-up doll, weren't you?'

I nodded.

He kept his gaze on me for several seconds longer than I thought necessary. He looked down and stared at the three-quarters full plate of lunch on the table before him.

'Look guys,' he said, 'I'm sorry about what happened to you that night.'

I snorted.

Williams raised his head.

'But I never emptied your credit card. I can't help you there.'

'Yeah right!' I said, trying to sound sarcastic.

'You use a non-bank ATM in the office of a brothel, and you think there's only one person who could have stolen money from your account? Any half-wit would know you don't use the in-house ATM at a brothel.'

His argument was, unfortunately, compelling. One of the many ongoing strains in Laird's and my friendship has its origins in the finances of that long-ago night. Because of the lack of available funds in my account, I couldn't pay the $1500 on-the-spot 'fine' imposed by the brothel management team as a result of Laird's attempt to kiss the sex worker. Laird, however, was able to pay the fine using his mother's Mastercard and I agreed, foolishly, to repay him half the $1500. It's important to bear in mind that at the time of making this commitment, I'd just narrowly escaped being beaten to death. Consequently, my gratitude may have been a little artificially pumped up.

Laird, on the other hand, had refused to contribute anything towards the $3500 theft on my credit card account on the grounds that this was totally *my* fault. Begrudgingly, he agreed to pay his half of the initial fee for the service provided by the sex worker—a service that thanks to Laird, I hadn't got to enjoy. This came to $300, which he subtracted from the $750 I owed him, but he held firm in his commitment not to give me any money for the theft.

In reality, the theft, and the subsequent financial impost had little impact on my life. Although it ushered in a period of belt-tightening, my deceased uncle's stipend saw me through the worst of it. It was the principle of the thing that irked me.

Williams' apportioning of the bulk of the blame on to me and my lack of ATM common sense would have been music to Laird's ears— had he actually liked music. He looked at me with an 'I told you so' expression on his smug face. As far as I was concerned, the matter was in no way closed. Even though I no longer held out hope of seeing any money from Laird, I continued to allow this blatant lack of decency to colour—vividly—my opinion of him.

'Why did you disappear?' I asked, referring to Williams' surreptitious departure from the bathroom of our room at the brothel just prior to the situation exploding.

'What do you mean?'

'Descending the wall..'

'Lucille Ball?'

'Why did you climb down the wall like that?' corrected Laird.

'I don't remember climbing down any wall.' He picked the loaded fork up from his plate and brought it to his mouth.

I moved closer to Williams. 'You climbed down the wall, went to the ATM in the office and, while we were distracted upstairs, you accessed my credit card account.'

'How much money did you lose?' he asked.

'$3500,' I shouted.

'Did you go to the police?' asked Williams, chewing his food.

'No.'

'Why not?' A grain of steamed rice escaped from his mouth as he asked the question.

'I didn't want to,' I said.

The fact was, had I filed an official statement with the fraud department of the credit card company, it would have drawn attention to the locations of the last two transactions, which were the adult bookstore

168

where I purchased the blow-up doll, and the ATM in the office of the brothel—neither of which I was particularly proud. Besides, I didn't want to hassle my credit card company who, on the whole, do a good job and often cop a pretty bad rap from the media. I'd felt ok about letting this one 'go through to the keeper'.

'What?' asked Williams.

'He didn't want to,' said Laird.

Williams looked at Laird and shrugged.

Laird nodded back to him, implying that whatever negative assessment Williams had reached as to my psychic health, he was in agreement with it.

I stormed off angrily in the direction of the escalator. At a distance of twenty or so meters, I looked back and saw the two men share a joke—most probably at my expense.

XI

I pushed open the front door of the apartment. It felt good to be back home. I'd left the mall straight after the meeting, foregoing a visit to *Cubist* and a planned conversation about donut robots. I was breathing hard, and it wasn't just from the exercise. I was angry.

I understood that things probably looked very different from Laird's perspective; after all, he hadn't been robbed of $3500, so it didn't matter to him if Williams was the culprit or not. Even if Laird *did* believe that Williams had robbed me, it would in no way influence his decision not to like him—my misfortune was, at best, irrelevant when it came to any decision making on Laird's part. Furthermore, Williams had nothing to do with the broken wrist he'd sustained, so he had no gripe with him on that account either.

I still believed Williams had stolen the money, but cracks were beginning to appear in that belief. Maybe it was just convenient for me to believe in Williams' guilt—I'd done it for so long I'd grown attached to it. Maybe I'd made him the villain because it provided an easy solution, a human face and body to blame rather than a void of anonymous abstract criminality. Had I, through laziness, continued to sully the reputation of an innocent man?

No, he was guilty, and Laird was a fuckwit.

I moved towards the bathroom.

I'd smelt it from the hallway, even before I'd opened the door. Standing in the half darkness of the unlit room, it was difficult to make out what it was. I switched on the light. The bathroom window was closed—that's what I noticed first. Then I saw the toilet seat lid, which was down. It looked like it had been painted. Then I saw the bath. Covering the lip of the bathtub perfectly was a one-inch thick deposit of bird shit—like cake frosting. Taking a second look, I saw that the 'paint' on the toilet seat lid was actually bird shit too, as was the overlay that covered the window ledge. There was not one drop of bird shit on the floor of the bathroom.

XII

'That's weird shit alright,' said Gary.

He stood behind the bar, polishing a glass with a bar towel. Outside, the evening peak hour traffic was waning.

'What did you do?' asked Bronwyn.

'I left and came here.'

We were, of course, discussing the mysterious arrival of bird shit in my house. I was seated at the bar with Doc, Bronwyn and, surprisingly, Kelly, the famed diarist, who I assumed was oblivious to Bronwyn's public reading of her work.

Upon making the bathroom discovery, my first instinct had been to get the hell out of there as soon as possible. I quickly phoned and left a message for Heidi, our cleaner, requesting one of her 'super cleans' ASAP. I taped off the bathroom door with masking tape and left a note for my mother on the kitchen table, telling her of the state of the bathroom and advising her to use the facilities of Mrs Barnes, our next-door neighbour.

I then hi-tailed it up to the Stella for a stiff drink and some much-needed company.

*

'The bird could have flown in through another window,' said Doc, 'done its business, then flown out. Did you check all the windows in the house?'

'The bathroom door was closed,' I said.

'The bathroom window was open, the bird flew in dropped its load and flew out again. The wind then blew the window closed.' This contribution came from Bronwyn.

'But there was hardly any wind today,' said Gary.

'Yeah, but it can get pretty swirly up where you are,' said Bronwyn.

Doc, Gary and I all shook our heads.

'I can't help but think Wendy, the Swans supporter, had something to do with it,' I said. 'Last time she was here she threatened me.'

'Does she know your address?' asked Doc.

'I don't think so. I've only spoken to her a couple of times.'

'Still she could've looked you up in the phonebook,' Gary said.

'True,' I conceded.

The idea of Wendy knowing my whereabouts and acting on that information was an awful one.

'What if the bird flew up the pipe,' said Kelly, her voice stripped of its charm by my memory of her written insults, 'then up out of the bath plug hole, then . . . '

'Maybe your mother did it,' interrupted Gary. 'I wouldn't put it past Megan's mum to pull a stunt like that—and not as a cry for help either; she'd do it to piss me off, first and foremost.'

The thought had crossed my mind that my mother might be the perpetrator. After all, our relationship had been under some stress lately. That the bird droppings had been deposited in the middle of the day, between my departure for the mall and my return home, a window of only three hours, pretty much gave her a watertight alibi. Nonetheless, I was in half a mind to make enquiries at Class Axe to make sure she'd put in a full work day.

'Megan's mum would use her own crap though, wouldn't she?' said Bronwyn. There were the makings of a smile on her face.

The remark instigated a hiatus in proceedings as we each turned over in our minds this new idea.

'No,' said Gary, after the pause. He looked defensive and confused, on the verge of anger. Bronwyn had crossed a boundary with her scat accusation. I'd learnt from past experience that, when it came to criticising his family, Gary could certainly dish it out, but if another person did it, he became protective and easily offended.

Bronwyn wisely decided to move the conversation away from Gary's wife's mother.

'It has to be someone breaking into your house,' she said.

We all agreed.

While we'd been discussing the various possibilities for the bathroom vandalism, Carter Highland, the MC from Gary's fiftieth birthday roast, had been losing big on the poker machines. He emerged from the gaming room ashen-faced, a perceptible stagger to his step.

He moved slowly towards the bar area, staring most of the time at the carpet, and deposited himself on a stool.

'Could someone get me a bloody Mary?' he asked, his voice pathetic and raspy.

'What's up with you?' Bronwyn asked.

Carter stared ahead. Eventually he let out a subtle, yet audible sigh.

'You ok, Cart?' asked Gary from behind the bar.

Carter sat looking at the floor

'You been on the pokies, mate?' asked Gary.

Carter nodded meekly.

Carter's meekness here was in stark contrast to his playing style on the machines. Some poker machine enthusiasts sit emotionless in front of the machine. Their subtle, almost expressionless movements give very little away as to the fortune being lost or briefly won back. Finally, they stand up from the stool, having lost the family home, and with little more than a shrug of the shoulders, make their way purposefully to the exit and beyond.

Carter was different. He wore the vicissitudes of chance on his sleeve for all to see.

Like most enthusiasts, he had his favourite machine, *The Dream Machine*. I can still picture him in my mind's eye: bloody Mary in his left hand, an unlit cigarette dangling from his mouth, his right foot balanced on the lower rung of the stool, his left leg dangling free. I'd observed the frenzied, downward swipe of his right index finger on the plastic buttons and the opera of facial expressions that ran the gamut of emotions: love; hate; despair; elation; belief; guilt; shame; pride; humour; childlike naivety; adult naivety; sarcasm; forgetfulness; self-deprecation; self-loathing; and general loathing—any human reaction you cared to name, over the course of a six-hour sitting, you'd see it.

All the while, he remained bonded to the machine, wheeling and dealing, doubling up, triple-lining, maxing out ... That is, of course, when he wasn't jumping for joy, having averted catastrophe with a big payout or pacing his immediate surrounds snarling at the cruelty of chance.

Like all good theatre, it built to a climax and word would spread through the pub that Carter Highland was losing big. In the final stages of a session there might be five or six of us crammed among the machines in the gaming room, transfixed as Carter vainly tried to extricate himself from a deep hole of loss. We rode with him through the highs and the lows; those brief moments of fightback and the more frequent moments of defeat, the little defeats that joined together to make the big defeat. Finally, there was that last spin, then ... nothing.

Empathy and compassion weren't nouns that sprang readily to mind at the Stella Maris. We tended not to ponder over the ramifications in the outside world of a loss at the poker machines. We'd commiserate with Carter—who wouldn't?—after a bad night's losses. One of us might buy him a Bloody Mary or lend him money for a taxi home, but the full extent of the devastation remained chiefly unexplored. Over the course of ten years we'd watched as he lost, first his house, then his flat, then his job, and then his wife and family. The last loss had been the hardest of all to take.

The indifference, on our part, was made easier to maintain by Carter's own behaviour. After each gambling catastrophe, he seemed to make a full recovery. Sure, he'd spend a couple of months in the doldrums, but then he'd be back, taking a leading role in the social life of the Stella such as hosting the weekly meat tray raffle, the annual darts tournament or the triennial men only wet T-shirt competition.

After losing the two homes and his job, Gary stepped in and agreed to monitor his gambling. To this end, it was decided that should Carter, in Gary's opinion, show signs of overstepping the boundaries of responsible betting, Gary, with the aid of the security staff if necessary, would physically remove Carter from the gaming room.

This system worked well until Gary took his family on a holiday to The Central African Republic and was away from the hotel for two weeks. In that fortnight, Carter shoved his marriage and custody rights through the coin slot of *The Dream Machine*.

But once again Carter bounced back—as evidenced by his upbeat performance as MC at Gary's roast.

Gary had sounded worried when he'd asked whether Carter had been on the pokies that night. It was a question he already knew the answer to. Carter's body language, as he moved from the gaming room to the bar, left no doubt that he was in trouble. Gary must have been feeling guilty for being behind the bar chewing the fat over a bathroom full of bird shit when he should have been in the gaming room looking out for his mate.

Some of us were disappointed too, no doubt, that we hadn't witnessed the spectacle of this most recent pokie binge—from the look on Carter's face, it must have been a doozie.

Underpinning these reactions was an obvious question: what the fuck did Carter have to lose and from where had he gotten it?

Gary placed the Bloody Mary on the bar top.

'On the house,' said Gary.

Carter stared into the middle distance. Eventually Bronwyn fetched the drink from the bar and brought it to him.

'Here you go,' she said, pressing the glass against Carter's chest.

Carter took the glass in his right hand, brought it robotically to his mouth and emptied its contents in one pull.

'Thirsty!' said Doc heartlessly.

'How much did you lose?' asked Gary.

' A lot,' said Carter staring at the floor.

'Where did you get the money?' asked Gary.

'Stacey's super.'

Stacey was Carter's ex-wife. She worked as a triage nurse at one of the bigger hospitals—tough, heroic work on the frontline; long, exhausting hours spent dealing with harsh reality as it came in bloodied and broken from all walks of life. Underpaid and underslept, she managed each month to put a little money aside for the day that would eventually come when she no longer had it in her to revive the over-dosing teenager, or tend to the stabbing victim, or restrain the violent meth addict; tasks that while commonplace, never got any easier; tasks she carried out hour after hour, week after week, year after year.

And now, somehow, a poker machine had swallowed a large chunk of this money. Somehow, Carter Highland had gained access to his ex-wife's superannuation account. How could he have managed to do this? That it was illegal was the least of it.

'Oh Christ!' said Gary.

Even Doc's tongue clicked in his mouth.

This was a truly appalling predicament.

I wanted to walk over to Carter, put my arms around him and tell him that whatever it was he'd done, it would be all right. I wanted to tell him that no situation was ever so bad that it couldn't be made good; tell him that we, his mates here at the Stella, would do whatever we could to help out; tell him that he was not alone in this world.

But then she walked in.

Amber.

Alone.

She was wearing the same poncho she'd worn the first night I met her. Outside, a dark, winter evening had fallen and, when she stepped into the hotel and stood under the interior fluoro ceiling lights, it was as if she'd walked on stage—waif-like, precious jetsam blown in from the uncaring world. And although she was smiling, subtle reflections on her two cheeks signalled that she'd been crying too.

She stood for a moment and gestured awkwardly with her arms, as if to say: 'well, here I am!'

I got up from my stool and walked straight over to her without saying a word to anyone, including Carter—who I never saw again.

'Amber!' I said, standing facing her.

'Hi!' she said.

'How are you?'

'I'm ok.'

'Wow, long time no see!' I noticed that my right hand was in my trouser pocket, jingling coins like her father had done. I quickly pulled it out, leaving it to hang limp and weird by my side.

'Could we go somewhere and talk?' she said.

'Sure, follow me.'

I led the way to the beer garden.

*

Although both pool tables were in use, the beer garden was relatively uncrowded. We sat at a table near the back wall, as far from the glass entry doors as possible.

I waited for her to speak, but she didn't.

Eventually I broke the ice: 'Did you get my letter?'

She nodded.

'Look, I'm really sorry about my behaviour the other night,' I said.

'So am I,' she said.

There was something a little too easy about her apology. Furthermore, was she apologising for her own behaviour or was she expressing sorrow at mine? We sat for a moment while I pondered the possible reasons for why she'd come.

Had she had a change of heart? Had she, after meditating on my correspondence, come to realize she'd been too quick to judge? Did she now believe I was a good man, solid and dependable, whose wisdom, accrued over many years, could provide the sturdy framework around which a good partnership is built?

Or did she just want to patch things up; re-establish a platonic semi-friendship in order to assuage her own guilt concerning the harshness of her response to my advances? After all, she did call me a 'fucking moron'.

This was more plausible, but much less attractive.

'Oh, I've got something for you,' she said, pulling from her bag a small brown object, which she handed to me. It was heavy, considering its size.

'I cast it myself,' she said.

'Oh!'

'Yeah, it's lead. It's a cicada.'

I looked at the small sculpture resting on my palm. It resembled more a burnt cocktail frankfurter than a cicada. Truth be known, its strongest resemblance was to human waste. Vaguely discernible were a head, thorax, abdomen, one crumpled wing and half of a leg. An artist's impression, I I guessed. But its heft was impressive.

'Wow, it's beautiful,' I said

'Thanks.'

The fact that she'd come bearing gifts, regardless of the quality, was, to my reckoning, evidence of strong emotions. But I knew not to get ahead of myself—this is a trout that must be caught with tickling, I thought, then instantly wished I hadn't.

She began to speak about a recent rehearsal for a dance piece she was working on (something involving someone being struck in the face with a cactus), but my mind was almost totally distracted by the new possibilities her visit represented.

Did she have any idea of the significance for me of her coming to the hotel? I had lunged at her amorously and now here she was, back for more! How could she not purposefully be trying to reignite the smouldering embers of my passion?

'I think it'll really shake them up at the Institute,' she said.

'Yes.' I agreed

She knew damn well what she was playing with—she was almost thirty for god's sake!

But what about Roderick? Where did he fit in? I remembered only too well the way she'd called him 'baby' that night. Maybe she was one of those 'two at once' women? By this I mean a woman with the emotional capacity to be involved in a mature caring relationship with more than just one man at a time.

Would I be willing to share her with Roderick?

Maybe, given the right set of circumstances.

'How's Roderick?' I asked, eager to test the waters.

'We've broken up.'

'Oh.'

I felt a weight lifted off my shoulders. Good lord! I wasn't the type of man who would share a woman with another. It didn't surprise me that they'd broken up. After all he was a conceited, overbearing knob.

'That's a shame,' I said, hoping it didn't sound sarcastic.

'Irreconcilable differences,' she said.

'It happens,' I said in an attempt at sounding worldly.

'He was too controlling. I needed to get away.'

I nodded.

'So, here I am!'

'Here *we* are!' I said. I made a sweep of the beer garden with my right hand.

'Yes, *here* we are!' she repeated, a fragile smile on her face.

I don't regret that night. I was following my instincts; what else could I do? As the evening progressed, the bar got more crowded and word spread that Geoff Maddox was with a woman. For the first time in a long, long while, I felt empowered as a man. I tried to control my drinking, but it was always going to be a struggle due to the generous vibe in the house towards me. Even Gary gave me a twenty per cent discount on local tap beer.

The symbolism of Amber's gift took hold of me. Wasn't I like the cicada, a creature that after many blind winters fruitlessly labouring under the cold, damp earth is suddenly liberated—airborne and beautiful—able to soar among the branches of trees? It wasn't so much that it had been a long time since I'd experienced the uplifting rush of being in, or on the verge of, a relationship; I'd actually *never* really experienced it—at least not a proper one with somebody like Amber.

And I played the part of the boyfriend well: paying for her drinks; introducing her to almost everyone; diligently including her in conversations; praising her dancing to the skies; going with her to the beer garden so she could smoke; waiting patiently for her outside the toilets—all this and more. I was a regular Don Juan.

At one point, Bronwyn, dark with booze, tried to intimidate her with a slab of gobbledegook she'd memorized from Heidegger. She obviously wanted to establish to the newcomer her position as top dog in the pub brains department. Noticing the nervous expression beginning to form on Amber's face, I quickly stepped between them, and bore the full brunt of Bronwyn's lecture. I toughed it out to completion, absorbing the predictable withering look of disappointment that eventually showed on her face when she got what she wanted, the confession of ignorance on the part of a listener.

Although I played the knight in mirror-polished armour well, I took care never to refer to Amber as my 'girlfriend'. No, she was just my 'friend.' I knew the dangers of 'over-egging the omelette' and frightening off a potential mate. Even though I hadn't yet earned the right to publicly designate her as my significant other, it didn't stop me from demonstrating, through body language, the romantic nature of our partnership. I sat close to her at all times and although I never went so far as to put my arm around her, I was nonetheless 'hands on' when it came to underlining important conversation points or offering to get her more drink from the bar. I trod the path extremely carefully here— I'd already cruelled the pitch back in Newtown, and I didn't want it to happen again. On the whole, I made do with a lot of lingering eye contact, smiling and the clenching and unclenching of both fists in front of my chest—an action I deemed suggestive of deep affection.

Amber and I were sitting at a table near the gaming room when Kelly lurched up, uninvited,

'So, when are you two getting married?' she asked. Her frivolous question was supplemented with a drunken stomach bump to the table that spilt Amber's and my drinks. It was obvious she'd been dispatched by a higher authority to ask us the question. Sure enough, Bronwyn, seated at the bar, was looking directly at us—her claret-fuelled grin did her face no favours.

It was about 12.30am and the pub was going off. Kelly's question had interrupted me as I was midway through telling Amber about the success of *Changes*, the jazz club; how it had completely changed the culture of The Rocks and how I would still be running it but for a deep desire to constantly be setting myself new challenges.

Although annoyed at having been interrupted, I was also interested to see how Amber would react to Kelly's lame jape—whether she would wave her hands in the air and say: 'oh no you've got the wrong idea!' or turn to me with a show of embarrassment before laughing nervously at the preposterousness of such a question and then ask me, theatrically: 'so Geoff, when *are* we going to get married?'

She chose the latter.

Kelly stood, swaying and smiling, unable to add anything further to the conversation. Eventually, realising her errand had been carried out, she headed back to the bar and to Bronwyn.

I had a strong desire not to expose Amber to Doc's toxicity. By keeping one eye on his movements—from bar to beer garden and back—I'd managed to steer clear of him for the entire time since Amber's arrival. After Kelly's departure, I successfully manipulated Amber into the poker machine gaming room, which, although cramped and noisy, provided safe haven.

The lighting in the gaming room was much darker than in the main body of the pub and the play of the constantly blinking lights from the machines produced a parody of enchantment—as did their clicking and spinning noises, which fused together to form a dismal mimicry of nocturnal wildlife ambience. Every so often this disenchanted forest setting was punctuated by the eruption of a beeping fanfare. Was this to be our love grotto?

'I don't normally come in here,' I said, lying.

We sat in front of *Rats of Tobruk*, a war-themed pokie positioned well away from the coin trough of *The Dream Machine*, which was full with what I assumed was Carter Highland's desperate urine.

I feigned ignorance about the workings of the machines, pretending not to know how to put coins in and asking for Amber's assistance. I didn't know yet what her stance on gambling might be, so I deemed it prudent to play it safe and come across as someone who only under rare circumstances might have a bit of a flutter, not a middle-aged man who regularly wasted hundreds of dollars on slot machines.

'Oh, I see,' I said, 'I press this button, and these buttons spin!' I infused the utterance with childlike astonishment.

'Are you making fun of me?' Amber said.

For a moment, I was seized with panic. I'd overdone it, my dishonest naivety had been misinterpreted as ridicule.

'No.'

She punched me playfully on the shoulder.

'You're such a kidder!' she said, laughing.

I relaxed.

Not only was I off the hook with regards to having offended her, I was now free to enjoy playing the machine properly. I quickly set about losing a $100 in about twenty minutes. All the while Amber watched on, enjoying my display of fearless betting. I got the feeling she liked being with a gambling man.

I was king of the world. I felt impervious to whatever life could throw at me. Let it take its best shot!

I was about to get up to go and break a fresh fifty-dollar note at the bar, when Laird and Jock Williams entered the gaming room.

It was impossible not to notice Williams sizing Amber up; it was downright offensive.

Rather than sit down, he and Laird remained standing, which meant Amber and I had to swivel our stools 180 degrees in order to converse with them—something that put a brake on my gaming.

'Buenas noches!' said Williams. His use of Spanish alluded to Amber's poncho. He was dressed as the wealthy farmer in the city— cream trousers, blue open-necked shirt and Blundstone boots. His right eye was covered with a dark leather eye patch. He reeked of after-shave, not a bad thing seeing as it was becoming clear Carter Highland had been eating asparagus shortly before his final pokie binge.

'*Buenas noches senor,*' answered Amber, bowing her head in mock formality—an action that annoyed me.

'*Yo hablo espanol muy bien,*' said Williams.

Amber nodded vacantly.

'Hi,' said Laird, 'I'm Laird.'

'This is Amber,' I said with pride and worry.

'And I'm Jock,' Williams said, grinning at Amber. 'You speak Spanish very well.'

'Thank you,' said Amber.

'*Ich möchte noch ein Bier,*' I said. It was the only complete foreign sentence I knew.

'What?' said Amber.

'I think it's time for another beer,' I said.

Williams bent down and appeared to study Amber's neck.

'What's the problem?' I asked

'You don't have a plug there do you?' Williams asked Amber.

'No.' Amber was confused.

I wasn't.

Let me take the opportunity to write here that although I did pur-chase a blow-up doll many years ago, the doll was left on the floor of an airport, deflated and unused. Never at any time since have I had the need or inclination to buy another such item.

'Sorry, it must have been the light,' said Williams.

'I don't have *any* piercings,' said Amber.

She didn't seem offended at Williams' question. Nor had she noti-ced Laird's snigger. For the moment, I was safe but I knew Williams could seriously hurt me here and I was beginning to squirm.

But then something occurred to me: if I'd read Williams' body language correctly, he found Amber attractive. Thus Williams would be facing a dilemma: if he continued using his Blow Up Doll jokes to embarrass me, he risked offending Amber whose non-understanding of the coded doll references was an important part of the humour. If she was to find out she was being used as a conduit for his smut, she would surely be insulted and his chances of coupling with her would be severely diminished. Part of me welcomed the competition for Amber's affections that Williams represented, because it put a gag on his schoolboy doll jibes.

But all that was predicated on the belief that he fancied her. Maybe I'd misread his sizing up of Amber. Perhaps he was more interested in pursuing his puerile humour and humiliating me than in impressing an attractive woman. Either way, I'd find out soon enough.

'I've never been into body decoration,' said Amber. 'I'm happy with what I've got.'

Williams stood with a smile broadening on his face.

He looked at me.

I looked at him

'Who'd like a beer?' he said. 'I'm going to the bar.'

He'd backed down, for the time being at least. On one hand, I was relieved; on the other, I now knew for sure that Williams was a rival and I was not relieved.

*

'I held his head in my arms as he died. I'd grown up with this pony— we were best friends. I'd had him since I was seven! I made a promise to myself that night in the barn that I would do everything I could to educate people about Equine Cushings Disease.' Williams was holding court and holding it well.

We were still in the gaming room.

'Wow!' said Amber.

I noticed even Laird nodding his head in approval.

'So you're a vet then?' asked Amber.

'I have skills related to equine medicine, but, no, I'm not formally qualified. I do know a lot about animals, being a fifth-generation landowner. You have to, to run a thousand head of cattle.'

Laird shook his head in a display of faux disbelief at the enormity of Williams' task—Laird and he were becoming a double act.

'Have you ever had to castrate a bull using your teeth?' I asked. I shouldn't have. Not only was it a cheap shot that stereotyped farmers as being boorish, but it also struck me that Amber might be a woman who appreciated this sort of behaviour in a man.

Williams chose not to dignify the question with a response, which made me think that perhaps he *had* engaged in the practice.

The question hung undignified.

'I used to love riding when I lived up the coast,' said Amber.

'Out on the property,' said Williams, 'I love to get up right at the crack of dawn, saddle up one of the mares and just go riding—all day sometimes. It clears my head.'

'I would love that!' said Amber.

'You should come out there,' said Williams.

'Sounds great!'

I couldn't compete with Williams and his horse stories.

Laird didn't help matters. Several times during Williams' description he made eye contact with me. His expression was one of ridiculing condescension that said: 'give up mate, you're outclassed.'

And maybe he was right. What on earth did I have to offer someone like Amber?

I could feel the first stage of a self-loathing mindset establishing
itself. I took a swig from my beer, got up and moved towards the exit
of the gaming room.

*

While Williams had been boasting in the gaming room, outside in the
lounge, a situation had been developing. Doc had told Kelly about
Bronwyn's public reading of her diary. And Kelly was none too pleased.

When I entered the lounge, things had escalated to the point
where Kelly, isolated over on the far side of the room, was wildly brandishing the Stella's commemorative cricket bat—a prized piece of pub
treasure upon whose surface the autographs of the 1981 New Zealand
and Australian cricket teams had been inscribed. It normally lived in
an imitation oak and glass display case, mounted on the far right-hand
wall next to the end booth.

Kelly was swishing the air with the bat and Gary was advancing
on her, forcing her backwards, using the legs of a bar stool to prod at
her—like a lion tamer with a chair. He was flanked by the two security
guards, Steve, on the left, Megan, on the right.

A small crowd had set up a chant of 'Kelly, Kelly Kelly . . . '

Gary had already herded her some distance using this stool method,
the general aim of which was to corral her into a confined space and
then wait for her to exhaust herself swinging, whereupon the two security guards would move in, pincer-like, and overpower her.

Some have wondered, given the potential for serious injury, why
the bat was kept in such an accessible place. This was chiefly due to
Gary's philosophy of not punishing the whole group for the sins of

the individual; why deprive the vast majority of non-violent drinkers the chance of viewing a rare item because of the behaviour of one or two delinquents? Very few people over the years had removed the bat from the cabinet. The vast majority of conflicts had been settled by way of the word, the fingernail or the fist.

Furthermore, it was more than likely a person would reach for the bat late in the evening, at which point they were generally so drunk and tired that only a weak and glancing blow could be delivered. (Occasionally, there was real timing and power behind the 'shot' as was the case with Ed Firth, who received a custodial sentence for grievous bodily harm inflicted on his brother Dale late one night, following a charity pie toss gone wrong).

On the whole, though, a bat assault was a harmless, festive occasion; a moment of high hilarity that inevitably came to occupy a sentimental place in the oral history of the hotel, without which history the idea of using the bat might never occur to patrons in the first place. Constituting damage to memorabilia, a bat escalation invariably resulted in a life ban for the batter. Sometimes he or she was a well-liked regular, pushed to breaking point, and consequently, amid the cheering and egging on of the crowd, there was also the melancholy understanding that this was a form of farewell; a swan song before moving on to another hotel—or, as with the Firth assault, prison. This wasn't so much the case with Kelly however, whose vicious diary entries had earned her no friends among the regular patrons of the Stella. In this instance, there was more a feeling of good riddance—at least that's how I felt and I think I'm a fairly indicative person.

As for the instigator of all this, Bronwyn, she was over by the bar, safe and smiling, enjoying the carnival of Kelly's hysterics, as were many other people in the room.

'Get a-fucking-way from me you arsehole!' Kelly snarled, stepping evermore backwards towards the front corner of the room.

It was plain that the target of her anger was now no longer just Bronwyn; Bronwyn had set her off, but now Kelly's rage had entered a deeper level. Her use of the bat had changed too, from being one of inflicting injury on Bronwyn to one of defence against the menacing advances of Gary and the two bouncers.

'Put the bat down Kelly,' said Gary, inching forward with the barstool.

'I'll put the bat down if you fucking back off!'

'Put it down,' he repeated.

The crowd morphed from the 'Kelly, Kelly...' chant into Put down the bat, put down the bat.' Its cha cha syncopation was highly infectious, causing more people to join in. The number of punters in the room swelled as patrons migrated from the beer garden into the lounge, eager to find out the cause of the commotion.

I found myself clapping my hands and chanting along.

Eventually, Kelly was coerced into the front right corner of the lounge. She stood, defensively moving the bat horizontally in the air before her while Gary and the two bouncers waited, uncertain as to how to proceed. It had the semblance of being staged; a tableau vivant of raucous pub life; a parody of indoor cricket.

The chant faded away sharply as we all became in thrall to the sudden intensity of the moment. Kelly was trapped like prey and the possibility of something truly horrible happening quickly dawned on us.

Megan, the security guard on the right, broke ranks first and made a charge at Kelly. She (Kelly) being right-handed meant the attack was on her weak 'leg-side'. Kelly managed to land a blow high on Megan's shoulder, its power harmlessly absorbed by both the soft padding of her Stella Maris fleece and the fat of her upper arm. The momentum of the swing, combined with Megan's forward movement, caused the face of the bat to slide up from Megan's shoulder and brush against her neck as she successfully placed Kelly in a bear hug, Once in the hug, Kelly could only manage to land soft, one-handed taps to the back of Megan's head. The scene reminded me of a batsman congratulating a teammate for having scored a century.

Kelly's shoulder blow and head taps were recorded by the pub's CCT facility, and would be trotted out in court as evidence in the subsequent assault hearing.

Quickly Steve, the other bouncer, joined his colleague and cricket morphed into rugby league as the two security guards wrestled Kelly to the floor.

The excessive force used by the bouncers was also recorded by the CCT and would be used as evidence in Kelly's counterclaim against the hotel staff.

Somehow, from the writhing mass of bodies, Kelly's arm poked out, her hand still clasping the bat. Gary put the stool down, strode over and wrenched the memorabilia from Kelly's grasp. He turned and walked back in the direction of the bat cabinet, leaving Steve and Megan to mop up.

And so ended Kelly's tenure as a regular at the Stella Maris. She was frogmarched to the exit and beyond by the two bouncers.

When the doors to the street swung shut behind the three people, there was sparse and brief applause. Twenty seconds later, when Steve and Megan re-entered the pub—without Kelly—they were greeted with boisterous whooping and cheering. They played to the crowd, bowing ironically and gesticulating comically with their arms.

By the time I got to the bar, Gary had already replaced the bat in its display case and was standing in his normal position behind the serving counter. All around, people were experiencing the high of a post-violent moment. Many were congratulating Bronwyn on her courage under fire. Apparently, there'd been a long and unpleasant build-up, prior to Kelly reaching for the bat, which Bronwyn had seen off without backing down. The fact that she was a good deal bigger in build to Kelly wasn't considered relevant in the appraisal of courage. Bronwyn was now wearing a wine-soaked shirt and had a scratched forearm—evidence of having survived an ugly struggle.

I bought a schooner of Resch's and headed back to the gaming room.

Amber was still there—on her own.

'What happened to Laird and the other guy?' I asked.

'Jock?'

'Yeah.'

'They left.'

'Oh.'

'Jock had to get up early in the morning.'

Having Amber tell me why Jock had left struck a sour note; it represented a level of complicity I wasn't comfortable with.

I looked over at the *Dream Machine's* coin trough and noticed ripples in the auburn liquid caused by the death throes of a stuck moth.

'What do you feel like doing?' I asked, sadly expectant of the answer.

'I'd like another drink.'

That was not what I expected.

'Hey,' I said, a newfound skip to my voice. 'Why don't we go back out into the lounge?'

'Lead the way!'

With the Kelly show over, things had begun to return to relative normality. All the people who'd come in from the beer garden had gone back to the beer garden, and the general buzz in the room had died down.

We made our way to a table in the lounge.

'What'll you have?' I asked, eager to fetch.

'A glass of white wine and a packet of Hume's.'

'What flavour?'

'Plain.'

'Hey, what is it with the crisps? You don't really look like someone who eats a lot of crisps.'

'Oh, I like the packet. I like the crisps too—I pig out but I like the packet.'

'The cylinders?'

'Yeah. I'm going to use them in a dance piece.'

I shook my head in order to show disbelief at the inventiveness of such an idea. I put my beer down on the table and set out once more for the bar.

*

'Who's the bird?' asked Doc.

I was standing at the bar, waiting for Gary to finish filling a wine glass from a six-litre cask of room temperature moselle. Doc was seated at a stool; the same one he'd occupied more or less continuously since the afternoon.

'Just a friend.'

'She's a bit of a looker.'

'I suppose so,' I said nonchalantly.

'How did *you* end up with something like that?' Doc asked. Even by his standards he was very drunk.

'Thanks Gary,' I said, handing him a ten-dollar note. 'Keep the change.' I don't normally tip, but I wanted to vacate the bar area as soon as possible—it was only fifty cents anyway.

I moved with determination in the direction of the lounge table.

'Hey,' Doc shouted from his stool, 'aren't you going to introduce me to your woman?'

I ignored him and walked on until I reached the table.

'Here you go,' I said. I handed the glass to Amber then I realised I'd forgotten the chips. I looked back towards the bar and watched as Doc staggered towards us, monstrously reminiscent of a child taking his first clumsy steps towards his proud father.

I didn't know how he kept his pants up. On one of his last visits to the men's room, Doc had decided not to do up the zipper of his jeans, nor the top button, nor the decrepit belt that seemed mouldy and cracked beyond function. The onlooker was presented with a white 'V' shape, whose base hung in the sub-crotch gap between his thighs, and whose extremities were implausibly supported on both sides just below his hips. I mused over the possibility that some substance acquired during the evening was at work, adhering Doc's skin to the inside of his jeans.

I say the V shape was white, (the factory setting of his underpants) but, in truth, it was more of an off-white, in places bordering on beige. With several of the lower buttons being either undone or missing, the bottoms of his short-sleeved shirt flapped openly in response to his stagger, teasing the audience with their covering and uncovering of Doc's underwear in a sort of hands-free *can can*.

At a point several metres from our table he stopped, bent forward and sneezed violently. Miraculously, he spilt not a drop from the three-quarters-full schooner of dark beer, which he held in his right hand.

I sat down, positioning myself so that the maximum amount of table stood between me and Doc, who quickly righted himself and resumed his approach.

'Hello,' he said on arrival at the table, bending over so that his face was uncomfortably close to Amber's. His missing teeth complimented the two thick strands of jelly that dangled from his nostrils.

'Hello,' said Amber, unavoidably.

'I'm, Doc. I might be old, but I know a thing or two.'

'I bet you do,' said Amber.

Doc grinned. It was a grin telegraphing the first stage in an absurd campaign to woo a prospective mate. I had witnessed similar from Doc on many previous occasions.

Amber smiled evenly in return.

The open-plan nature of Doc's attire allowed for the developing bulge in his crotch area to be easily viewed.

Doc dragged a chair into position and sat down.

'Long night!' he said.

Neither Amber nor I said anything in response.

'Reminds me of a night I once had in the navy.'

'You were in the navy?' asked Amber.

'Many years ago now,' he said.

'How old are you Doc?' I asked.

I reckoned him to be in his early sixties, even though he possessed the spring in his step of an 80-year-old.

'Old enough to know better,' he said, trying to wink at Amber. The effort caused a trombone-like noise to sound in the near distance.

'You're a character!' said Amber.

'I aim to please!' said Doc.

She laughed and play-punched him on the shoulder, a similar gesture to the one she had performed with me, back in the gaming room.

Subsequent to Amber landing her punch, Doc made quick eye
contact with me. I don't know if Amber noticed it, but the message
was loud and clear: 'pay attention junior and see how it's done.'

Doc playfully rubbed his shoulder, feigning injury.

'Steady on! I'm an old man. You shouldn't punch an old man!'

Doc found this utterance extremely funny and, after a raspberry of
saliva and remnant beer, he began to hiss, catlike, with uncontrollable
mirth.

His laughter morphed seamlessly into a coughing fit that had him
rocking back and forth in his chair for almost thirty seconds, at the end
of which he proceeded to wipe his face across the entire length of his
bare forearm before taking a long restorative drink from his schooner.

'I'm sorry,' he said. 'I haven't laughed like that in years. You're a
funny girl.'

'Funny ha ha or funny peculiar?' said Amber.

'Both!' said Doc, who once more laughed. This time he managed
to tame it before it developed into a hacking fit.

'So, are you a vet?' Hadn't she asked Williams the same question?

'I don't want to talk about it,' said Doc, clearly wanting to.

He took another pull from his drink.

He placed the glass back down on the table, then picked up a beer
coaster, sodden from the evening's spillage, and while holding it above
his lap, began, grim-faced, to slowly tear it into strips, obviously wishing to convey the impression of a man haunted by troubling memories.

I had witnessed Doc use tales of his time in the navy for the purposes of picking up women before. In essence, the ploy had rational

foundations: stories of heroism are versatile instruments in the tool-box of romance as are those designed to create sympathy.

Doc's problem however was that the evidence for the hard lessons he'd received during his brief stint protecting our way of life was scant on the ground.

Gary had first called his bluff one night when Doc refused to pro-duce official material to support his claims of having 'witnessed things no man ever should'. So too had Yolanda, Bronwyn's friend, herself a naval officer who'd served as part of Operation Slipper in Afghanistan and who, very early on, in a failed courtship attempt by Doc, had noticed that things didn't add up.

In terms of conveying passion, Doc was on slightly firmer ground with his other main topic of conversation—medicine. His eyes filled with tears when he spoke of his time at medical school and the unfair-ness of a system that caused him to finish his studies prematurely (before the end of first year); his voice faltered convincingly as he recounted tales of injustice and corruption at the highest levels of the medical fraternity.

But, in Doc's mind, this wasn't nearly as sexy as the fabricated accounts of his life in uniform.

Over the years, I've grown sympathetic towards Doc's looseness with the truth; if anything, I find it rather sad. So what if he needed to invent a back-story that was unable to withstand the most cursory of interrogations? Aren't we all guilty of exaggeration and prevarication at moments when the urge to impress grabs us?

But tonight, things were different; I had no room for the luxury of sympathy. I'd be mad to think Doc posed any substantive threat to my prospects with Amber; it was more that his sentimental sob story would eat into the diminishing amount of time I had left with her. At

2.45am, the bell would be rung, ceiling lights would begin to flash, last drinks would be called, and I would turn into a pumpkin.

'Are you ok?' Amber asked Doc, much to my disappointment.

Doc closed his eyes and sighed.

'I'll be all right,' he said, trying to sound stoic.

Readers who find the actions of the various players in this account unbelievable, should realise that it was now well after 2am. Drunkenness is a poorly performed drama written by an incompetent playwright. I'm telling it how it was.

Right on cue Doc scrunched his face. Waterworks!

I'd be the first to admit to the use of tears for carnal gain (unsuccessfully) and I also admit that Doc's tears, although not related to any Naval memory, probably had real origins in his life-damaged psyche, his ability to be able to bring them on at will notwithstanding. But I was in no mood for empathy.

Doc brushed the coaster confetti he'd been making from his lap onto the carpet. He folded his arms, placed them on the table and, having rested his forehead on his uppermost forearm, he began to roll his head from side to side.

'My buddies, my buddies . . . ' I heard him say.

We were well on the path towards having the rest of the evening hijacked by 'Doc care'—a dread reinforced by Amber, who'd begun to rub the back of Doc's neck!

I had an idea: there was an outside chance I could use cigarettes in order to rupture the continuity of Doc's compassion ploy. I knew his smoking habit was such that sooner or later he would need to go out to the beer garden. If I introduced the subject of smoking and thus got him thinking about cigarettes, I just might get him to act on his desire. . .

'How much is a packet of cigarettes these days?' I asked.

'About $20,' said Amber.

'Wow! That's expensive. I can remember when they were only $2.50.'

'Most of it goes in tax,' said Amber.

'Wow! If I smoked nowadays like I used to, I'd be spending about $6000 a year on cigarettes!'

I noticed Doc had stopped sobbing.

'Boy, you must have smoked a lot,' said Amber, who had stopped the neck massage.

'About 20 a day.'

'That's a lot!'

I nodded.

'I can even remember that ad,' I said.

'What ad?' asked Amber.

'You'd be too young to know it. How did it go?'

I began to sing:

Join the club,
Join the club,
Join the Escort club.

Doc shifted his head, his eyes now met my gaze—a snake in a basket.

Thirty-five cents and you're a member.

'Who was the guy who sang that?' I asked

Amber shook her head.

'It's on the tip of my tongue . . .'

Doc sat up straight.

'Tony Barber,' he said.

I had successfully coaxed him into an upright position. 'It's times like these I really miss smoking,' I said. 'There's nothing like that relaxation at the end of an evening, when you've got a beer in your hand and you're talking with friends.'

I was laying it on thick, but subtlety would be lost on this audience.

'Why don't you have one?' said Amber

'Oh, no. I can't. It's been ten years. If I had one now, I'd have to have another one, and then another one. I'd be right back on them.'

'Maybe you'd be able to control it more, now that you're older,' said Amber reaching down for her bag. I tried to ignore the covert reference to our age gap.

Meanwhile, Doc had pulled from his pocket a packet of cigarettes—the health warning cover image, a close-up of a mouth motley with sores and missing teeth, could have been mistaken for a poorly-framed selfie he'd taken.

'I think I'll go and have a cigarette,' said Amber rising from her chair, a leather tobacco pouch now in her hand.

'Me too,' said Doc.

Doc's emotional outburst must have had a sobering effect on him; he got to his feet, did up his trousers and shirt buttons and wiped his face with his forearm. He was now all spruced up for his smoking date with Amber. My tactic had backfired. Rather than separate the two of them, I'd joined them together in the fellowship of smoking. Doc even managed to get his arm around Amber's waist as they made their way towards the glass doors leading to the beer garden. I watched as Doc chivalrously held the right-hand door open for Amber to walk through.

If I followed them out to the beer garden, it would look a little bit too much like I thought Doc was a competent competitor in the quest for Amber's attention. It was better to play it cool and make her come to me. I took out a ten-cent coin and, flicking it with the nail of my index finger, spun it on the table's surface.

*

'It must be getting late,' said Amber.

She'd returned from the beer garden with Doc. He stood next to her, smirking.

'I think it's about 2.40am,' I said.

'Time for a nightcap,' said Doc. He turned to Amber, 'what'll it be?'

'Oh, I'm all right thanks Doc,' she said, sitting down. 'I don't think I can drink anything more.'

'Ok, I'll be back in a tick. Don't go away!'

'I won't,' she said to his departing back.

We watched him trying to jog to the bar. I needed to move us before he returned.

'Can we go outside to the beer garden?' I said.

'But I've just come back from there.'

'I know, but I'm starting to feel a bit claustrophobic, I wouldn't mind some fresh air.'

'Ok,' she said, puzzled. 'You're not ill, are you?'

'Never felt better,' I said trying to smile.

*

We sat where we'd sat earlier in the night when Amber had given me the cicada jewellery that I now felt weighing down my left trouser pocket

'Amber, I was wondering,' I began.

'Yes?'

'Well . . . ' This was the moment I had been both looking forward to and dreading all evening. I wanted to sound sincere, but I didn't want to sound sappy. I wanted innocence without ignorance; naivety without gullibility. I wanted to show strength of character without being overbearing; straightforwardness without seeming facile. In the end, I settled for being the real me. I think.

'Would you like to see me again?'

'Geoff, I need to take things slowly,' she said, shaking her head slightly. 'I've just broken up from a long-term relationship. I need time.'

'Of course,' I heard a rasp in my voice. 'I understand.' I didn't. Why had she given me the metal insect?

We watched the dregs of a pool game being played out on the table nearest us.

'I mean,' I said, 'I totally understand, but it'd be great to meet up and talk a bit about your work sometime.'

Amber looked down at the ground. Several large cockroaches were scavenging for leavings on the surfaces of the paving stones.

Through the glass doors leading back to the lounge I could see Doc. He was standing, scanning the room, glass of beer in hand, yet to realise where we were. It wouldn't take him long.

'I don't know, Geoff.'

I had to work fast.

'I mean, we could meet up for coffee or something.'

Doc had seen us and was making his way towards us.

'Just for half an hour . . . ' Doc pushed open the doors and stepped onto the brick paving of the beer garden. Amber was still looking at her footwear. ' . . . in the afternoon.'

Doc looked angry.

'I don't know,' said Amber.

Doc was only ten metres away now.

'How about Tuesday?' I was now blurting.

'Ok,' said Amber

'Howdy folks!' Doc called out.

'Smarties café. 2pm,' I snapped.

She nodded.

'You can't get rid of me that easy!' said Doc. His forced smile was grotesquely lit by the flames of the portable gas heater standing nearby.

'We weren't trying to get rid of you,' said Amber. 'Please, come and join us!'

Doc sat down, drinking from his glass as he did so. At the moment his backside met the wood of the chair the bell sounded and the lights in the awnings above the pool tables began to blink; it was now 'last drinks'.

I stood up. I'd gotten what I wanted and was thirsty.

'I might get myself one last drink,' I said. 'Do you still not want one, Amber?'

She shook her head.

As I walked past the pool table, a tall man in his early thirties slammed the eight ball into the bottom left pocket to win the game. I put my hand in my left trouser pocket, closed my fingers around the lump of metal Amber had gifted me and entered the lounge.

I purchased a schooner of beer at the bar, left Gary a generous tip and returned to the beer garden to find Doc sitting by himself.

PART 3
The Wind of My Breath

I

The knocking had transcended the narrative of my dream to become a phenomenon for my now awake senses.

'Mr Maddox,' said the female voice. 'Are you in there?'

Judging by the distance from the branch-shaped shadow projected onto the carpet to my bedroom chest of drawers, it was around 2pm.

I got out of bed—actually *off* the bed. There was no need to get dressed as I was still in the clothes I had on the night before. I opened the bedroom door.

It was Heidi our cleaning lady, although 'lady' implies someone much older than she was. She'd been recommended to my mother by Lionel, another instance of his ongoing influence in our lives. At first, I'd baulked at the idea of paid domestic help, it being anathema to my ideals of egalitarianism. But I'd since softened my stance. After all, she needed the money to support herself while she completed her science degree (honours in Zoology) and to this end, apart from cleaning houses, she also tutored high school students, gardened and worked several shifts at a *Mister Minute* key cutting outlet.

She stood in the hallway looking frightened and angry.

'You don't pay me enough to clean up stuff like that!'

She was of course referring to the bird faeces in the bathroom. I had purposely not been clear in my phone message as to what the 'clean' might entail.

My head felt like I'd eaten detergent-flavoured ice cream too quickly. I tried to adjust to the light in the hallway as memories of the final stages of the previous evening came back. Gary, Bronwyn, Doc and I had kicked on at *The Beard*, after the Stella closed. I couldn't recall the taxi trip home but I did recall seeing the taped bathroom door and deciding to celebrate the dance of life on one of the garden beds outside. (I hoped none of the neighbours bore witness). I vaguely remembered dawn breaking.

'This is hazchem territory,' she said. 'I should be wearing a mask and a jumpsuit.'

She had a point. The state of the bathroom was confronting. Recently she'd told me that at some point she was moving to Berlin to join up with her muso boyfriend. I wondered if I'd just brought forward the date of her inevitable resignation from chez Maddox.

'How much extra?' I asked.

'I want $300 to clean this up. What is it anyway?'

'Pigeon shit.'

Bursting out of the bathroom, Heidi's Alsatian, Fonzie, bounded down the hallway eager to be with his mistress. Once alongside, he jubilantly shook his body, and sprayed the nearby environs with the material in which he'd just been rolling.

*

'That wasn't pigeon shit,' said Heidi.

We were standing in the kitchen, the clean-up completed. It hadn't taken that long, certainly not $300 worth of long. Heidi had scooped most of the stuff into a bucket, which she'd emptied outside in the garden—'does wonders for the soil,' she'd assured me. The remainder she'd wiped up with paper towels before flushing them down the toilet.

My heart sank as I braced myself for some truly awful news.

'It's got to be a bigger bird,' she said. 'I think it's swan shit. I took an avian unit last year. We studied black swans.'

'That's interesting,' I said. 'How many swans would have been needed?'

'To get that amount?'

I nodded.

'In one day?'

I nodded.

'Probably 90.

Hey Amber,
Great night last night! Had a bit of a headache this morning!
Just confirming Tuesday. Smarties is down near Church Street,
opposite the hardware. I'll see you there at 2pm. Can't wait to catch
up and hear about all your work.
xxx
Geoff

Believe it or not, this email took over two hours to construct. With darkness falling outside, I pressed send. It was dinner time. I emerged from my room and sat at the dining table. A vaguely oval-shaped piece of crumbed veal was positioned on the plate before me between a mound of boiled peas and a mound of coarsely mashed potato.

'So, how was your day?' I asked my mother, who joined me at the kitchen table, her meal a replica of my own.

'All right,' she said.

'Well that's good.'

My hangover had lifted and I was eager to tell her all about Amber.

It was early days in our relationship—if indeed that was what it was—and I knew I shouldn't be getting too carried away, but I also thought that my mother's life might be brightened by news that her son may have (at last) been tamed. The days of bachelor carousal and aimless nihilism gone, to be replaced by the stable nurture of a good woman. Who knew? If my mother played her cards right, she might even get to enjoy the fruits of our pairing in the form of a joyful grandchild or two bouncing on her knee.

I needed to keep a lid on these wild flights of fancy. I pushed a three-layered pile of veal, peas and potato I'd built on my fork into my mouth and began to chew.

But then again, in this day and age, anything's possible. It wasn't unusual at all for men in their late forties to start families. And here at the townhouse I had the perfect set up. Amber and I would be in my room with the baby, until it got older, and then we'd partition the living room and turn it into a nursery. My mother would be out most of the days, but at nights she'd be able to babysit while we . . .

I forked another load into my mouth.

I really did need to keep a lid on things. After all, I was only having coffee with her and talking about her work—something I was now actually quite interested in. My exposure to dance had been limited, but if what I saw in Mona Vale was anything to go by, she definitely had talent. More importantly, she seemed to have her head screwed on the right way. There was no reason why she couldn't make a go of it. Of course, juggling a career with having a family was a perennial problem for creatives, but what with mum here to anchor things down, Amber could have considerable freedom to spend the necessary time abroad, collecting all the accolades she wanted.

Another fork load was delivered.

There were of course Amber's own parents to ease the burden. But something inside me was reticent to go down that road. I got the feeling Amber's father and I mightn't see eye to eye on certain things and, from what I'd seen at the institute that night, things could get ugly. Better to sail well clear of that dangerous coastline!

I took a drink of green cordial from the glass in front of me.

'I've met someone,' I said.

She looked at me with an expression of condescension and disbelief.

'She's a dancer.'

'A dancer?'

'Yes. She's studying at the institute.'

'How old is she?'

'She's in her late twenties.'

'Isn't that too old to be studying dance?'

'Not these days.'

She got up from the table and walked to the foot-operated kitchen tidy bin that stood against the section of wall below the window. She placed her foot on the pedal, flipped the lid open and with the help of her knife she slid the remnants of her meal off the plate and into the bin. The thudding sounds as the objects hit the bottom were mixed with the brief rustling noise of the plastic bin-liner. She took her foot off the pedal and the lid snapped shut. She walked over to the dishwasher, pulled down the front door and placed the plate and cutlery inside. She closed the door and left the kitchen.

*

I lay in bed, looking up at the luminous dots of light. It wasn't an accurate star atlas; in fact, the dots were just randomly placed dabs of glow-in-the-dark paint I'd applied to the ceiling as a teenager. Yet they successfully conveyed the illusion that I was sleeping in an open field beneath a sky full of stars.

I thought about the night I'd spent in the garden of the activity centre in Newtown and the sound of the crickets there, chirping together. It was strange how some insects chirped at night while others like cicadas . . .

Cicadas!

I leapt out of bed like a man with a cramp in his calf.

The decorative cicada that Amber had given me!

For the whole day I'd had this feeling that something was missing. I just couldn't put my finger on what it was. Now I knew. It was the weight—or lack of it—in my left trouser pocket; the pocket that had held the sculpture of the insect.

I turned on the light and began to rummage.

*

'So, you have no record of a taxi fare from King Cross to Lane Cove?'

I was talking on the phone to a woman at the taxi call centre.

'No sir.'

I hung up.

Outside, the first stirrings of a dawn chorus had begun. Prior to leaving for *The Beard,* at 2.30am, I'd conducted an extensive search by torchlight of the property grounds, paying particular attention to the garden bed I'd recently fertilised. I'd then combed an area of footpath, nature strip and gutter, ten or so meters either side of the presumed taxi drop off point. I'd then phoned all the taxi companies.

I knew I'd had the lead weight in my pocket when I'd entered *The Beard* with Gary and the others, and I *thought* I'd had it when I left, but given things had been extremely blurry then, I wasn't one hundred per cent sure.

No one had handed the cicada in at *The Beard,* at least that's what the night manager told me. I believed him. It wasn't the sort of thing a person would covet for themselves unless they knew Amber or myself. Furthermore, should a punter have seen the object lying on the floor, they would probably have been reluctant to handle it. So, unless a cleaner had scooped it up and thrown it away, there was a slim chance it might—24 hours later—still be lying in a dark and uncleaned corner of the room. My search proved fruitless.

On my return home, I performed another phoning round—after all there might be different personnel with different abilities and, hopefully, different answers.

Using a large fishing sinker and the recliner rocker in the living room, I'd simulated the possible cab ride. Sure enough, given enough time and suitable hip movement, the object had easily escaped the confines of my trouser pocket, and had fallen snug and hidden between the seat cushion and the chair's arm.

All the evidence pointed to the taxi scenario.

I picked up the phone again.

*

By 7am, having conducted several more searches of the garden and kerbside as well as numerous ring-arounds, I gave up. All the phone calls, searching and pacing had come to nought.

The cicada was lost.

I went to bed.

II

I woke as daylight dwindled—crepuscular, melancholic and judgemental. After the long night spent searching for the lead cicada, I had
slept through most of the day. Although this wasn't the first time I'd
woken at sunset, I was mindful nonetheless of feelings of shame and
guilt.

I needed to *do* something.

*

It was 6.30pm. The mall was packed. Office workers, shop keepers,
mothers, fathers, infants, school kids, entertainers, sports stars, homeless
people, men in love—all moving through the atriums, walkways, food
halls and escalators; all of them, whether they liked it or not, playing
their part in the service and protection of the queen bee of capitalism.

I'd come to purchase a gift for Amber. After all, she'd given me the
now lost cicada and I felt it incumbent on me to reciprocate. Through
the act of giving, I also hoped to distract her attention from the potential problem of desire deficit and focus it more on material gain.

I paced back and forth alongside the gleaming shopfronts thinking
hard about what form my generosity would take. I wanted to get her
something of lasting substance. I ruled out jewellery or items of clothing. These courted the danger of differing subjectivities as to what
constitutes beauty—hadn't I just experienced this very thing with the
cicada?

I wanted to make a bold statement and 'knock her off her feet'. It was time for me to take control.

*

I strolled confidently through the main exit of the mall wearing the sunglasses I'd impulsively pampered myself with. Inside the string-handled paper bag I carried in my left hand was what would soon be Amber's Tag Heuer *Aquaracer* watch. This would require a bit of austerity in the short term, but I was in this for the long haul and was ready to make any sacrifice if it meant strengthening the bond I shared with her.

The levels of stress surrounding the meet-up for coffee had grown considerably with the purchase of the watch. An important meeting deserved a successful gift, which, in turn, required a successful meeting in order to make the gift purchase worth it. I chuckled inwardly at the Escher-like circularity of it all.

Also, buying the watch had somehow made me feel better about having lost the cicada.

To make sure there'd be no stuff-ups the next day at the handover, I decided to conduct a dress rehearsal. I hailed a taxi and ordered the driver to take me to Newtown.

*

'That's fascinating, Amber. Oh, by the way, I bought you something I thought you might like.' I pulled the box from the paper carry bag at my feet (I would have a proper shoulder bag come the real meeting) and placed it on the table.

No, it wasn't quite right—I didn't like the 'I thought you might like' part.

I was sitting at a window table in *Smarties*, doing the run through. The café was almost empty and so long as I kept my mutterings to a whisper, I could conduct the rehearsal undetected.

I put the box back in the carry bag and repeated the practice exercise.

'Wow that's really interesting, Amber. Oh, I almost forgot, here's a little present.' Once more I placed the gift on the table.

'A little present' somehow sounded lecherous. 'Here, I've got something for you.' That was better.

I reset.

'That's really fascinating, Amber. Oh, here, I've got something for you.'

I wasn't confident I could pull off the 'oh, here.' It could easily sound wooden. I needed to be easy and natural and not push things. I should let the gift do the talking.

Tomorrow the café would be more crowded. I might have to raise my voice.

'Wow, that's really fascinating, Amber.' I placed the gift on the table again. 'Here's something I got for you.' I waited, picturing in my mind Amber's response.

'Go on, try it on. It's yours now.'

III

To make sure of getting the chosen window table, I arrived at Smarties at midday. The table was free when I arrived, a good omen. I duly seated myself.

I ordered a coffee and a brownie.

A man at a table nearby asked me to stop jiggling my leg. I stopped.

When my brownie arrived it was a melted mess. I explained to the waiter that having mud cake heated up should be an option requested by the customer, not the default mode requiring cancellation. I turned down his offer to fetch me a room-temperature replacement, preferring to play the martyr to poor service by only eating a third of it and sullenly poking with my fork at the remainder.

Again, the man at the nearby table asked me to stop jiggling, which I did. I took out a coin, and managed a few spins on the top of the table before the jiggling-sensitive man asked me to stop that too.

In the pages of a pink and yellow glossy magazine taken from the rack near the counter, I read an article about the extraordinary post-birth weight loss of a prominent American actress. I took in most of it.

Time moved slowly, but it moved.

At 1.50pm, having drunk five coffees, eaten two muffins, a third of a brownie, and half a lamington, I began to feel nervous. We were in the 'zone'; she could arrive at any moment.

I wanted to get up and pace. But if I got up, I'd lose the table.

Attached to the back of the entrance door was a brace of small bells that jangled whenever the door was opened. With every new jangling of the bells, I felt my stomach tighten. Could it be her?

2pm came.

2.10pm came.

2.15pm came.

What if she didn't come? Would it really matter all that much? Wouldn't it just be more of the same? A big FAIL—cue the Bronx cheer. The waters of a dark current began pulling me towards a precipice. I'd manufactured this whole thing. I'd seen only what I'd wanted to see and had made the rest up. She was never going to turn up—who was I kidding?

But there she was. Having been successfully conditioned to not respond to the jangling entrance bells (enough non-Ambers had come in by this time), I no longer looked up when they sounded. I was staring at the half-eaten lamington on the plate in front of me, absorbed in my meditations.

'Hi!' She was standing next to the table, 'sorry I'm late.'

From the sweatband around her head and the over-the-shoulder sports bag she was carrying, I deduced that she'd just been exercising.

I stood up too quickly.

'Don't get up,' said Amber, too late.

'How are you?' I asked, midway during the process of sitting back down. My overdone smile flexed beyond my control.

'Pretty good,' she said, taking her place on the opposite side of the table. 'I like your sunglasses—they suit you.'

'Thanks.'

'Have you come from the gym?' I asked

'What?'

I lightly pinched the skin of my forehead with the thumb and fore-finger of my right hand—a mime signifying her sweatband. 'The gym.'

'What?'

I performed once more my sweatband charade.

She looked bewildered, bordering on offended.

'The gym,' I said, persevering with the hand gesture. 'The headband.'

'Oh this!' she said touching the band, having finally understood. 'I'm sorry, I'm a bit slow today. No, I've got a stretching class at 2.30pm.'

It was now 2.20pm.

'Sorry,' I said, pointing at the partially eaten lamington. 'I started without you.'

'That's ok.'

'What'll you have?' I asked.

'You know what, I think I'm ok. I've already had two cups of coffee today. I'll be speeding off my head if I have another!'

'What about a herbal tea or something? I'll pay.'

'No really, I'm fine. You know, I remember reading somewhere that green tea has just as much caffeine in it as coffee.'

'Wow, that's fascinating Amber. I've got something for you.'

I pulled the box from the carry bag at my feet, and placed it on the table.

'Go on, try it on. It's yours now.'

'What is it?' she asked. The look on her face was not one of grati-tude, more one of fear.

'Just a little something I thought you might like.'

She reached forward and picked up the box.

'It's a watch!' she said in response to having seen an image of a watch on one of the sides of the box.

Her look of fear subsided and was replaced with a smile—inchoate but maturing fast.

'Wow, it's beautiful,' she said, removing it from its packaging and rolling it gently from one hand to the other like a weirdo fondling a tarantula.

'Geoff, you shouldn't have! This must have cost a fortune.'

'Well you gave me that beautiful cicada.'

'I . . . I don't know what to say.'

'You don't have to say anything.'

Slipping her hand through the black leather watchband she began to strike various arm poses, assaying her new acquisition.

I noticed the 'jiggling Nazi' looking at Amber.

'It's amazing! Thank you so much! Thank you!'

She manoeuvred the watch face so that it caught the weak afternoon sunlight that shone through the window of the cafe. She twisted her wrist and the beam from the reflection glinted in my eyes.

'The spotlight's on you, Mr Maddox!'

We laughed.

Although it had been brief—seven minutes to be exact—the coffee meet-up had been highly successful; the watch had been worth every cent. The only slightly less than perfect thing had been her use of my surname when she'd shone the sunlight in my face. I understood that she'd used a rhetorical device, a mock formality that ironically conveyed a familiarity, but would she have called me 'Mr Maddox' had I been her own age?

I also couldn't remember telling her my surname.

But this was small change compared to the goal I'd kicked with the quality timepiece. And before heading off to her stretching class, she agreed to let me take her out to dinner the following Thursday.

IV

In the nine days that spanned the coffee meet up and the proposed dinner date my moods swung full and frequent between a smug sense of achievement and a doomed sense of failure—a state not substantively different to my normal animus but made much more vivid due to the recent amorous activity.

Life went on at the Stella.

Laird continued to constantly advertise the trappings of his wealth. But I no longer found this irritating. Ironically this was partly due to the boasting itself. Had I liked Laird, I might have been concerned that his incessant braggadocio would be giving others the idea to develop their own ticket hustles in direct opposition to his. So eager was he to feed his ego that he didn't see the inherent danger. But I didn't like him, so I didn't worry.

He was now going on about having a 'working holiday' in Melbourne and was even threatening to take his scheme international.

'Why not?' he said pugnaciously one night after several drinks. 'Why shouldn't I make this thing work for me? I've always wanted to see the world. This skill is portable.'

Calling this flimflam a skill was absurd. The idea of Laird as any sort of craftsman was a smack in the face to vocational training of any kind.

*

Doc, true to form, was able to inject some quality negativity into proceedings. On Friday evening, I miscalculated and wound up sitting next to him at the bar. It was early, around ten or so.

'What was the name of that girl who came in here the other night?' he asked.

'Amber?'

'She was nice. You wouldn't happen to have her phone number?'

It would have been delusional for Doc to have expected me to fulfil his request for information. Although he was no stranger to delusion, there was something about his facial expression during the asking that pointed to something more malicious. Was he trying to wind me up? By positioning himself as a competitor in the quest for Amber's attentions, was he snidely pointing out that his obviously impossible ambitions were no more unrealistic than my own?

Maybe I was overthinking things and endowing him with a sophistication he didn't have. Perhaps I was getting paranoid in my old age. Intentional or otherwise the barb hit home, not least because, in truth, I still didn't have Amber's phone number. And he did seem a little too satisfied with the blush I couldn't stop from spreading over my face.

'No, I don't, actually,' I answered.

*

On the whole, though, I felt optimistic about the future. After all, I had a lot to be happy about. The situation with my mother was improving, the girl of my dreams and I were almost going steady (no matter what Doc may have thought), and I still had my health.

I didn't even mind being smacked down by Bronwyn at the conclusion of a brief and one-sided discussion on the Sunday night. In her cups and eager to show off her smarts, she was going on about Walter

Benjamin and something called the 'Dialectical Image'. This somehow related to Gary's cricket bat and its new significance following Kelly's use of it. I was fairly certain Bronwyn wasn't using the term correctly. As per usual, the monologue ended patronisingly. She moved her unclenched right hand backwards in the air above her scalp whilst making a *shuuum* sound to represent her concepts travelling over my head before walking away.

*

There was one thing that was really bugging me, however. The thought of it lingered on, constant and uneasy, like a threat. The swan shit. There seemed to be no logical explanation for it save for someone breaking into the apartment. And yet, how could they? Was Wendy capable of this?

*

'Go ahead, open it,' I said.

I'd taken Amber to *Swallow*, a vegan restaurant in Newtown specialising in mock meat dishes. We'd ordered and were waiting for the first course.

It would have been way over the top to replicate the expense of the first gift I'd given her; I thought an ipad mini was a perfect follow-up.

'Oh my god—it's an iPad!' said Amber. 'I've always wanted one of these!'

'Turn it over,' I said.

A delightful expression of nervous apprehension showed on her face as she dutifully turned the object.

Engraved on the back of the iPad was a *fleur de lys* design and written underneath it were the words: *To Amber from Mr Maddox.*

Amber gazed at me with a look of appreciation that, in hindsight, should have included moist eyes. It seemed, nonetheless, as if she was reacting to a truth revealed for the first time.

'Well, thank you Mr Maddox!'

'My pleasure, Miss Lockhart!'

'Don't call me that.'

Her four words extinguished the warm glow of received generosity we'd been enjoying. I was taken aback by the hardness of her face, a hardness that instantly brought back to me the dreaded night in her kitchen.

'What?'

'Miss Lockhart—please don't call me Miss Lockhart.' At least she'd said please the second time through. 'Call me Amber, or Amber Lockhart , but not Miss Lockhart.'

'Oh.'

'It reminds me of being at school. It makes me feel ill.'

'I'm sorry, I didn't mean to . . . '

'I know, I know you didn't mean to.' She paused, taking a breath before continuing: 'Look, I shouldn't have reacted the way I did. I'm sorry too.'

Part of me was disappointed that the vibe had been ruined, but another part was relieved. In an earlier draft of the engraved text I had written: *To Miss Lockhart From Mr Maddox*. I'd dodged a bullet.

'It's a bit smaller than a real Ipad isn't it?' she said, testing the weight of the device in her hands.

*

By the light of the moon, we walked among the ruined gravestones of Camperdown cemetery. It had been my idea. On leaving *Swallow* we'd gone on to *Klonimus* where we each had one cocktail before Amber said she was tired and wanted to go home. I quickly suggested a stroll in 'the old boneyard' to add a dash of colour to the evening and hopefully revive her flagging spirits.

'Sometimes I think I could give all of this away.' I had no idea why I'd said this; it was an empty statement made chiefly for the purpose of displaying what I considered to be macho rhetoric. For most of the evening Amber hadn't really said anything and I'd run out of topics to the extent that I was now talking in meaningless slogans.

'Give what away?' she asked.

'All of this.' I made a sweeping hand gesture.

'Me too.'

We passed by a damaged memorial. Rendered in stone, the base section of a tree trunk 'grew' upwards from the plinth while next to it an arm holding a garland emerged from the ruins of what had once been a kneeling woman.

'In the end, you've got to learn enough to teach yourself,' I said.

'Unless you already know it.'

'True.'

We had reached the entrance to the cemetery.

'Thanks for a wonderful dinner,' I said.

'Thanks for the ipad.'

I moved towards her, my arms readying themselves for a hug; I tried to keep my preparations covert.

Amber thrust out her right hand. I grabbed it with both of mine, and began shaking it; a display of warm platonic friendship that left open the possibility for something more substantial to happen at some time in the future, should both parties agree.

'You make me feel like a good person,' I told her.

'You make me feel good too,' she replied.

'Hey, would I be able to get your phone number?' I tried to sound as relaxed and off the cuff as possible.

Straightaway, a look of concern crossed her face. 'I've just got a new phone, which I stupidly left on the dresser back at the house, and I can't remember my number.'

'Can I walk you home?'

'I'll be alright, thanks.'

She turned and strode away. I walked back to *Klonimus*.

V

I sat alone at *Muffin Siesta*, coffee and muffin—mugged and plated—on the table before me. I could see the clock on the wall behind the counter of *Pearl River*. It showed 1.05pm. It had been four days since our graveyard farewell and Amber hadn't replied to a single email. There had been six—all of them friendly invites for meet-ups.

I tried to give her the benefit of the doubt. Maybe she was way too busy with term papers. Maybe her email provider was off line due to important maintenance being carried out. However, try as I might, it was difficult to stave off the growing suspicion that I was a sad, aging loser and had no right to expect someone like Amber to harbour anything but contempt towards me.

From out of the melange of shoppers traversing the mall emerged Laird.

'Thought I'd find you here,' he said, pulling up a chair. 'How are you?'

'Ok,'

'I'm just taking a break,' he said in response to a question I hadn't asked.

I nodded.

'Things have been really good for me,' he continued. 'Now that Jock's come on board, we've almost tripled our intake. He's a good worker.'

I bristled at the mention of his name, a subtle movement that Laird picked up on.

'Yeah, I asked him to come on board with me.'

It took me a moment to process this.

'What about his farm commitments? Doesn't he run a thousand head of cattle?'

'He's got a manager looking after it for him now. He says he wants some new challenges.'

I was unable to stifle my snigger. Laird looked at a point midway between us on the table and smiled.

'He also wants to spend more time in Sydney with Amber.'

I also looked at a spot midway down the table and smiled. My leg began to jiggle.

'By the way, Amber says to say hi.'

*

'Another schooner thanks Gary.'

I put the $8 on the bar top, four $2 coins stacked one on top of the other.

'Put her out of your mind, mate,' said Gary. 'You're better than this. You're twice the man this other guy is.'

I was fairly certain Gary hadn't exchanged more than several words with Williams.

'Consider yourself lucky, mate. You don't want to end up like me. You know what Megan wants to do now?'

He handed me the beer as I shook my head.

'She wants her mother buried in the back garden. Can you imagine that? Every day I'll get up and the first thing I'll see when I sit down for breakfast is this whopping great big headstone!'

'Is she ill?' asked Bronwyn.

'Who?' said Gary.

'Megan's mother.'

'Strong as an ox.'

'I just want some truth,' I said, returning to the subject of Amber. 'I don't like being dicked around like this.'

I was drunk and I knew it wasn't good to be blurting out stuff about Amber and me. When Gary had hijacked the conversation to his own domestic hell, I should have let it rest. But I couldn't.

'Maybe I'm just too old for her.'

'Here, here!' said Bronwyn.

'That's ridiculous, mate,' said Gary, ignoring Bronwyn. 'You're in the prime of life.'

Bronwyn sprayed her foreground with mirth-propelled wine.

'Hey Bron,' said Gary. 'Tone it down. Show some sensitivity.'

'Sensitivity? What's happening to *him*,' she said, pointing her wine glass at me, 'has been happening to women for thousands of years. I get so tired of hearing that it's always the woman's fault!' She looked directly at me: 'Fucking get a life. You're an old man. Of course she doesn't want you!'

'Hey! That's really out of line Bronwyn,' said Gary, his jaw thrust forward in righteous anger.

'It's the truth! He said he wanted to hear the truth—well there it is!' She was almost shouting, but grinning at the same time.

'She's right, Gary,' I said. 'I'm an old fuckwit.'

'There's nothing wrong with aging,' said Bronwyn, 'but sitting around feeling sorry for yourself because of it; that really sucks. Angst before death is merely a fucking epiphenomenon of bourgeois loneliness.'

She stood up from her stool.

'I'll be back in a minute.'

She put her drink down on the bar and walked off towards the toilets.

'Just ignore her, mate,' said Gary.

I nodded.

*

My knees were wet; again the dampness in the soil had been transferred to my skin through the fabric of my jeans.

As before, the light in the front room bled through the gap between the edge of the blind and the window frame. The hall light was also on.

From the intersection a block away, I'd seen Amber enter the house just before 5pm. At 6pm, I'd taken up my normal position in the activity centre garden. She'd been inside now for three hours and in that time no one had either come or gone. I deduced that she was either in there alone or with a person or persons already present before the start of my surveillance at 2.30pm.

There was of course the possibility that someone could have come in via the back entrance, an area I obviously couldn't watch while kneeling in the activity centre. This inability somewhat undermined the effectiveness of my observational efforts. Nonetheless, I continued watching the front of the building, it being the best bet for possible visitor action. It somehow seemed right that I should be out here, on a cold winter's night, suffering like this.

Nine pm and no exits or entrances. I decided to inspect the rear of the property. I turned into the back alley and there he was—Williams. The white trousers and the boots identified him straightaway. He was standing with both hands clasping the top of the fence, a metre apart.

His chin rested at a midway point between them. He was peering into the backyard. I was struck by the lack of dignity the scene showed.

I ducked back up the alley.

VI

My credit card stopped working. I could hear it being slowly forced back out of the mouth of the ATM while I took in the significance of the words 'Insufficient Funds' displayed on the screen. I was transported back to the Redfern brothel and the night of the blow-up doll. This time, however, there was no criminal involved, the watch and iPad had done it. I was still two weeks away from the next interest payment on the term deposit bequeathed to me by my uncle. I estimated I had enough in cash reserves to last me three days. After that, I was homebound. Grounded.

The fact was, now more than ever, I needed money; money to get myself around; money to socialize properly; and money to gather information in order to ascertain exactly where I stood with the only woman who had ever meant anything to me.

Desperation dressed me in an ill-fitting suit and took me to Lithgow and a regional NRMA branch. I'd chosen an out of town venue in order to make sure I wouldn't be working a room that Laird might have already visited. It also seemed a good idea to get my chops up in a more relaxed, semi-rural environment. It was midday and I was clutching a handful of queue tickets—waiting for the right moment to start working the room.

The branch wasn't anywhere near as crowded as the Medicare centre where I'd watched Laird work his magic. This meant that the gap between the numbers displayed on the screens and the numbers on the fresh tickets being pulled out of the dispenser was never more than about 30. And because 20 of those numbers were in my hand and not in the hands of actual customers requiring service, their screen time was very short. Consequently, I had roughly only a four-minute wait time with which to play.

The lowest number I held was 362. Number 353 was called. I approached a woman with three small kids, followed by a guy in a suit and then a man of the cloth—all customers who looked like they were in a hurry.

Nothing.

On my second attempt with the woman, she shooed me away and threatened to notify management. I waited beside the ticket dispenser for one of the others I'd targeted to change their mind—but the time needed for that to happen was longer than the wait for their number to be called—at which point, of course, my tickets were useless!

I kept having to restock every ten minutes with fresh tickets, an undertaking requiring me to monopolize the ticket machine for an overly lengthy period of time, causing further irritation amongst my potential client base.

An outcome I hadn't expected, however, was that a significant number of people in the room saw what I was doing as outright begging. As a result, several people gave me small change without actually taking a ticket.

I'd been working the room for three quarters of an hour when a large male employee tapped me on the shoulder and asked me to leave.

My earnings? A dollar seventy-five Australian and two Croatian Kuna. The return train fare cost me $17.

*

Location, location, location—for a successful ticket queue scheme, it was crucial to pick the right area. To this end, I chose, on the next day, a CBD branch of Services NSW at which to practice my new profession.

Now this was more like it! Midday; a packed, standing-room-only space, under-staffed with screaming babies and exhausted parents, high-powered professionals (one barrister even had her wig still on!) and harried tradespeople. All of them hoping like hell to get in and out asap.

I took my twenty tickets from the dispenser.

So great was the backlog, there was even time for me to grab a cup of coffee before approaching people, and so I began to thread my way through the mass of impatient customers towards the exit. I was flushed with a feeling of independence. I didn't need my uncle's money. I was going to make this work—fuck, if Laird could do it, so could I!

Suddenly, I felt two sets of hands grab me from behind and before I knew it, my feet had ceased to influence the direction in which I was travelling; I was being frogmarched out of the centre.

I expected the two assailants to be uniformed security guards, but, when I was finally released on the pavement outside, I stood before two men dressed in pale coloured chinos, blue cotton shirts and Blundstone boots. They both looked to be in their early twenties.

'What the fuck do you think you're doing?' one of them, the slightly taller one, said.

'Nothing. What is this?' I asked.

'You don't come here again—ok?' said the shorter one.

'I was renewing my driver's li—'

'No,' said the taller one, 'you listen to me. You come here again, and we're going to break every fucking bone in your body. Do you understand?'

'You understand?' said the shorter one.

'I guess so.'

'You guess so,' said the shorter one again.

I didn't see the punch but I heard the sound—and then I couldn't breathe.

The taller one stood over me as I lay gasping on the footpath. Behind his head, between the tops of several skyscrapers, I could see patches of blue sky.

'Don't come here again,' said the taller one.

The shorter one kicked me in the ribs. He could have kicked me harder.

VII

I woke with a jolt. Had I just shouted out loud? I tried to grasp the strands of narrative that had frightened me, but the relief of waking was fast dissolving them.

Wendy had been in the dream, her and Gavin; they were holding hands. She was laughing of course. Someone was tied up in a chair, was it me? She was calling me a saint. I was naked. She had Laird's deluxe vaping mod. The crowd at the Stella was chanting: '*she's got a mod, she's got a mod, she's got a mod . . .*'

She broke off holding hands with Gavin and came towards me, the mod in her hand, grinning and saying: 'Saint Geoffrey, Saint Geoffrey, poor Saint Geoffrey.'

By my reckoning it was still morning, barely. I got out of bed and straightaway felt the stabbing pain in my ribcage. It had been almost 24 hours since the assault, and the pain still seemed to be growing in intensity.

I'd dined at home the previous night and, although I'd like to boast that it took a superhuman acting effort on my part to hide the injuries from my mother, the truth was that she paid little attention to me at dinner these days; my groans and winces elicited no inquiry whatsoever as to their possible cause. She was a tough crowd.

I breakfasted on the usual: microwaved coffee and on-the-cusp-of-use-by-date muffin.

Dear Mr Maddox,
Sorry I haven't written in a little while. I've been so busy with stuff.
I need to see you. Can we meet at Smarties, tomorrow? How would
2pm be? I really hope you're well.
Love
Amber.

I brushed a fly off the computer screen and re-read it.

I walked out of my bedroom and on through the hallway to the kitchen. I turned around and walked back to the bedroom. The email was still on the screen, I had not been dreaming. I brushed away another fly and began to construct my reply.

Amber,
Great to hear from you! This would be great! I'll see you there!
I hope you're well too!
I can't wait to hear all about your work!
Love,
Mr Maddox

A fly buzzed close by—its fast crescendo caused me to smack my ear hard with my hand. Once again, I walked out to the kitchen and back, savouring the moment.

Two flies were on the screen when I returned. I waved them off and, positioning the cursor over 'send', held my hand so that it hovered a few inches above the touch pad.

A fly landed on the back of my hand.

I pressed down on the mouse, sending the email.

Amber and I were back on!

An attempt at punching the air was aborted mid-way through due to rib pain.

There were now three flies on the computer screen, which I shooed away. I absentmindedly observed the flight path of one of them as it spiralled upwards.

The pattern on the ceiling was geometrical—and it was the pattern, more than the number of flies that was so disturbing. They were in grid formation, evenly spaced—three or so centimetres apart—covering the entire bedroom ceiling; a grim, elaborate parody of my glow in the dark stars.

I left the bedroom for the safety of the hallway, where I stood looking back into the room through the open door. The few flies still airborne were like loose threads on the side of an intricate tapestry. Every so often a fly would leave the grid and fly down into the room; straightaway, an already airborne fly would take its place, landing in the exact same spot on the ceiling.

*

Bronwyn didn't believe me. She allowed that there may have been flies, but not that they were in any sort of pattern.

'Flies are like cats; you can't herd them,' she said, pleased with her witticism.

I was about to laugh sarcastically when I saw Laird come in off the street. Being 3pm, it was an unusual time for him to frequent the Stella. He looked pissed off, which pleased me.

'Bourbon and Cola,' he barked on approach to the bar.

'Coming right up,' said Gary.

'Geoff here's had another occult experience!' said Bronwyn. Her mouth and eyes were wide open as she shook her hands, palms out, on either side of her face and groaned. The mockery was poorly executed and embarrassing.

'Great,' said Laird, who stood at the bar waiting for his drink.

'With *flies*!' The way she emphasised the word 'flies' was off-kilter. The sport she was having at my expense wasn't warranted, yet it was perfectly in keeping with the conclusion I'd reached some time ago: her way of dealing with the major, systemic disappointments of her own life was through the time-honoured tradition of belittling some-one else.

'The ceiling in my bedroom,' I said, 'completely covered in flies. Each of them evenly . . . '

'Doesn't surprise me,' said Laird. 'Your place is a fucking pigsty.'

'Steady on,' said Gary, handing Laird his drink.

Laird took his drink and moved towards a vacant stool.

I heard a small voice inside me telling me not to take the bait, not to let Laird press any of my buttons.

'It's the truth,' said Laird, sitting down.

'It's not the truth,' I said. 'I keep the place relatively clean and tidy.'

'Give me a break,' said Laird. 'I've never seen you lift a finger. Your poor old mum works all day. She hasn't got time to clean the house—and you, you do nothing.'

'It gets cleaned professionally once a fortnight,' I said, referring to Heidi.

Laird's mother didn't have to work. She'd inherited a fortune when her husband had passed away and was happy to spend her time keep-ing an immaculate household, which allowed Laird to lead a largely chore-free existence. It was deeply offensive for him to criticise me for failing at something he'd never had to face.

It might seem that every male regular who drank at the Stella lived with his mother. This wasn't the case. It was true that both Laird and myself supported our respective aging parents and Gary shared digs with his mother-in-law, but the only other male regular to adhere to the traditional family setup was Doc, who lived with his mum in a duplex—a once large house divided (by his mother) into two autonomous living spaces. It was always amusing to hear Doc proudly proclaim that he'd moved out of home thirty years ago, never letting on that he still lived under the same roof as his 85-year-old mother and slept in the same bed he'd slept in as a 10-year-old.

Now *his* place *was* filthy!

By bringing the subject of my mother into the conversation, Laird had achieved what he'd set out to. I got to my feet and headed in the direction of the toilets. With both hands, I pushed a stool out of the way, making it crash against the metal base of a lounge table.

As I walked past the ATM—the same ATM where I'd caught my first glimpse of Amber—my anger evaporated. Laird might be a dickhead and my flat might be squalid, but Amber, off her own bat, had invited me on a date!

I was all smiles as I reapproached the bar.

'Did you wash your hands?' said Laird.

'How come you're in here so early?' I asked, ignoring his puerile jape. 'Business slow?'

Up at the bar, Bronwyn and Gary were having strong words over the size of her last serving of red wine.

'Business is great,' Laird said unconvincingly. 'How come you're walking funny?'

'I fell down some stairs. Where's Jock?'

'Why do you ask?'

'You two seem to be inseparable. Isn't he your business partner now?'

'I don't want to talk about it.'

VIII

We sat in the living room, I was on a large club sofa in need of repair, she was on a green recliner rocker in upright mode. I'd made the trip up the North Shore to Killara for a consultation with Sonia Rocklin, a personal friend of Gary's mother in law and a woman in possession of 'the gift'. It had come about through Gary's urging. He didn't strike me as the superstitious type, but the fly incident combined with the swan shit had creeped him out and he felt I needed professional advice. I was sceptical, but thought I may as well go up there; who knew, I might get a good story out of it to impress Amber.

Set back from the road on two acres of poorly kept grounds, the house was of Tudor design and huge, six bedrooms minimum. She lived alone. A tarred driveway pocked with half-metre-high weeds led from the front gate to the garage on the side of the house. Clearly, it had been many years since a vehicle had made the journey.

Painted portraits and photographs of numerous children hung on walls and stood atop various sideboards and bookcases positioned around the room. I took the subjects of these portraits to be her off-spring who'd now grown up and left the nest. An impressive portrait in oils hung directly above the unused marble fireplace. It was of a man in military uniform. The square-jawed look of determination on the sitter's face was testament to a life of discipline and rationalism. This was her husband, Brigadier David Rocklin DSO, who had died sometime in the early eighties. Various items of south-east Asian art were also on display around the room—evidence of overseas post-ings. A grandfather clock stood idle in the corner nearest the doorway through to the kitchen.

Having briefly described to her the happenings back at the flat—the bird shit and the flies—I waited as she pondered the information.

She sat forward in the chair.

'Has anything like this ever happened before in your flat?' she asked. Her voice was soft but authoritative. I suspected she'd done her fair share of military dinner party hosting.

'Never.'

'Have you been in contact with any person or thing that may have triggered these events?'

I told her about Wendy and the game of pool. I omitted the details concerning her trouser removal demand and merely said that I'd accused her of cheating and that consequently she'd reacted extremely negatively.

'And how did you react to her reaction?' Sonia asked.

'Well, I stood up for myself. She cheated.'

'How did you stand up for yourself?'

'I called her a name.'

'What name?'

'A moron.'

'A moron?'

'A fucking moron.'

'OK,' Sonia said. She leant back in her chair and absentmindedly stroked her chin with her right hand.

'Can you describe Wendy's appearance to me?' she asked.

This was a tough ask. The closest I could get to a physical descrip-tion of Wendy was that she resembled the Skipper off *Gilligan's Island*.

'Alan Hale?'

I nodded.

'Did she have any markings? Tattoos or piercings?'

'She had a star shaped thing on her arm.'

'Here?' With her left hand she clutched her right arm just above the elbow.

I nodded.

She breathed in hard through her nose and leaned forward once more.

'This is bad.'

'You know her?'

She nodded.

'It's a relatively small crowd of us here in Sydney. I avoid her though.'

'Why is this bad?' I asked, meekly.

'Well.' She took a deep breath. 'Wendy is a very angry soul. A troubled person. Wounded.'

'There was one other thing,' I said. 'She spat at me.'

'Spat?' she was more alarmed than inquisitive.

'Yes. And she told me she was looking at me with her third . . . '

'OK,' Sonia said, cutting me off. 'Did she manage to get hold of any personal items of yours. A handkerchief or a piece of hair or skin?

'No.'

'Any coins you'd handled, a glass you'd drunk out of?'

A gust of anxiety blew through me; I'd left my half-drunk schooner on the table in the beer garden when I'd stormed off. Wendy would have had access to it.

'I left my glass of beer outside,' I said as if confessing to a crime.

'Alright, listen to me. You're in real trouble. You've offended some-one with considerable power to cause you harm.'

I swallowed hard.

'What can I do?'

'Not a lot.' She stood up. 'I can *try* and do something, I have a few options at my disposal, but you have to realise . . . ' she looked hard at me, 'she's strong.'

'But surely she's got better things to do than torment someone she hardly knows.'

'Not really. To her you're a man who called her a fucking moron, that's all she needs to know. And for her to do what she's doing doesn't really require much effort, she only has to set something in train and tend to it occasionally. The flies and the bird shit were mainly for her own amusement. Her main goal is to make you suffer in ways you may not be aware of, or attribute to paranormal activity. She wants you to go downhill. She wants to ruin your life.'

'So, there's nothing I can do?'

'Apologise. Next time you see her, grovel. Buy her a drink, com-pliment her—do whatever it takes to redeem yourself. But don't men-tion anything about the flies or birds. Make her think you're doing it because it's the right thing to do. OK?'

'OK. '

'Now, do you have a personal item on you that I can keep?'

My right hand grasped the cloth balled up in my trouser pocket. It had been a while since I'd freshened my handkerchief and having, extracted it, I saw that there was a large blood stain clearly visible.

'Hang on,' Sonia said. She walked over to the sideboard next to the fireplace, opened the doors and extracted from its interior an empty instant coffee jar. Whilst walking back over to me she unscrewed the plastic lid.

'Drop it in here,' she said holding the jar in front of me.

*

I had a lot to think about on the journey back down the highway. To begin with, there was the receipt I held in my hands, for $440. Fortunately, the night before, Gary had lent me $1000 in cash—at a reasonable interest rate—until the arrival in my bank account of the next instalment of my uncle's stipend. I could cover the cost of the consultation, but it still stung.

While I waited at the top of the driveway for my taxi to arrive, I was passed by a man carrying an angry two-year-old child. He turned into the driveway and continued briskly towards the front door of the house. He was having difficulty restraining the infant, who was hissing and cursing in what sounded an awful lot like fluent Latin. Sonia must have been raking it in.

I wasn't sure how seriously I should take this Upper North Shore voodoo. A lot of hysterical people seek miracle cures for things that probably only require common sense to fix. Her bill had left a sour taste in my mouth. Surely someone with the gift wouldn't have need of money; they'd be able to magic up whatever they wanted whenever they wanted it. A real clairvoyant would do their stuff for free, because it would be the right thing to do, wouldn't they?

IX

The large Thursday afternoon crowd meant that our window table at *Smarties* was taken, so we had to make do with sharing a table next to the toilets. Amber had ordered a chai with almond milk. I followed suit.

'I need money,' Amber said. She was wearing the poncho, the jeans and the Ugg boots.

Apart from saying hello to each other, deciding which table to sit at and ordering the chai, these were the first words either of us had uttered. I appreciated her getting right to the point.

'Oh?'

'Yes, my father has refused to pay for next semester and the people at the institute say if I don't come up with the money, I'll have to leave the course.'

'That's terrible.'

'Yes!'

Our teas arrived.

'How expensive is the course?'

'$10000.'

'$10000 for one semester?'

'Yep.'

'Expensive,' I mused bringing my cup to my lips. 'Why's he doing this?'

'He thinks it's a waste of money. He wants me to do nursing.'

'Can't you get a loan from the government?'

She smiled and shook her head.

'It's not an accredited tertiary institution,' she said, making mocking quotation marks in the air with her hands. 'I have to pay upfront or no course.'

I took another sip from my cup.

A small but noticeable part of me was enjoying the feeling of empowerment the situation imbued me with—a feeling missing in our dealings with each other up to this point.

There was also the fact that until now, my generosity had been largely unsolicited and consequently unattached with strings. This here was different. By responding positively to Amber's request, I would have every right to expect some sort of reciprocation.

There was, however, the problem of my maxed-out credit card.

I brought my cup once more to my lips.

'It would just be a loan. I'd pay you back,' said Amber.

The possibility of me wedging my way into her life in such a spectacular fashion as a $10000 loan was inspiring. It inspired me to come up with a plan very quickly. The cheque account. My mother had a chequebook, which she kept in the safe in her bedroom.

'When do you need it by?'

'Monday.'

I took a deep breath. The moment had come when I needed to ask the question I'd been dreading; a question the answer to which would determine whether or not I proceeded with the course of action forming in my mind.

'What's going on between you and Williams?'

'What?'

'You and Williams, are you seeing him?'

She tensed up. I'd like to think she was taken aback by my manly forthrightness.

'No!' she said, breaking into a frowning smile and shaking her head to show she thought the question ridiculous.

'If you really want to know,' she continued, 'he makes my flesh crawl.'

Had Aretha Franklin herself been sitting there singing, her voice would not have sounded as mellifluous as Amber's had just done.

'Really?' I asked, embarrassed at my infantile tone of voice.

'He's revolting!'

I burst out laughing, flooded with glorious feelings of relief and *schadenfreude*.

'Come on, he's not that bad!' I said.

We held each other's gaze.

'Well, come to think of it,' I continued, 'yeah, he is that bad.'

'Yeah, he *is* that bad!' she agreed.

'Sorry, I hope you don't think I was prying. I mean, it's your life. I don't really have any business asking you something like that.'

'It's ok. I don't mind.'

I sat back in my chair, well satisfied, then remembered the money.

'Look,' I said, 'it should be ok—the money. I can get it to you by Monday. Shouldn't be a problem.'

I had never before been the recipient of a look like the one Amber gave me at that moment. It was a look that said I am truly humbled by your generosity, you are a very special man. It was a look that seemed to grow in intensity as she fathomed the depths of the gift put before her. It lasted only several fleeting seconds but its brevity didn't detract in any way from its power; duration is a paltry measure with which to gauge the importance of such instances.

'Thank you so much! You have no idea how much this means to me.'

She leant across the table, and put her arms around my neck. I stood up in order to lean in closer. I felt the pressure of her forehead on the top of my shoulder, and the ticklish brush of her hair on the side of my nose. With my right hand, I began to pat her back and felt the fibres of the poncho against my palm. We stood subtly swaying, locked in this embrace, for several seconds.

Was this the happiest moment of my life?

It occurred to me that it might well have been the first time I'd ever hugged a woman under forty sober; the fact that it had happened in broad daylight was also a personal best.

X

My mother's safe was in her bedroom. She'd had a strongbox of some description for as long as I could remember. It was something I felt uncomfortable with as it represented the existence of areas in her life to which I was barred access; something that qualified the unconditional love generally expected of a mother.

The safe was the size of a small esky. On the front was a key pad similar to a telephone however, instead of the '*' and '#' signs, there were the letters: 'A' and 'B'

On my return from coffee with Amber, with mum still at work, I tinkered around with the keypad for half an hour or so, randomly pushing buttons in the hope I might strike it lucky. I didn't.

*

My mother had an antique writing desk in her room where she'd pursued her hobby of writing poetry—back in the days when she'd had more time on her hands. The desk had belonged to her great-great grandfather's great uncle, a gallant Scottish captain during the Napoleonic wars, the news of whose death, reportedly, had brought tears to the eyes of the Duke of Wellington. One sad day in the (hopefully) distant future, when my mother passes on, it will belong to me. But at that moment it was the possible repository of the combination for the safe that contained the cheque book that could win for me the heart of the only non-blood-related woman I'd ever cared for. I felt sure my ancestor, Allan, would approve.

The desk had three drawers. I pulled open the top drawer which contained a row of pigeonholes on either side of which were sets of small interior drawers.

Pay dirt! The bottom interior drawer on the left-hand side held a small pamphlet for the *Firelord Personal Safe*.

To open the strongbox, explained the instructions, a four-digit code needed to be keyed in, followed by the pushing of button 'B'. There was no four-digit number code written anywhere on the pamphlet.

I searched the other interior drawers and cubicles of the desk several times over, to no avail. My mother had chosen a less predictable hiding place for the pass code.

I couldn't blame her.

*

'There's a guy in Drummoyne who does that sort of thing,' said Gary from behind the bar as he presented me with a beer on credit. 'Megan's brother met him through a work mate.'

'Oh?' I said.

'Yeah, he and Megan wanted to have a look at some certificates in their mum's strongbox.'

I hadn't realised how many people had personal safes these days.

'It was a while ago though,' continued Gary. 'Five or six years— when Barbara was still living in Castlecrag.'

This was the first time I'd ever heard Gary refer to his mother-in-law by her Christian name. It was strangely humanising.

The influx of after work drinkers at the Stella had out-fluxed as early evening passed into night. I was seated at the bar with Gary, Doc, Bronwyn and Laird.

'What's it for?' he asked.

I was prepared for this question.

'I've forgotten the code to my safe.'

'You've got a safe?' asked Doc.

'Yeah,' I said defensively.

'What do you need a safe for?'

'Just stuff I have.'

'What sort of stuff?' asked Doc.

'His old porno DVDs probably,' interjected Bronwyn

'No, he keeps those in his bedroom chest,' said Laird. 'He's got so much of it, it wouldn't fit in a safe.'

Rather than laugh at Laird's quip, the three of them merely nodded in disdain.

'Where's your friend Williams, Laird?' I said, changing the subject.

'Why do you want to know?' he said.

'I don't know, I'm just curious. You two were as thick as thieves a while back.'

'Don't get him started,' said Bronwyn. 'He's been talking to me about it all afternoon and I'm fucking sick of hearing about it.'

'Thanks Bronwyn,' said Laird.

'Well let's face it, you fucked up,' she replied.

Laird nodded.

My mood, already good, received a bonus fillip with the sight of Laird's hangdog expression.

'What happened?' asked Gary, himself smiling.

And so Laird explained to us why his relationship with Williams had gone sour. An all too familiar story: a person forms a partnership with another and the latter ends up taking over and squeezing the former out. Sometimes this sort of thing happens slowly over time, and is caused by the gradual revealing of innate character traits— one person being more apt to dominate, the other more apt to be dominated.

In this instance, the takeover had happened in a matter of days. Williams had very quickly sized Laird up as an idiot and when Laird boasted to him about his scheme early on in their friendship, Williams moved in.

In his telling, Laird painted himself as being the victim of an extraordinarily unlucky set of coincidences that had allowed Williams to gain a foothold at the executive level of the operation. It was obvious, however, that Laird had been a pushover; he was no match for Williams' brute cunning, physical prowess and experience.

He'd generously schooled Williams in the ways of the ticket scheme, teaching him how to wait for the right moment to begin, whom to target and when to leave the premises. Even though Williams could never be as proficient at it as Laird (or so Laird told us), he nonetheless was successful enough to earn cash amounts that rivalled those of Laird's.

The biggest change in circumstance was when Williams, under the guise of helping some young guys from the country get started in the city, brought in his own people. He claimed they were cousins of his, but Laird suspected they were hired thugs. Very soon Williams had monopolised all the Service NSW, Medicare, Consulate and NRMA offices in the Sydney metropolitan region.

Laird was no longer needed.

I now knew who was responsible for my sore ribs. I could add this to the $3500 he owed me.

'Wow, that's terrible,' said Gary, clearly finding Laird's travails amusing. Laird however appeared to believe Gary's condolence to be sincere.

'What can I do about it though?' he said.

'Go to the cops,' I said.

Gary was unable to keep his snigger internal.

'Or one of those current affairs shows,' said Doc, joining in the fun.

XI

I'd worked it out using the key pad on the telephone in the living room. I could key in 20 four-digit numbers, 20 'B' keys and write the digits down on a piece of paper in approximately two minutes and 10 seconds—or 130 seconds. This meant that each possible code entry and recording took 6.5 seconds. There were 9999 possible four-digit codes with which to unlock the safe. To enter *all* of them would take approximately 18 hours and three minutes. I was expecting the code for the safe to be a number a good deal less than 9999.

It so happened that my mother was working a seven-day week at Class Axe. It wasn't unusual but it was a serious stroke of luck as it meant, with Saturday and Sunday now available, I had ample time to 'crack' the safe. I felt it to be a good omen; a vindication of my decision to lend Amber the money. It then occurred to me that an actual good omen would have been finding the code for the safe in the writing desk. But we play the cards we're dealt with.

It was 11.30am on Friday. If I did six hours a day of code entering I would comfortably open the safe by Monday at the latest. That was, of course, if I didn't make any errors.

Carrying a mug of microwaved coffee, I walked to my mother's bedroom, opened the wardrobe, sat down on the floor in front of it, placed the mug on the floor, brushed aside the several long coats and robes hanging in the wardrobe that were crowding the box, cracked the joints in my fingers, positioned the wad of blank paper beside me, placed the ballpoint pen in the centre of the topmost sheet of paper, took a sip of coffee, put it down again and began work.

After two hours, I had entered 810 incorrect codes—at a speed of 8.9 seconds per entry. At this rate I was now looking at a 24 hour, 41-minute turn around.

I worked productively from 2.30pm to 4.30pm, reaching the number '1540'. This meant a rate of a number plus 'B' pressed and logged every 10 seconds. The slower time I attributed to having to get up and straighten my back more often than expected. I was also beginning to seriously rethink the six-hour working day. Knowing my mother, she'd no doubt have set the code in the high 9000s. If I were to have any chance of getting the cheque to Amber by Monday, an eight or even ten-hour day was looking likely.

I took another break. Getting back to work at 5.30pm, I laboured till 7:10pm, reaching 2205.

Day two of the safe heist saw me reach 5350. I'd worked from 10am till 7pm. It was a definite improvement on the previous day's figure, but still short. I had hoped to be in the high 6000s by then.

*

There are few things more satisfying after a hard day's work than the first beer of the night: the feel of the glass rim against one's lower lip, the uppermost section snug against the bridge of the nose; glass and human locked together in a held kiss. And then the slight cock of the head backwards to bring about the first deep pull—a pull constructed from multiple swallows—and the receiving of the glass's fluids. It's the only time of the night when drinking beer has two functions: to satiate by the quenching of thirst, and to gain access to the realm of festivity. This nexus of the somatic with the spiritual is in itself intoxicating. The golden river courses its way down the throat and on into the digestive system where it gifts its load of alcohol to another river, the blood stream, which carries the message that the working day is finished to the far-flung regions of the neural network.

It had taken me several minutes to drain my first schooner of the evening. Gary was up the other end of the bar serving another customer. It was 9.15pm. The pub was moderately crowded. Bronwyn was at a table nearby, lecturing someone about something.

Wendy and Gavin entered from the street. Both of them were draped in Sydney Swans regalia and had painted their faces in the team colours. It was the first time I'd seen them since the pool game.

Having despatched Gavin to fetch drink, Wendy took her place at their favourite booth on the right-hand side of the lounge.

'G'day mate,' Gavin said on arrival beside me at the bar. Had he forgotten my name? A thick red 'V', bordered in white, covered a large part of the right side of his face. Contained within the red 'V', was the profile of a swan's neck set against the backdrop of the Sydney Opera House.

'Hello,' I replied. 'Did you win?'

'Slaughtered them,' he said. The paint on his face problematised the reading of his facial expressions. I assumed he was looking happy.

Gary returned to our end of the bar.

'Right, who's next?' he asked.

Both Gavin and I pointed at each other,

'You go,' I said.

'No, you go,' he said.

'No, really, you go,' I said

'Ok,' he said reluctantly.

*

No sooner had Gavin departed with his bourbon and cokes, than Gary spoke: 'Did you confront him about the bird shit and the flies?'

I hadn't yet revealed to Gary any details about the consultation in Killara with Sonia. Ever since I'd seen Wendy and Gavin enter the pub, a looped sequence of Wendy's spit had been playing in the cinema of my mind. I was surprised at the intensity of feeling the images still provoked in me.

I wasn't drunk enough to engage in conversation with Wendy yet.

*

With five schooners under my belt and three missed opportunities to discuss the matter with Gavin, at Gary's urging, I got off my bar stool and headed for the booth.

Not much more than an hour had passed since my first beer of the night and as I made my way over to the booth, I felt decidedly wobbly. I was midway between the bar and the booth when Gavin said something funny to Wendy. She erupted in cackling laughter the sound of which sliced through the ambience of the lounge. But it was more the sight of her that stopped me in my tracks.

I've got nothing against the painting of one's face in support of a sporting team. I myself, given the right set of circumstances, could don greasepaint should I feel a strong affiliation to a particular group of professional athletes. But there was something truly awful about Wendy's makeup. Her face was chiefly painted white. Written roughly, in untidy red capitals across the top of her forehead was the word 'BLOODS'. Surrounding both her eyes were triangular areas of unpainted skin. Positioned symmetrically around her mouth was a bat-shaped expanse of red, which brought to mind the clown makeup worn by the serial killer John Wayne Gacey. It was difficult to make out the exact contour of her mouth while it moved in accordance with her laughter—it was as if her lower face had become a screen upon which played an animated cartoon of a bat flexing its wings!

Fear and revulsion gripped me, as well as (mysteriously) faint stirrings of tumescence. I quickly sublimated this fear into anger and disbelief. There was no way in the world I was going to apologise to *that*, that low-life specimen of bullshit suburban sorcery. Wendy and Sonia Rocklin could both go to hell (not that there was one). I retraced my steps back to the barstool. I didn't think Wendy had noticed me but, with hindsight, I'm not so sure.

I spent the remainder of the evening focusing my thoughts on *real* world events such as my various predictions (all extremely positive) concerning Amber's reaction to the money I'd be giving her once I cracked the *Firelord* safe.

At around midnight, I watched as Wendy and Gavin migrated from the lounge to the beer garden. I left the Stella shortly after.

*

I'd set the alarm for 10.30am, but after five snooze commands, I shut the thing off and slept through till 12.30pm. Being Sunday, it was the last full day I had to work on the safe before my rendezvous with Amber. I needed to be somewhere over 8000 by day's end, a feat requiring an 11-hour workday. I would then have Monday morning to finish off, should I need it.

I opened the door to my mother's room.

There she was, sitting up in bed. She hadn't gone to work.

'Why have you come in here?' she asked.

'I heard a noise and thought I should investigate.'

'Do you come in here when I'm at work?'

'No, never.'

I noticed a bucket on the floor beside the bed.

'Not feeling well?' I asked.

'I feel terrible . . . food poisoning . . . the meat . . . been up all night.' Her voice was thin and croaky.

'That's no good.' My concern at her illness was quite real. 'Does this mean you won't be going in to Class Axe today?'

She nodded.

I went back out to the kitchen, sat down at the table and gazed out through the window at the craggy, leafless limbs of a garden tree.

*

'Shouldn't you see a Doctor?' I asked, standing at the doorway of the bedroom. 'I'm worried about you.'

She shook her head. 'I'll be alright. I'm over the worst of it.'

'You don't look like it. How about I give Dr Laurie a ring?'

Once again, she shook her head.

I went back out to the kitchen.

*

'Is that you?' she said.

'What?' I was on my knees in front of the wardrobe. I'd tried to open its door and had caused its hinges to creak. Whatever other incapacities my mother may have been experiencing, loss of hearing was not one of them.

'What are you doing down there on the floor?'

'I think I dropped something when I last came in here.'

My plan had been to remove the box from the wardrobe and to relocate it to my bedroom. It had been based on the faulty assumption that, with her body locked in battle with the food poisoning bacteria, she would be dozing in and out of sleep.

I crawled around, briefly, at the foot of the bed.

'I must have dropped it outside.'

I left the room.

*

'Hello, I'd like to speak with Dr Laurie please,' I said into the mouthpiece of the telephone. Dr Belinda Laurie was my mother's GP who'd recently moved her small practice into a large family medical centre not far from the mall.

'I'm afraid Dr Laurie isn't in today,' said a female voice on the other end of the line.

Of course, it was Sunday.

'Would you like to make an appointment?' she asked.

'Is there anyone at the centre I can talk to now?'

'I'm afraid they're all with patients at the moment.'

'It's a bit of an emergency.'

'Sir, if this is an emergency, you should call 000.'

'Oh?'

'Otherwise, Dr Laurie will be in on Monday between 10.30am and 4pm. Would you like to make an appointment?

'Thank you, I'll call you back.'

I hung up and went back out to the kitchen.

'Mum,' I said standing at the foot of the bed, 'I really think you ought to go to hospital.'

'Hospital? Don't be silly.' Her voice had a happy tone to it, touched no doubt by the level of my concern. 'I'm alright,' she continued, 'a couple of days in bed and I'll be back to normal.'

'I believe it's food poisoning,' I said into the telephone mouthpiece.

'Is the person conscious? Can she walk or will she require assistance into the ambulance?' said a female voice on the other end.

'She's drifting in and out of consciousness and she needs assistance. She doesn't want to go to hospital, but I think under the circumstances it would be the best option. I'm very worried.'

I wasn't being dishonest. This was not the prank call of a juvenile. I was making sure my mother received the best possible medical care for a condition that could easily escalate. Nevertheless, memories of teenage hi-jinx involving emergency service departments and fake pleas for help came to mind.

*

'Come on Mrs Maddox,' said the female medic, 'we're just going to slip you onto this trolley.'

The trolley was standing at the foot of the bed, at right angles, forming a capital 'T'. I was impressed that they'd managed to manoeuvre the device into the bedroom.

My mother was shaking her head violently, frustrated at not being listened to.

'Go away!' she croaked. 'I'm not going to hospital.'

Standing next to me at the doorway of the bedroom was another medic, a man. I turned to him and shrugged, an attempt at a 'see what I mean' type of statement.

'Mum,' I said, turning back to her, 'you're very sick. They're just trying to help you.'

'No!' she shouted.

'Grab her legs!' ordered the female medic to her colleague.

The man moved towards the bottom right-hand side of the bed, reached under the sheets and began to grapple with my mother's feet.

Bent over in this fashion he was vulnerable and, sure enough, my mother managed to free her left leg from his grip and landed the heel of her foot squarely on his jaw. He was propelled backwards over the footboard of the bed, and fell against the base of the gurney, pushing it backwards into the wardrobe. He ended up sitting on the floor with his left arm entangled in the upper crook of the trolley's x-framed undercarriage and his right hand massaging his jaw.

The female officer removed a syringe from her medical bag. My mother saw it and screamed, 'Nooooo!'

I felt like I was witnessing an exorcism.

'Calm down, mum,' I said.

She was now standing up on the bed. Her feet sank into the mattress as she shifted her balance from one leg to the other in readiness for an attack.

'Help me Roger,' the medic said to her colleague on the floor.

I didn't need to watch this. I went out to the kitchen, trying not to visualise what my ears were hearing.

*

I walked with them out to the street and watched as the gurney's wheeled undercarriage collapsed upwards into the bed base before the whole thing was slid into the back of the ambulance. My mother remained parallel to the ground at all times. She was sleeping peacefully.

I praised Roger and the other medic for their professionalism but declined the invitation to ride with them to the hospital. I watched as the ambulance pulled away from the kerb, relieved that my mother was now in safe hands.

Her bedroom bore witness to the violent struggle that had taken place: bed sheets and pillows were strewn about, the mattress was

CHRIS ABRAHAMS

halfway on, halfway off the bed and the antique standing lamp lay toppled over on the floor, its shade severely dented. As I opened the door of the wardrobe, I noticed that the impact of the trolley had chipped a sizeable chunk of wood off its corner.

At 2.45 pm, I made myself comfortable on the floor in front of the safe and set about the day's work. '5,3,5,1,B ... 5,3,5,2,B ... 5,3,5,3,B ...'

The winter afternoon gave way to a winter dusk before finally settling into a winter's night. By 9.30pm I'd reached 7770, my best effort thus far, but there was little to rejoice over. True to form, my mother had set the code high, as if she'd predicted a time when I'd be in need of access, sitting with sore back and aching fingers, tapping out for whole days at a time the fucking codes on the keypad of her strongbox.

My eyes were swimming in their sockets, fatigued by the constant squinting required for accuracy inside the dimly lit wardrobe. I was mentally tired from the mind-numbing repetition of the five-button-press and concluded that continuing on would be pointless, indeed detrimental; accidently keying in a wrong four-digit number or making an error in recording the number could spell disaster.

With my already poor cash-flow situation heavily compromised by Sonia's service fee, I decided to borrow money from my mother's purse and treat myself to a well-earned, after-work drink at the Stella.

The purse was in her handbag, which would normally have accompanied her to work. Owing to the events of the morning, however, the bag was still under her bed, her designated hiding place for it. There'd been other times in my life when, strapped for cash, I'd been forced to take matters into my own hands. These had required stealth and planning and were usually carried out in the early hours of the morning by exploiting her pill-induced slumber. The ease with which I *now*

264

pulled the handbag from its hiding place—without recourse to either a stomach crawl (a movement that required painstaking synchronization with the breathing pattern of the sleeping woman), or a fidgety hour spent kneeling near the doorway with fishing rod, line and hook, trying to snag and drag the handbag out into the hallway—made me feel strangely uncomfortable.

I placed the handbag on the kitchen table, opened it and removed the purse. From the purse, I fished out two 50-dollar notes. I would tell her the money was used to tip the ambulance people.

There were various compartments inside the purse for cards and such. I took out her Medicare card and absentmindedly rubbed the underside of my thumb against its raised lettering—I probably should have handed this to the ambulance people. I replaced it and fished out another card—her old librarian staff card. Why would she hang on to that? I was struck by how young she looked in the photograph. She also had a current driver's licence. Why?

I put the cards back in their slot, snapped the purse shut and began to stuff it back into the open handbag.

I noticed something inside the handbag: a small notebook about the size of a pack of playing cards. I'd seen it before, on the other occasions when circumstances had forced me to borrow money, but I'd never bothered to open it.

On the first page was a poem:

How I'm letting things slide now!
Just slide towards the edge
Taking the brake off
Blaming now
Let it go
Gone

It was interesting that my mother was still writing her poetry and part of me was relieved that her work schedule hadn't totally squashed this outlet for her creativity.

I turned the page. There was another poem:

I will watch the bruises on my arms
Develop like photographs
Then he will tap me on the shoulder and say
'It's time to go.'
And I will go to the coast.
And I will sit upon the rock.
And I will let another energy take over.

I turned the page.

All the steps have brought me here
To the last room
Where I will atone
Trade waste for waste
For the first time
Responding to need
Simple and deep
Worse to come
Sweet and thick
Numb then stung
With hatred on the tear

I turned the page once more:

Safe
3567

At first I didn't realise the significance, thinking it was a poem that incorporated numbers. Then, bang! It dawned on me.

I rushed back into the bedroom and knelt on the floor in front of the safe. I keyed in the four numbers and pressed 'B'.

Straightaway I heard a new click sound coming from inside the strongbox—something gave. The door popped forward slightly. I pulled it all the way open and sat back, looking into the dark interior space.

Then something else occurred to me—the numbers: 3-5-6-7 or 3/5/67.

It was my date of birth.

XII

We sat at the window table in *Smarties*. Outside on King Street early afternoon winter sunlight infused everything with a laidback feeling. It felt good to be alive, relaxed and in control.

'Oh, before I forget," I said, reaching down to the back pack on the floor. 'I've got the money.'

Amber's face showed relief when I sat back up, the chequebook in my hands. I placed it on the table before me and pulled from my coat pocket grandad's Eversharp Skyline.

'To whom should I make it out?'

'I didn't know it would be a cheque. I thought it'd be cash.' Her look of relief had been shoved aside by one of worry.

She stood up.

'I just need to make a phone call. To the uni.'

She made her way to the exit door, opened it and stepped out onto the footpath. The door swung closed behind her, causing the string of bells attached to clang briefly.

Even though I didn't yet have a name to enter into the 'Pay' space on the blank cheque, I began to fill in what I could. I entered the amount in words and then numbers, then the date, and then I forged my mother's signature. Although the nib of the pen felt a bit scratchy, its elegant heft instilled the proceedings with gravitas. I regretted not filling out the cheque under Amber's gaze.

'Look, it should be alright,' said Amber, sitting down. 'Just write 'cash' in the pay space.'

'Ok.' I picked up the pen and entered the word. I tore the cheque from the chequebook and, holding it several inches from my mouth, began to blow on it to dry the ink. The slim page flapped to the wind of my breath. Unfortunately, the image of Wendy kissing Gavin's chips, back at the Stella Maris, came to mind.

'Nice pen,' said Amber

'Yes, it belonged to my grand-.'

'It's ten thousand right?' she asked.

I nodded.

'There's a bank just up there on the corner,' she said, pointing across to the other side of King Street.

'Are you in a hurry?' I asked, leaning forward and offering her the now dry cheque. She didn't reach for it, her hands stayed under the table.

'Here's the cheque,' I said, somewhat redundantly.

'I think it'd be better if you cashed it. I've never really used a cheque before.'

How times had changed!

'You've never seen a cheque?' I asked, sensing the opportunity to engage in a 'when I was young, there was no . . . ' type conversation.

She shook her head.

'When I was young, this,' I shook the cheque in the air, 'was all there was if we wanted to move large amounts of money. We didn't have ATMs—imagine that!'

I placed the cheque down on the table before continuing: 'I did all my banking with a passbook account. I'd go to the bank and the teller would fill the book out by hand and then stamp it. There were so many more tellers back then.

Amber's lack of engagement showed her clear intention to starve the conversation of air in the hope it would soon peter out. I, on the other hand, was determined to get my money's worth, even if it meant a lonely monologue. I now see that I was talking in order to distract myself from thinking about what I was doing.

'There wasn't any Internet either,' I went on. 'You know, I can't begin to imagine life without the Internet now! Have you seen those new SD cards? You can fit a terabyte on them. I can remember my first Mac—a Classic. It had two megabytes of RAM. But then again, they landed on the moon with only a quarter of a megabyte of RAM.'

She remained unresponsive, her mouth closed.

'In terms of the Classic's hard drive capacity,' I continued, 'compared to these SD cards, I'd need half a million Classics to get the same hard disk space.'

Amber gave up maintaining eye contact with me and was now looking at her watch, the one I'd given her.

'And then there's the Cloud! But then, thanks to Snowden, it now looks like all this new technology has come at a price to our privacy and freedom. Every click, every search, it's all logged, somewhere. All our personal details are now . . .'

'Sorry Geoff, I've really got to get moving, otherwise I'll be late for my class.'

I looked at the cheque on the table. I got to my feet.

'Ok. Let's go.'

'You know what?' she said. 'I think I'll stay here. The bank's just over there.'

Once again, she pointed across King Street in the direction of the bank, as if she thought I might have already forgotten it.

*

Five minutes later I was back. 'Here you go.'

I placed the envelope containing one hundred $100 bills on the table in front of her and sat down. She picked it up and put it in her shoulder bag.

'Aren't you going to count it?' I asked.

'I trust you Mr Maddox.' She stood up. I stood up.

'I've got to fly,' she said.

'When can I see you again?'

'This week's pretty hairy—I've got a 500-word essay due that I haven't started yet.

'How's about Friday?'

She appeared to be doing mental calculations.

'Email me—or I'll email you,' she said.

We stood looking at each other. Her smile seemed stale, unconnected with any emotion.

I moved forward and put my arms around her, a clumsy hug that amplified her lack of responsiveness.

She wriggled out of the embrace.

'Ciao!' she said, backing away.

I stood and watched as she left the cafe, jangling the fucking door bells in the process.

XIII

'It's called queue harvesting,' said the woman on the screen, 'and it's the latest public nuisance coming to a Medicare or NRMA office near you.'

For once a television monitor at the Stella showed something other than sport. Gary, Bronwyn, Doc, Laird and I, along with a several other regulars, were watching the screen that was mounted on the wall next to the cricket bat cabinet.

The woman wore a high-shouldered, red power suit and was positioned in front of a vacuous blue office space. Every so often a shadowy worker would traverse the out of focus hinterland, pausing beside a computer monitor in order to signify dutiful fact gathering.

'Eric Stevens brings you this exclusive report.'

'Turn it up!' shouted Laird.

From behind the bar, Gary obediently pointed the remote at the monitor. An establishing exterior shot of a busy Medicare centre came on the screen. The camera then cut to a mid-shot of an exhausted looking young woman. She was standing next to a large pram around which two small children were chasing each other.

The camera stayed on the woman while a voiceover began: 'Queues!' said the male voice, 'who needs 'em? And they just keep getting longer—that is unless you're willing to pay.' The voiceover was delivered in a television journalist's drawl whereby every sentence ended in a wooden downward inflection. 'Here at this Medicare

Centre, if you've got the money, well, you can simply buy your way out of the wait.'

The camera cut to a uniformed security guard.

'They come in,' the security man said, 'take a whole lot of tickets from the dispenser, and then they on sell them to customers.'

The camera cut to the reporter, Eric Stevens, a young man in an ill-fitting suit and too large spectacles. Behind him, the Medicare centre was in full swing.

'There's not a lot of skill to this lurk,' he said, speaking directly to camera. He walked over to the dispensing machine. 'You simply come over here, to this machine, take a handful of tickets and then you wait a while.'

On screen, a man in a business suit appeared: 'I'm a busy man, so yes, I've bought tickets in the past. But I don't condone it, really.'

The camera panned slightly to the right, bringing Stevens into shot. He was standing next to the businessman, holding a micro-phone. 'Would you do so again?' he asked.

'Yeah, probably.'

The report cut to Stevens, now in wide shot, in front of the mill-ing throng. Again, he addressed the viewer: 'So just who are these people—these 'queue harvesters' as they've become known—and why are they proving to be such a nuisance.'

The camera showed a darkened office space. In profile sat a man, similar in build to Laird and wearing similar clothes to Laird. His head was extremely pixelated but easily recognizable as belonging to Laird.

On the soundtrack, a pompous drum loop and a low synthesiser drone added stark criminality.

Stevens' voice was heard in voice over: 'Geoff, an ex-harvester, agreed to speak with us, on condition that his identity be kept secret.'

'I could clear six grand easy,' said the digitally disguised man who was clearly Laird. His voice had been pitch-shifted down.

'That's every week?' asked Stevens, off camera.

'I made six grand every week, on average,' said Laird.

'You sound like you're proud of this,' said Stevens.

'If I didn't do it, someone else would have.'

'Why did you stop?' asked Stevens.

'It got hard to look at myself in the mirror.'

The program cut back to the security guard: 'Yeah, some people benefit I guess—those who are prepared to pay. But their gain comes at the expense of the other customers, the ones who maybe can't afford to fork out money for tickets. It adds even more time to their wait.'

The businessman came back on screen: 'Look, they should put more staff on. This wouldn't happen if these places were properly staffed.'

The video cut back to the office and Laird: 'I'd target the single mums first, then the professionals, then the tradies.'

'Let's get this straight,' said Stevens, out of shot. 'You'd go after the single mums; the most vulnerable?'

'I'm not proud of myself.'

Onto the screen burst grainy black and white images of the Medicare Centre shot by a CCTV camera—a time counter ticking away in the top left hand corner. Stevens's voice, accompanied by the pompous drum loop and bass synthesiser, intoned: 'Peak Hour has obtained exclusive surveillance footage of a queue harvester in action.'

The video showed a man wearing white pants, a dark cotton shirt and an eye patch—Williams—approaching a woman waiting with a pram. The woman shook her head in response to Williams' enquiry.

Laird's voice was heard in voiceover: 'He's picked her out, and she's refused—most people do the first time.'

The video was then sped up to show Williams moving away from the woman to go and stand at the dispenser. The onscreen counter sped quickly through three minutes of recorded action; the fast motion *mise en scene* had a comical look.

The video returned to normal speed and showed the woman begin to push the pram towards Williams.

Laird's voiceover continued: 'Ok, she's changed her mind.'

'She's going to buy a ticket?' asked Stevens.

'She's going to buy a ticket.'

The woman reached Williams. At the moment when she handed over the money for the ticket, the music stopped and the video froze. Using the trope of a photograph being blown up, the camera performed a staggered zoom with each stagger accompanied by exaggerated old-fashioned camera shutter noise. A barely decipherable close up of the middle section of a crumpled banknote—held on one side by Williams and on the other by the woman—was the end result. '$10' appeared in bold white lettering on the bottom of the screen.

'He's just made himself $10,' announced the pitch-shifted Laird.

The manager of the Medicare centre seated behind a desk appeared on screen: 'It's not a staffing issue; the staff here work very hard and do a great job. We don't get any complaints.'

Stevens now returned to the screen speaking directly to camera: 'Earlier today, we received a tip off that there would be a queue harvest at this branch and we weren't disappointed.'

We were then shown Williams, this time caught on high-definition video, attempting to sell a ticket to a soldier.

'Excuse me sir!' shouted Stevens still off camera, 'Did you just sell a ticket to this soldier?'

The video became jerky as the person holding the camera moved quickly into position.

Williams smiled and shook his head.

'Well how come,' continued Stevens, 'you're holding all those tickets in your hand?'

Williams continued to grin at the camera.

'Sir,' said Stevens 'can you answer the question? How come you've got all those tickets in your hand?'

Williams maintained his grin.

Suddenly, his right hand veered directly at the camera lens, growing enormous and blocking out the light. Noises of scuffling and bleeped swearing could be heard. In a frenzied eruption, light returned to the screen but the readability of the images disintegrated into a riot of tumbling shapes and smeared colours. Legibility finally returned as a result of the camera having ended up lying on its side on the floor.

Then the branch manager, in his office, was back on: 'We're putting on extra security and we're determined to make this a thing of the past.'

The video cut to the security guard: 'My advice to people? Just don't buy a ticket. It's actually an offence to buy a ticket from a harvester and people who do so are liable for a sizeable fine, and we *will* prosecute. We are determined to break the harvesters' business model.'

'So just be patient?' said Stevens from off camera.

'Just be patient and wait your turn,' said the security guard.

The businessman came back on screen: 'As long as there are queues like these,' he gestured with his hand at the packed room, 'I'll buy tickets. I just don't have the time.'

We then cut to an older woman, frowning and shaking her head.

Stevens spoke in voiceover: 'But there are some customers who definitely aren't onside with the harvesters.'

The older woman spoke: 'I think they should be strung up by their ...' A bleep censored her final word .

The surveillance footage of the mother buying a ticket from Williams was replayed in slow motion, accompanied again by the eerie drum and synthesiser soundtrack. Over the top came Stevens's voice: 'But whatever you think of them, there's one thing that's for certain: life just got a whole lot harder for the harvesters.'

The music swelled up underneath the footage. Just like before, the video froze at the point where the $10 note changed hands, and the staggered 'zoom-in' was repeated. The blown-up image of the note stayed on the screen while Laird's voice came up, in voiceover: 'It got hard to look at myself in the mirror.'

The image faded to black and the music came to an end with a delay-effected drum hit vanishing in ominous echo.

The female anchor was back on the screen: 'That report from Eric Stevens. We contacted the health minister for his response, but he declined our invitation to appear on the program. Back with more after the break.'

The *Peak Hour* logo barged onto the screen along with a quick sting of theme music.

'Can we switch this crap off?' asked Bronwyn, having happily watched the whole segment.

Gary pointed the remote at the screen and instantly a scene involving a family eating processed cheese was replaced by one of ten hungry greyhounds chasing an artificial lure around a dirt track.

'Did you make that yourself?' asked Doc, turning to Laird.

Bronwyn laughed.

'I brought it into being,' said Laird.

XIV

It was sometime around 3.30am when the taxi deposited me at the front gate of our apartment. From Smarties, I'd gone straight to the Stella where, having been forced to watch Laird's *Peak Hour* episode, I'd stayed until the bell was rung.

The balcony light was off. I fumbled around in the darkness, trying to get the key into the keyhole of the front door. Having succeeded, I pushed open the door and walked into the living room. I collapsed into the recliner rocker, causing the springs in some part of its internal workings to vibrate for a noticeably long time.

The walk up the path from the taxi had cleared my head. For the first time in many hours I thought about Amber and her lacklustre reaction to the $10000. The way she'd said 'ciao' irked me. It was a word I'd never heard her use before. It was strange how surety as to the rationality of an action can be turned on its head by the utterance of one syllable. Her 'ciao' had done just that.

'What the fuck have you done?' I spoke the words aloud. The answer was horribly simple; I'd stolen a shit load of money from my mother and had given it to a dancer I hardly knew.

I tried to console myself with the memory of Amber's promise that the money was considered 'loaned', not 'gifted', and Amber did seem like an honest person. But when other memories such as having to cash the cheque myself and her subsequent lack of demonstrative gratitude came to mind, the palliative quality of the loan rationale evaporated.

And what if Amber was lying about the uni fees? One thought that provided a modicum of positive spin on the whole thing was that even if I never saw the money again, at least I'd have helped a struggling young artist achieve her dreams. But what if even that was bullshit?

Feelings of anxiety began to escalate.

I could no longer comprehend the subjectivity that had taken hold of me in the days prior to giving Amber the money. Automatically, I engaged in another soothing exercise, one of trying to imagine myself *prior* to cashing the cheque; of trying to picture myself walking out of the bank with the cheque still in my hand.

I stood up from the chair.

'You know what,' I said out loud, 'I've changed my mind. I'm keeping the money.'

I spoke to an empty lounge room sofa upon which I superimposed a fabulous Amber, a mind ghost plucked from the previous afternoon at *Smarties*.

The exercise brought with it brief pockets of artificial relief, enough to make me repeat it over and over. But the illusion was impossible to sustain. The suspended reality came crashing back down time after time, forcing me to confront the abject nature of my predicament, whereupon I'd be compelled to sit back down in the recliner rocker and utter the words 'why the fuck did you do it?'

I segued into a different genre of relief: the atonement that can be wrought from self-flagellation. I got up out of the chair and walked to my mother's bedroom, whispering to myself: 'you are such a fucking idiot, you are such a fucking idiot, you are such a fucking idiot.' The use of the mantra provided a small amount of highly perishable comfort.

I used the light from the hall, it lit the bedroom enough for my purposes. The doors of my mother's wardrobe stood open so that the safe, even in the half-light, was clearly visible, its door ajar. I placed the chequebook in the strongbox, closed the door and pressed button 'A.'

*

I wrote in a hurry, my sentences interrupted by regular and involuntary glances upwards towards the bedroom ceiling in fear of another fly plague. The act of composing the email had a calming effect on my stress levels.

> Dear Amber,
> It's Mr Maddox here. Hope you're well. It was great to meet up this afternoon at Smarties. Look, I don't really know how to put this, but (takes deep breath!) I think I was a little bit too hasty with the money thing. The fact is, something's come up and I'm going to have to ask if it would be ok for me to get the money back. This is very embarrassing. I sincerely hope that it won't cause too much inconvenience for you. If it's ok I could swing by your place tomorrow and pick up the money. How would 2pm be? Or we could meet at Smarties—your call. One idea that came to mind for getting you your fees, was that maybe we could organise some sort of fundraiser at the Stella Maris—a pie toss or something? Anyway, once again, I'm very sorry about all this. BTW I saw that there was an interesting dance piece on at the Performance Space next weekend. I'd pay for the tickets if you were interested in going. I hope everything's going well for you.
> Love, Mr Maddox

I clicked 'send' and went to bed.

XV

The 15 minutes of morning that remained when I woke were greeted with a much greater sense of optimism. Things weren't nearly as bad as I'd imagined them the night before. The buffeting gusts of despair, logical in their causation, had somehow given way to a calm and sunny nihilism. It really didn't matter all that much. Nothing really mattered. Even if Amber didn't pay me back—something I wasn't expecting—I could handle the debt. Ten thousand dollars was not a lot of money.

There was no response to my email from Amber on my computer, but this didn't surprise me—she probably hadn't read it yet.

I went to the kitchen.

Due to my mother being away receiving great medical care, the breakfast pickings in the fridge were scant.

*

'My cousin,' answered Laird.

We were at *Muffin Siesta* and I'd just asked him how he'd managed the *Peak Hour* report.

'He's a producer on the show,' Laird continued. 'I just rang him up. He loved it.'

'How does Williams feel about it?'

'Not too flash I expect.'

I felt disappointed that the story of Laird's ticket scam—having ended so dismally for him—contained an empowering epilogue. I'd just gotten used to having the surly and unpleasant Laird back, and now, here he was, sitting opposite me, contemplating a life in television journalism.

'Maggie May' by Rod Stewart was being pumped through the myriad sound-conditioning outlets of the cavernous mall interior.

'Apparently, it was the highest rating episode they've ever had—that's pretty good, isn't it?'

'That's great.' I nodded. The absurdity of this question quashed any feelings of jealousy he hoped to instil in me.

'I heard about you and Amber,' he said. The compassionate tone he was trying to inject into his voice was truly horrible.

'From whom?' I asked

'Bronwyn.'

'Look, mate,' I said, 'I really don't want to talk about it.'

'If I were you, I'd forget about her.'

'Yeah, well actually Laird, you're not me.'

No advice from Laird was welcome, let alone advice concerning the topic under discussion. However, the curtness of my last utterance belied defensiveness, which in turn belied hurt—hurt which Laird, in his post-ratings-bonanza-fuelled condescension, seized upon. I got the feeling he thought he was Dr Phil, now that his pixelated mug had been on TV. Nothing would bring him more pleasure than the sound of his own voice doling out life advice.

'You can't always get what you want,' he said sagely.

I made motions to get up from my chair. Sensing this, Laird quickly continued: 'She said you made her flesh crawl.'

'What do you mean?' I asked.

'She finds you repulsive. I didn't want to have to tell you this, but … you're a mate. I care about you.'

This was a double whammy. On the one hand was the news about Amber's professed disdain for me; on the other, the monstrous hypocrisy of Laird who, under the Trojan horse of mateship, had just delivered a king hit to the fragile belief I held in my competence as a man. Whatever snippet of gossip Laird was peddling, it was being used for the sole purpose of causing me pain.

'Who told you that?' I spoke as flatly as I could.

'Who do you think?'

'Williams?'

Laird nodded, well pleased at the upper hand he had attained in this contest of ideas.

'Well she told me that *Williams* made her flesh crawl,' I said, before a much-needed brain to mouth filter could be put in place.

XVI

The headlights shining on the parked cars caught my attention. Roderick's Getz pulled up directly in front of Amber's house. He got out of the car, walked to the front door, opened it and went inside. Several seconds later, both he and Amber emerged from the house and walked to the parked vehicle. Roderick flipped the boot and motioned to Amber to help him remove something, a cardboard box about the size of a bar fridge.

'It seems bigger than the others.' I heard Amber say, before a car drove past, covering Roderick's reply.

They lifted the box out of the car and began to carry it towards the house, with Amber having to shuffle backwards. They'd almost reached the front gate when she lost her footing and stumbled, letting go of the box in the process. It landed on its bottom edge and I heard a clanging sound.

'You fucking idiot!' hissed Roderick.

'I'm sorry, I couldn't help it,' said Amber. 'It's fucking dark, you know.'

Amber picked up her end of the box and continued towards the house. She was now limping, having twisted her ankle.

Just before he passed the threshold of the entranceway, Roderick said: 'we're going to have to use that fucking Acepromazine again.'

I heard Amber say something in a worried tone of voice before the door slammed, kicked shut by Roderick's heel.

*

The chair opposite the man was empty, as it had been when I'd ventured into *Klonimus* on the very first surveillance evening in the neighbourhood centre.

As before, various sheets of paper, black with ink, were spread on the table before him; the jottings of the haphazard calculations of his genius.

I watched as he poured his beer from one glass to the other and then back again.

'Why do you do that?' I asked, chiefly to see if he would remember me.

His pour complete, he put the empty glass down on the table and took a long pull from the full one still in his hand. He opened his mouth and executed a post-drink exhale brimming with satisfaction.

'You asked me that question once before,' he told me.

I was impressed. The benign smile on his face suggested to me that he knew the reason why I had repeated my inquiry. The smile I took to be an invitation for me to talk.

I was wrong. He pointed at a place on one of the sheets of paper.

'This is a fractal, its individuation is the same as its totality, the son of man repeated in all men. Don't worry about this,' he said pointing to a cluster of Greek letters and arithmetical symbols. 'The first sin led to knowledge of nakedness, we all knew that, but . . . '

I shrugged my shoulders, 'if you say so.'

' . . . it is nowhere listed among the orthogons of Wersin—here look.' He directed my gaze towards one of the sheets of paper. 'The Eigen value—love—can be balanced using partial differentiation.'

I let the man talk on, using the smooth flow of complex nonsense as background muzak over which I considered what I'd witnessed while kneeling in the garden of the activity centre.

Roderick and Amber must have reunited, or indeed had never broken up. The way Roderick had called her a 'fucking idiot' was proof they were an item.

The man opposite me repeated his bubble-destroying beer-pouring ritual while explaining an arcane connection between the Kirnberger III tuning system and the Gordon Rugby Club.

If they (Amber and Roderick) hadn't broken up, then Amber had lied to me back at The Stella and a lot of things followed on from that lie.

*

I paused before knocking, my knuckles inches from the translucent glass of the front door. Inside, many lights were on and through the glass I could make out the shadowy forms of Amber and Roderick as they moved about industriously.

At *Klonimus*, my meditations on the significance of Amber's lie had forced me to my feet and brought me here, to confront her, to be a man.

A gap of some five inches separated my hand from the glass and the instigation of my quest for answers. I knew there was only a small time frame in which I could act before momentum evaporated whereupon I'd walk away and pace the darkened back lanes of Newtown, attempting to regain my *cojones*—an activity that could last until sunrise, before probable failure.

The decision to proceed was made *for* me; my bulk at the door was just as visible from inside as the two indoor people had been from the outside.

'There's someone at the door.' It was Amber speaking. She was in the living room.

The sound of Roderick's voice coming from the kitchen at the back of the house was harder to hear, but I believe he said something along the lines of: 'get rid of them.'

Footsteps got louder. The door opened.

'Hello,' I said, pre-empting Amber who now stood before me, her mouth slightly open.

'What the fuck are you doing here?' she asked.

'Just passing, thought I'd drop in.'

'It's 2am in the fucking morning. What do you want?'

This was an obvious but awkward question. I had under-strategized. I didn't want to go straight to the hub of it and accuse her of lying to me; I needed to *properly* escalate things in the hope of finessing out the details of her duplicity.

Behind her in the living room, on the floor underneath the table, was an empty Hume's Crisps canister.

I pushed past, accidentally shouldering her into the hall wall, which I apologised for as I continued forwards into the house.

'What the fuck?' said Roderick, stepping into the living room from the kitchen. He had in his right hand what appeared to be a doll—a very colourful one with a blue head.

'You can't just barge in here like this,' said Amber, limping up behind me.

I could see past Roderick into the kitchen where, on the table, several other dolls were lying on their backs amid various lengths of bubble wrap. Stacked up on the floor next to the table were wiry metallic structures.

They weren't dolls; they were birds, either dead or unconscious. The wiry structures were cages and in them were other birds—similar but conscious.

Parrots.

I became aware of a pungent smell.

I quickly surveyed the living room. On the coffee table in front of the sofa, half a dozen opened Hume's cylinders stood upright like oversized candles. I moved quickly, picked one up and peered into the opening. I saw the azure-coloured cranium of a parrot.

It was obvious that something illegal was being undertaken in the house; something to do with parrots.

'How many can you fit into one of these?' I asked.

'Are you a cop?' asked Roderick.

'Oh fuck!' said Amber as if some horrible yet obvious fact that she should have been aware of had just been revealed.

It was of course absurd for anyone to think I could have manipulated Amber into borrowing $10000 from me so that I could then execute some sort of sting. After a moment's contemplation, Amber appeared to reach a similar conclusion, the look on her face of panicked regret dissolved.

'He's not a cop,' she said, looking at me with a disdain whose heavy implication was that I had neither the discipline nor ability to undertake any form of professional activity, let alone crime fighting.

'He looks like a cop,' said Roderick.

A part of me felt complimented that Roderick still thought I could be plain-clothes detective material. (Indeed I'm confident that, had I so wished, a life on the force would have been a fairly easy accomplishment.) I almost thanked him out loud.

'He's not a cop,' repeated Amber.

'How can you be so sure?' I asked, sensing an opportunity to inject some doubt into the proceedings in order to gain leverage. What I would do with this leverage was unclear to me. I was acting on instinct, and instinct told me to muddy the waters.

'Show us your badge,' demanded Roderick.

'I left it at home,' I said.

'Do you have a search warrant?' asked Amber.

'I don't need one,' I said.

'Like hell you don't need one!' said Roderick.

There was something about Roderick that told me he knew what he was talking about.

He put the parrot he was holding down on the living room table and moved towards me with intent to manhandle.

'Look,' I said, holding my hands in front of my chest, palms facing him, 'I was only having a joke. Of course I'm not a cop. I mean, really— me? Come on!' The backs of my legs were in contact with the edge of the coffee table,

My hand gesture was enough to pause Roderick's advancement.

'Ok,' I said, taking a deep breath, 'the reason I came over is that I needed to talk to you, Amber.' I gestured behind me at the Hume's packets. 'I have absolutely no idea what any of this is about.'

'What should we do?' Amber asked Roderick.

Before he could answer, a rustling sound was heard.

'Fuck!' said Roderick.

He rushed back into the kitchen.

The sound of frenzied activity followed. I heard wings flapping and chairs scraping and Roderick saying: 'Come here you little fucker,' followed by 'Christ!'

A panicked bird flew out of the kitchen across the lounge room and onwards into the hallway towards the front door.

Roderick stood at the entrance to the living room, a tail feather in his right hand.

'You didn't close the fucking door!' he said.

'Oh shit,' said Amber, who straightaway made a dash to the hallway to correct the oversight.

'And I almost trod on one,' said Roderick.

He looked at me as if it were my fault.

Amber came back from the front door.

'Why the fuck are they waking up?' she said.

'It's the Acepromazine,' said Roderick

'We've got to get back to the Ketamine,' said Amber.

This was a different Amber to the one I'd fallen in love with. She
seemed stronger, tougher, more in control. The girl-like tone to her
voice had been replaced by a more womanly one. I didn't find this new
Amber as attractive. In fact, I found it intimidating.

'Can I ask a question?' I interjected.

Roderick and Amber looked at me.

'Why are you putting these birds into these crisp cylinders?'

'We have a comedian in the room with us,' said Roderick.

'Is this what you wanted the $10000 for?' I asked Amber.

I was hoping that, by reminding her of the considerable amount of
money I'd quite recently lent her, I might repair some of the damage
my uninvited visit may have caused.

'No,' she said.

'Sit there on the sofa,' ordered Roderick.

I obeyed.

'And don't move.'

Roderick moved towards the staircase. I could feel the vibrations
caused by his footsteps on the wooden steps as he passed above me on
the way to one of the upstairs rooms.

'How many rooms have you got upstairs?' I asked Amber.

She turned and walked back down the hallway.

I heard her fiddling with the lock on the door.

Roderick began to talk on the telephone, his muffled and distant voice was impossible to understand.

Amber went to the kitchen.

I picked up one of the canisters standing on the coffee table in front of me. The can had no lid on it. I held it up to my right ear; the inhalations and exhalations of a small animal were faintly audible.

I looked down into the cavity of the tube and began to slowly rotate it. A mirror-less kaleidoscope, the blue, red and grey of a bird's head and neck were visible against the gloom of the further interior.

I upended the can onto the sofa beside me. A sleeping parrot fell with a small thud onto the cushion. It rolled down the slope formed by my body's indentation on the sofa cushion and came to rest face down against my thigh.

It was a strange and nasty world.

Gently, I put the animal back in the crisp tube and placed it back on the coffee table. Amber re-entered the room. She carried half a dozen plastic tube lids and a bill spike.

'Here,' she said, handing me the items, 'make yourself useful. Punch some holes into these lids.'

'For air?'

'Yes, for air.'

I set about perforating the plastic lids with the spike. She turned to walk back out to the kitchen.

'Is this what you do for a living?' I asked.

She paused at the entranceway.

'At the moment, actually, it is.'

'What about your dancing?' I asked.

She looked at me, a grin forming.

'What the fuck do you care about my dancing?'

'Ten thousand dollars' worth of care,' I said, pleased with my repartee.

'You didn't give me the money because you were interested in my dancing. You gave it to me because you wanted to buy me. Well you've done it! You've bought me. Congratulations!'

'Actually I lent it to you.'

It was clear that by referring to her dance I'd hit a raw spot and as a consequence something of the Amber I knew and loved had been glimpsed through the dark facade of this new parrot-smuggling incarnation.

Roderick came bounding down the stairs.

'Ok,' he said having reached the ground floor, 'we leave as soon as Jock gets here.'

Jock was not a common name.

Roderick turned to me.

'You're coming with us.'

With the bill spike, I continued to puncture breathing holes in the plastic lid I was holding, while ruminating over the new information.

'Come on, let's get the rest of these birds packed,' Roderick said.

Both he and Amber stepped into the kitchen.

I put the spike and the lid down on the coffee table. I stood up and walked on the tips of my toes to a point adjacent to the hallway.

'Hey!' I heard Roderick's voice.

I took off for the front door.

'It's deadlocked,' said Amber from the kitchen.

It was deadlocked.

I felt Roderick's hand on my right shoulder. He swung me around so that I was facing him. With both hands clasping my shoulders, he forced me, back first, against the hall wall. I offered little resistance.

He grabbed my throat with his right hand and pushed. My head hit the wall violently as he pinned me against it. The webbing between his thumb and index finger exerted uncomfortable pressure against both my carotid artery and windpipe.

'Listen pal,' said Roderick, 'you're not doing yourself any favours. Do you want me to hurt you?'

I shook my head as much as I could under the circumstances. I got the feeling that my eyes were bulging.

'Get back in the living room and stay on the sofa.'

I nodded meekly.

He let go his grip, allowing me a relieving inhalation of air. I turned and began to walk back up the hallway towards the living room.

The shove of his hands high up on my back was too powerful for me to absorb and remain upright. I staggered forward before crashing, right shoulder first, into the edge of the living room table. Among the objects on the table dislodged by the collision, was the unconscious parrot Roderick had earlier placed there and forgotten, which rolled off the edge and fell to the floor.

It was a good job they had carpet, I remember thinking.

'Hey, what the fuck are you doing?' said Amber.

'Sorry,' said Roderick, walking past me.

He picked up the bird.

'He'll be ok,' he said, optimistically.

Having placed the bird back on the table, he bent down once more and crawled under the table to retrieve a canister lying on the floor. Once back on his feet, canister in hand, he picked the sleeping bird up with his free hand and dropped it, tail first, into the cylinder.

Skilled labour! He stood the tube upright on the table and went into the kitchen.

Presently, I got up off the carpet and went back to the sofa, deciding it prudent to resume my puncturing.

*

The sound of a hand knocking against the glass pane of the front door interrupted my lid piercing.

From the kitchen Roderick said, 'here he is!' His tone was joking and familiar, like the announcement of the arrival of a popular guest at a party.

'I'll go,' I heard Amber say.

She emerged from the kitchen holding a key and moved briskly across the living room to the hallway.

Once in the hallway, she was out of my line of sight, but I judged, by the frequency of the sound of her footfalls, that the last two or so metres of the journey were accomplished by skipping.

She fiddled with the lock before opening the door.

'Hello!' said the male voice. It was Williams.

'Hello Mr Williams!' said Amber.

There were muffled sounds of breath and moisture; the slitherings of viscid surfaces conjoining and breaking part.

'God damn,' I heard Williams say, 'you're a fine smelling woman!'

It occurred to me that Amber was indeed one of those 'two-at-once' women. For a brief second I mused over the possibility that she might be a 'three-at-once' woman, a thought that, to this day, I feel shame at having ideated.

They emerged from the hallway holding hands.

'Where's your boyfriend?' asked Williams, loudly so that Roderick could hear. He playfully smacked Amber on the backside, in response to which she play-punched him on the arm.

'In here bro!' called Roderick from the kitchen.

'Better get in that kitchen, babe and put his mind at rest. We wouldn't want him getting jealous.'

'Shut up,' said Amber playfully.

She made eye contact with me. Even though it lasted no longer than a second, her look conveyed embarrassment. It showed she was aware she'd lied to me and that, to some extent, it mattered.

'What the fuck?' said Williams, registering my presence in the room. 'What's he doing here?'

'Hi Jock,' I said as I finished perforating the last of the tube lids.

Roderick came out of the kitchen: 'He gate-crashed and now we don't know what to do with him.'

'Boy, you really get around!' said Williams. 'What happened? Did your regular girlfriend run out of air?'

All three of them laughed at the joke. Fortunately, I had the memory of Williams' recent television appearance with which to lessen much of the intended humiliation.

'Ok, Romeo,' said Roderick to me, 'get up. We're going for a drive.' He turned to Williams: 'my car or yours?'

*

We drove in Roderick's Getz south along the Princess Highway. I was sitting in the back with Williams. Roderick was driving, with Amber sitting in the front passenger seat. In the boot compartment were twenty or so canisters packed loosely into three cardboard boxes.

Why I needed to be with them hadn't been stated. My uninvited visit had forced them to improvise, so there was a good chance that none of us in the car knew what was coming my way. It was still unclear as to just how hard-line these people really were. The goings on back at the house had bordered on slapstick and gave the impression that they were new to the game. The comfort I drew from this idea passed quickly; the unpredictable novice could be as dangerous as the hardened sociopath.

I suddenly thought of Wendy. Was she watching with her third eye, chuckling at my present predicament? If I had dropped my trousers after the pool game, would any of this be happening?

*

We drove south for an hour until we passed through the outskirts of Thirroul, a small village on the coastline between Sydney and Wollongong. Roderick parked his Getz opposite a large, fenced-off area of cleared land. I could make out heavy machinery and mounds of earth silhouetted against the moonlit sky.

All four of us got out. I stood and watched as Amber hugged first Roderick and then Williams. She broke from Williams, took a step backwards and spoke to them both: 'you be careful out there, you guys.'

She got back in the car without wishing me well.

Roderick opened the boot, pulled out a cardboard box and gave it to Williams.

We walked away from the back of the car until we reached the first cross street. We turned right. A long narrow road lay before us, trailing off into the darkness.

*

'There's no light on,' said Williams.

'He'll be up, don't worry,' said Roderick.

We were standing at the foot of the brick steps leading up to the front door of a small fibro house, the last one on the street. To the right of the house, a steep gully was fenced off. Thirty metres away, the fence connected at 90 degrees to the railing of a single-lane road bridge that crossed over the train line below. We were now about half a mile from the car.

Roderick walked up the steps and knocked on the front door which was duly opened to reveal a man the size of a jockey dressed in tracksuit pants, T-shirt and runners. In his right hand glowed a burning cigarette. Considering the season and time of day, I was impressed by the lightness of his attire.

'Raff, my man!' greeted Roderick. 'How's it hanging?'

'Good mate, good,' said Raff. 'Come on through.'

Roderick signalled for us to follow him inside.

*

We stood in a dimly lit room at the back of the house. It had originally been a veranda. At some point in time, the owner, or owners, seeking to capitalise on the investment by creating a cheap extra room, had enclosed it. The aluminium-framed windows, which probably afforded views of an ill-kept backyard, were covered with blackout curtains coarsely fashioned from dark-coloured bed sheets and doweling rods.

Fortunately, Raff's smoking did much to block out the stench of mould, beer and urine in the room. The urine may have come from the bull terrier lying asleep next to what I assumed was the back door. It was strange that it hadn't woken up.

Seated on a vinyl couch was a man watching *Shocking Asia* on a flat screen TV that was perched on a small bamboo and glass coffee table in the centre of the room. The volume had been turned down low which rendered the voiceover incoherent and this made me think the video was being played less for focussed entertainment and more for backgrounding ambience.

Against the wall opposite the couch an oblong Formica kitchen table stood cluttered with ashtrays, magazines, newspapers, DVDs and numerous glasses and bottles containing dregs. Whoever the film buff was, Italian splatter seemed to rate highly. Copies of *Cannibal Holocaust* and *Tenebrae* were conspicuous among the jumble.

'I should introduce you to my friends' said Roderick. 'This here is Jock.'

Having cursorily cleared an area of the larger items, Jock placed the box down on the table and held out his hand to shake with Raff. Raff took the hand and engaged it in manoeuvres of intricate twisting, the climax of which involved a finger click and a high five—some kind of local 'street' handshake. Williams tried to get down but ended up looking awkward, I thought.

'Sorry about your eye, man,' said Raff alluding to Williams' eye patch.

Williams nodded and shrugged.

'And this here is grandad,' said Roderick pointing me out.

'Your grandfather?' asked Raff.

'Amb's grandad.' The fact that I was around the same age as Roderick in no way hindered him in his pursuit of this ageist gag.

Raff gave me a quick once over with his eyes.

'Good to meet you mate.'

The handshake I received was a straightforward clasp and shake, something for which I was both relieved and slightly offended.

Also offensive was that Raff seemed to believe Roderick regarding my biological relationship to Amber.

'Well this here mate of mine's called Happy.'

Raff signalled for Happy to get to his feet, something he did reluctantly. He was a well-built individual with a shaved head. I took the nickname to be ironic. All three of us acknowledged him with various mutterings along the theme of 'Hey Happy!'

'You got something for me?' asked Raff now that the introductions were out of the way.

'We got eight Blue Bonnets—just like you asked for,' said Roderick.

He pointed at the Formica table.

Raff moved towards the table and placed his hand on top of the box. He drummed the fingers of his right hand briefly on the cardboard. He turned to Roderick.

'I asked for nine, mate,' he said, taking a drag on his cigarette.

The ninth blue bonnet, I concluded, was at that moment in a tree somewhere in Newtown.

'I'm sure you said eight,' said Roderick.

'It was eight,' said Williams.

Happy shook his head.

'It was eight,' I said. My utterance had been involuntary but when I thought more about it, it wasn't such a bad thing to have said.

'No mate it was definitely nine,' said Raff, looking at me. He moved away from the table.

'Is there a problem?' asked Roderick.

'I told the buyer we'd have nine birds. They've got to be out at Mascot in an hour and a half.'

'Well, now there are only eight birds,' said Williams.

'So I was right then, we agreed on nine birds,' said Raff.

'No, we agreed on eight,' said Roderick.

'It was nine,' said Happy.

The conversation had gotten bogged down.

'There's eight birds,' said Roderick. 'Take them or leave them.'

Raff stood thinking.

'Come on,' said Roderick to Williams. 'Let's go back to the car.' He turned to leave. Williams picked the box off the table.

'Hold on,' said Raff. 'We'll take the birds.'

'Ok,' said Roderick.

'I'm not paying for nine birds though,' said Raff.

'I wasn't expecting you to,' said Roderick.

'And, because you've fucked me around, I'm going to pay you for seven birds.'

'You pay me for seven birds, you get seven birds,' said Roderick, logically.

'Eight birds for seven birds,' said Happy, grim-faced.

'Here's $3500,' said Raff, pulling an envelope from under his T-shirt.

I couldn't help but muse over the idea that the envelope had been stuffed down the top of his jeans and parts of it had possibly rubbed against the upper strands of his pubic hair. Raff began to tear at the top of the envelope

'I want $4 K,' said Roderick. 'Like we agreed.'

'We agreed on $4500 for nine birds,' said Raff.

'No we didn't,' said Williams.

'Ok, then,' said Raff. 'The deal's off.'

'Ok!' said Roderick.

'Ok!' repeated Raff.

'We go back to the car then.' Roderick turned while shaking his head in disbelief, then moved towards the door that led to the front of the house. Williams motioned to me to follow suit.

We got to the foot of the outside steps when Roderick stopped.

'Oh what the fuck,' he said and began to walk back up the steps. 'Stay here,' he ordered Williams and, by association, me.

The thought of making a run for it crossed my mind. But I realized it would be a no-contest, the repercussions of which were too grim to contemplate. We stood in silence while Roderick re-negotiated with Raff in the back room. After several minutes, we heard a human whistle, which we took to mean our presence was required once more in the back room. We heeded its call.

'Ok grandad,' Roderick said to me. 'You're going to stay here with Raff and Happy.' He turned to Williams: 'Jock, you and I are going back to the car.'

They left the room.

It was heartening to see Williams in such a subservient role.

'You guys grow up in Thirroul?' I asked Raff and Happy.

*

Roderick returned with a small parcel wrapped in newspaper. 'Ok, here's another bird.'

'What's this?' asked Raff, lighting a cigarette.

'Like I said. It's a bird,' said Roderick.

'It's not packaged,' said Happy.

'We don't have any more tubes with us,' said Roderick.

'We can't give it to the client wrapped in newspaper,' said Raff.

'Well, go to a Seven Eleven, buy a pack of crisps, eat the crisps and then *voila*, you've got yourself a bird case!' explained Williams.

Raff took the package from Roderick, placed it on the floor and began to unwrap the newspaper. It was as if we were about to have some strange, indoor fish and chip picnic.

He finished unfurling the pages of the tabloid and a sleeping bird lay exposed atop the crumpled newsprint. Raff removed a smartphone from the pocket of his tracksuit pants and shone a bright light on the parrot. The result could have been in an art gallery.

'Magnificent,' muttered Raff, unpredictably.

He turned to Happy: 'Wrap it up again, and be careful.'

Happy got down on his knees and began repackaging the animal.

'Ok then,' said Roderick. 'That'll be $4500.'

The way the transaction had been going, I was expecting there to be another hitch but, surprisingly, Raff handed the envelope over to Roderick without complaint.

Happy finished his task with the newspaper and was on his feet holding the parcel in his right hand.

'It's been a pleasure doing business with you Raff, my man,' said Roderick.

Raff nodded.

We filed out of the room.

We'd walked about fifty metres from the house. With the approach of dawn, visibility had improved. Overhead, the deep blue colour of a cloudless sky was rapidly lightening.

'Hey Rod, mate.' Williams said. 'Give me the money.'

The rhetoric was so low key that, had it not been for the gun in Williams' hand, it could have been an innocent request to simply hold the cash to enjoy its heft, before handing it back.

'What the fuck?' said Roderick.

'Give me the money.'

'You're kidding me.'

A sedan approached. It pulled over to the curb, about ten metres in front of us. Two men got out—the same arseholes from the Medicare centre. They walked back down the footpath towards us.

'Eric,' said Williams, 'take the money off him.'

The shorter one moved towards Roderick.

'This is fucked up!' said Roderick as he handed the envelope over.

'Don't try to follow us Rod, if you know what's good for you.'

'You fucking cunt.'

'And as for you,' Williams said, turning to me. 'I've got some advice: don't fucking ever . . . '

A small flash came from behind Williams and I heard the sound of a firecracker.

'Jesus Christ!' said Roderick.

Then I was on the ground, on my side, watching the backs of Williams and the two other men as they ran for the car, got in and drove off.

Then blackness.

PART 4

Becoming a Habit

I

There were and will be some who were and will be disappointed at my survival. I'm certain Laird, for instance, would have experienced a frisson of pleasurable excitement had I passed away. No doubt he would have put it to good use, twisting the tragedy into verbal fodder for impressing upon others the vastness of his own life experience. I can picture him now, boasting to all and sundry about how his 'best friend' had been gunned down on the mean streets of his complex and dangerous world. My death would be callously employed to position Laird as being a man who'd seen it all. He might have even tried to make some god-awful documentary about it. Pathetic really.

As it turned out, Laird's ambitions were thwarted by my bear-like constitution and the trajectory of the bullet, which managed to miss any vital organs or bones. My collapse on the footpath in Thirroul came about more as a result of shock than of injury. That's not to say I didn't suffer any damage; a small chunk of flesh from the outer thigh of my right leg was taken out by the bullet and I now have a scar that will accompany me to the crematorium.

I came to in the back of the ambulance.

Hearing the gunshot and subsequent screeching of tyres as Williams and his accomplices fled the scene, a local resident had called the police, who'd arrived within minutes.

Roderick had managed to escape on foot.

The paramedics had no idea how serious my injury was. I was

rushed to Wollongong hospital, siren blaring, and afforded all the emergency perks that a bona fide life-in-the-balance shooting victim would enjoy. Lying on the gurney, I was wheeled down shiny corridors from one room to another, X-rayed by radiographers, scanned by Ultrasound, CT and MRI technicians, examined by numerous triage specialists and, finally, stitched up by an on-duty surgeon. I didn't mind being the centre of attention.

After the tests and scans had determined my medical state was satisfactory, I was told I'd be kept for a couple of days for observation.

Owing to the circumstances surrounding the injury, I was given my own room, no doubt to provide ease of access and privacy for the police interviews. I was given a few hours' rest before the interrogation began—time enough to get my story straight.

Williams had been mid-sentence when the taller of the two goons had shot me. From this I deduced that he hadn't intended for me to be shot—at least not at that moment. It was the result of a rush of blood to the head, an over-excited impulse from an inexperienced hooligan. And, unless the shooter was legally blind, he hadn't wanted me dead. From that range, to have only just nicked me, meant that it was probably more of a warning shot than anything else. As bad as the incident was, I was not the survivor of a premeditated attempted murder.

It might sound strange, but I didn't feel angry. In fact, I felt a sense of calmness and by the time Detective Sergeants Bradley and Chambers arrived to ask me about who shot me and why, I had my story pretty much nailed down.

I told them I was the victim of a drive-by shooting. I'd caught the early morning train down to my favourite place in Australia to experience the magnificent Thirroul sunrise. My mother being ill, I'd hoped that witnessing such beauty would lift my flagging spirits. I'd been walking along the road when a 2004 Mitsubishi Starwagon pulled over. Two youths, unknown to me, got out and one of them shot me. It was, I argued, a botched thrill kill; one of those absurd crimes that occur as a result of systemic failure in society.

Sitting up in bed, with a police laptop, I used a digital identikit program to render bodies and faces that bore no resemblance to either Williams or his underlings. I even said that the person who shot me was a woman.

'Are you or have you ever been a member of an outlaw motorcycle gang?' asked Bradley, a serious looking, mid-career agent of the law. He gave the impression he thought the idea absurd but had to ask for formality's sake.

I shook my head.

*

The initial interview was one of many conducted over the weeks. I stuck steadfast to my story. There were good reasons why I chose not to let on about what really happened.

The shooting had been a 'kick in the pants'; a 'wakeup call' for me to bring to an end to my association with Amber, Roderick and by extension Williams. The idea of continuing the relationship by way of the judicial system was something I wanted to avoid at all costs.

If I pressed charges against Williams, his arrest would soon follow—the professionally shot video of him selling queue tickets would aid in his apprehension. With Williams in custody, the parrot-trading would soon come to light. And if Roderick and Amber were to go down, I'd soon follow. I reasoned that they'd assert I was an integral part of the whole enterprise and it would be difficult for me to disprove them. The staffs at *Smarties* and *Swallow* could all testify to having seen me on numerous occasions enjoying Amber's company in the weeks leading up to the shooting. I had also cashed a $10000 cheque and handed the envelope full of money to Amber in a crowded café. It could easily be made to look as if I'd bankrolled the whole thing. There was also the matter concerning my finger-prints being all over the bill spike I'd used to puncture breathing holes in the crisp tube lids back at *chez* Newtown. All in all, there was a mountain of evidence linking me to Amber and Roderick. My shooting would be seen as being in some way connected with my membership of a wildlife smuggling network—the end result of a deal gone wrong.

Bradley had his doubts about my statement. He got hung up on the fact that I'd been shot on the inland side of the train tracks. Why wasn't I on the beach side if I'd been going to watch the sunrise? I told him I'd heard a dawn chorus start up and had made a detour to inves-tigate. We returned to this several times over the course of the inter-views. I never felt he completely bought the story. There wasn't much he could do about it.

*

I haven't laid eyes on Williams since the shooting. I imagine he and his crew are still active somewhere. It's not unusual for crims to walk away scot free with charges not pressed. The majority of fraudsters, armed robbers and murderers get away with it because the seeking of justice is just too complicated and expensive for the victim. For me too, revenge was a luxury I couldn't afford.

Nor have I seen Amber or Roderick. Sydney's a big town and if you don't actively look for something in it, you won't find it. Whether they are together or apart depends on the wash up from the double cross, I wouldn't be surprised if Amber has moved back home to Clifton Gardens.

Following the shooting, there'd been a brief period of media interest. Footage of the taped-off crime scene outside Raff's house, complete with uniformed cops strolling around, as well as interviews with residents were shown on various commercial TV bulletins. My name was suppressed, however, as was my suburb of domicile. This meant that neither my mother nor anyone at the Stella ever knew I'd been shot in Thirroul.

To this day, a small nagging knot of pain remains resistant to my best efforts to dissolve it. I still harbour feelings for Amber. I know this sounds stupid, but a part of me—tiny though it is—still holds out hope that Amber might, sometime in the future, turn her life around. Maybe she was just a naïve 28-year-old who got mixed up with the wrong crowd and maybe my shooting acted as a catalyst for her to focus on her art and achieve the success I wished for her. Was it possible that this now serious, successful Amber might one day decide to revisit the man who'd believed in her when all others hadn't? Who knows? Extraordinary things happen.

But as soon as I picture Amber as a focused and successful dancer, I'm swamped by other, much darker scenarios. It's highly possible that she and Williams planned the doublecross together; planned to rip off Roderick and also to diddle me out of ten grand.

And then the pendulum swings back. I remember the Amber who'd arrived alone that night at the Stella Maris dressed in her poncho, her wrists ringed by bracelets and her cheeks shiny with tears. The Amber who was so vulnerable, so needful of support.

But then again, maybe she was just a crappy dancer with poor fashion sense.

Several months after the shooting, I happened to be visiting Newtown when I inadvertently found myself strolling past her house. I watched as a young woman pushing a pram arrived home, unlocked the front door and entered. It was around lunchtime. A suited young man, who I assumed to be the husband, returned from work at around 6pm. It pleased me greatly that the sordid avian enterprise conducted within the walls of the old terrace house had now been replaced by the honest strivings of decent folk.

I'd been lucky with the bullet and I was lucky with the payout—yes payout! As part of a victims' compensation package to cover loss of income and provide for on-going counselling and physiotherapy (neither of which I needed) I received a considerable cash payout. Of course, the ambulance-chasing legal firm that worked the case for me pocketed most of the winnings but I still managed to get enough money to restock my mother's cheque account and then some. I'm hoping she doesn't look too hard at the transaction history, but should that day come, I'm confident it can be dealt with.

Another interesting thing that happened after the shooting was that I began to enjoy jazz. I listened to the many records in my collection and even purchased, at an exorbitant price, a second-hand copy of *Boiling Point* on the internet. My mother too seems to have made peace with jazz.

It turned out my mother's sickness had been a lot more serious than we'd thought—something to do with her lymphatic system. Thank God I'd got her into hospital when I did. Although the diagnosis was, of course, worrying, it also meant she was grateful that I'd acted quickly—so extra brownie points for me. She's on the mend and back at work now.

II

A light breeze rustled the leaves of the trees as they cast their long shadows across Lionel's front yard. Over half a year had passed since Sky's birthday party and it was now approaching the end of Summer. As we walked down the path that led to the front door of the house, I could feel the weight of the harmonica in the box I carried under my left arm.

My mother had done a lot of the 'leg work' by contacting Lionel and laying it on thick as to how I was deeply remorseful etc . . . Being Lionel's aunt and the sole surviving sibling of Lionel's deceased mother she felt obliged to repair the rift between us. I stood behind her when he opened the door. Our eyes made contact and it was clear that my appearance brought him no pleasure. I nodded; he nodded.

'Come in', he said solemnly. We followed him inside.

We stood in the large vestibule of the house. My mother spoke first.

'So, Geoffrey's got something to say,' she said, motioning to me to begin.

'It's an apology to Sky as well,' I said. 'And I brought a new present for her.' I pointed at the box under my arm. The clumsy linking of the 'sorry' speech with the harmonica, made me aware of how nervous I was.

'Well Sky's not here this afternoon,' said Lionel.

'Of course,' I said.

I bobbled my head in overly aggressive agreement, trying to show that I understood this to be absolutely expected under the circumstances.

'Well, I said,' trying to regain composure. 'I just want to say sorry for my behaviour at the birthday party. I don't know what came over me, but whatever it was, I'm deeply ashamed. I've had to do a lot of soul searching in recent times and I've come to realise how much you and your family mean to me. I would hate to think I'd done something to jeopardise our relationship.'

I looked at my mother. She nodded for me to go on.

'I know it's going to take time to heal the wounds that I inflicted on our friendship, but I hope that one day soon we . . .'

I noticed something lying on the carpet on the far side of the vestibule, near the entranceway to the main hallway. It was brown. At first I thought it was a large cockroach, but it was too big for that.

'Go on Geoffrey,' said my mother.

'Sorry?' I asked, momentarily thrown by the mental work of identification proceeding involuntarily.

'Continue with what you were saying,' she said.

'What was I saying?'

Lionel spoke: 'You hoped that one day soon we would do something,'

'Ah yes,' I said, taking up the thread. 'Yes, I hope that one day soon we can be the friends we once were.'

I handed him the harmonica and walked over to the object. I could tell it was non-organic.

'Don't turn your back on us and walk away,' said my mother in the reproving, disappointed tones that I'd grown to love.

I knelt down on the carpet to get a closer look.

There was no mistaking it, it was Amber's cicada.

I stood up, with the metal sculpture in my hands.

'Where did you get this?'

'What?' asked Lionel.

'This cicada.'

'I've never seen it before,' he said.

'Finish your apology, son,' said my mother.

'So, anyway,' I said quickly. 'I'm really sorry.'

Having formally concluded the grovel, I went straight back to the matter at hand.

'This is fucking weird,' I said. 'I left this in a taxi about seven months ago.'

How on earth had it ended up here?

There was new writing engraved on what I took to be the underside of its abdomen. Most of it was tiny and illegible. Whoever had engraved it had obviously known what they were doing; six rows of elegant script arranged verse-like. Although the bulk of the text was too small for the naked eye to read, I was nonetheless able to make out one word, which I took to be the title. The word was: 'Fotze'. It seemed like some sort of diminutive nickname; a term of endearment for a partner or relative.

'You're not taking it home with you,' said Lionel. It was obvious he felt I'd fabricated the taxi story in order to bags an item in his house that might have material value.

'Believe me,' I said. 'I don't want it.'

*

It was 6.30pm. The Stella Maris was sleepily moving into another Wednesday night.

'And Sky doesn't know where it came from either,' I said. 'It's appeared from out of nowhere. There's no logical explanation'

'She's lying,' said Gary from behind the bar. It was clear he'd been drinking. Several days had passed since my olive-branch visit to Lionel's house. With prompting from my mother, Lionel had agreed to let me apologise in person to Sky over the phone the night before. This gave me the opportunity to ask her about the cicada. She hadn't seen it prior to her father showing it to her on the evening of my visit.

'Why would she lie?' I asked.

'It's what they do,' said Gary sagely. 'Megan couldn't . . . whatever . . . useless,' he spluttered, desperately trying to construct a viable sentence with which to convey the hurt caused by his wife's mendacity. Eventually, he settled for a muddled account of an incident that had occurred some years previous at a petrol station.

My mind was elsewhere.

*

'Thank you,' I said as Lionel handed over the small yet heavy object.

The taxi driver had kept the car motor running. It was parked against the curb several meters away with the passenger door hanging open.

I'd phoned Lionel again and had persuaded him to part with the cicada. Tellingly, the meeting took place on the nature strip outside his house. I had not yet been granted solo visitation rights.

'It's horrible,' said Lionel. 'Glad to be rid of it.' This was rich coming from him after he'd refused to part with it for less than $200!

'I know,' I said.

We stood for a moment looking at the metal insect I held in my hand.

'It's probably poisonous too,' he said, no doubt referring to the lead content.

I nodded.

'Do you know anyone called Fotze?' I asked.

He shook his head.

I gave him the four 50-dollar notes and asked him once again if he was one hundred percent certain that neither he nor Sky had any idea where the cicada had come from or how it had gotten into the house.

'We have no idea,' he said.

He was telling the truth.

I hadn't wanted to repossess the thing for several reasons, not least was that it reminded me of Amber. Nonetheless, I needed to find out the meaning of the verse engraved on it.

I placed the object on its back on my bedroom desk and positioned the lamp to achieve maximum illumination, I set about photographing the abdomen with the smart phone I'd recently given myself. I was then able to magnify the image, in the process making the text legible. Antonioni himself would have been proud of my ingenuity.

The words were in German.

Fotze
Mit der Axt, die Sühne
Frühen Morgen Holz fein zersplittert
Nie wieder die Vögel und die Fliegen oder
Träume von Liebe und Kugeln
Du bist vorbei

I typed the verse into Google translate on my computer. It came out as follows:

Cunt
With the axe, the atonement
Early morning wood finely splintered
Never again the birds and the flies or
Dreams of love and bullets
You are over

Apart from its title, it read like one of my mother's poems. The birds and the flies were obvious references to my recent experiences with avian faeces and dipteran ceiling murals. The words love and bullets also resonated with important and recent life events. The last line was disturbing in its clear evocation of mortality. But there was something else; something in its construction that seemed contrived and functional.

Then I saw it. It was an acrostic. The first letter of the first word of each line: W-E-N-D-Y.

*

I heard the rustle of a key in the front door lock. From the sound of the push open, my mother had a spring in her step even though it was 8.30pm. I rose from my desk and made my way to the sitting room to greet her.

At first I thought the object she held, snug in its brown leather case, was a hockey stick. She placed it on the sofa before unburdening herself of her backpack, which she then placed beside it.

'Look what they gave me!' she said.

She picked the gift up off the couch, unzipped the case and removed a tomahawk.

'You're looking at Class Axe's February 'Employee of the Month',' she said.

I could not recall having ever seen her look so joyful. And it was infectious, this wonderful burst of happiness. A surge of glorious relief passed through me. It was as if the circle, begun years before, with my idea to start the music venue, had been completed. Here stood my mother, tomahawk in hand, a proud woman once more, satisfied with life.

She even did a little dance in celebration.

My face began to feel squeezed and I soon felt the fluid form behind my eyes. A pear-shaped droplet slid down my face. I let it slip over my top lip. I caught it with my tongue and swallowed it, savouring its saltiness.

But with the taste of salt, the beautiful moment disintegrated. A thought came potent and sudden: a tomahawk was a small axe. The words of the poem had specifically mentioned an axe. We now had one in the flat.

III

Sonia Rocklin arranged it all. Through her connections, she'd managed to contact Wendy and invited her to a 'meet up' at the Stella. Had they once been friends? It seemed implausible that such a well-heeled figure as Sonia Rocklin would be seen drinking with someone like Wendy at a grungy suburban hotel. But the metaphysical gifts they shared might override the facile differences bestowed on them by normal mortality. In any case, it was all she could come up with—and Wendy bought it.

I'd managed to get an emergency phone consultation with Sonia to discuss the discovery of the cicada and my mother's award. She was adamant that I needed to act fast. My mother and I were in extreme danger.

I confessed that I hadn't followed her advice of the previous year.

'They never do,' she mused. 'Listen to me. If Wendy wants that cicada to fly through the night and into that house, it will.' Sonia said. 'And if she wants your mother to win such a prize, this too will happen. She's a strong one.' Her words were ostentatious, like those of a fundamentalist preacher. The situation obviously called for a rhetoric more dramatic than the one I'd witnessed at her house.

I told her it was time for me to eat humble pie and admit I'd come up against something I couldn't handle. I needed to man up and ask for forgiveness, something that was becoming a bit of a habit.

'Yes,' she said.

It was expensive. She charged me for both the phone consultation and the email she'd written to Wendy. Time spent researching Wendy's whereabouts was also factored into the final price of $1320. Fortunately, she deemed it unnecessary for her to physically attend the pub meet-up which meant I dodged the added cost of what would have been an after-hours house-call with weekend loading.

*

I took a pull from my schooner. Outside, dusk was almost over. I sat by myself at a table near the gaming room. Months had passed since I'd last seen Wendy and Gavin. Their frequenting of the Stella was predicated on prior attendance at Swans' games. The summer months, empty of football, had robbed us of their company.

As per usual, on entry, she and Gavin made their way to their favourite booth. I watched as Gavin was dispatched to get drinks, at which point, I set out towards the booth, schooner in hand, passing him at a point roughly midway.

*

Her friendly smile gave the impression that she didn't remember me.

'Hi ya darlin', she beamed.

I tried to smile, kindly.

'Look. I don't know if you remember me,' I said, sitting down opposite her in the booth. 'I'm Geoff.'

'You're the jazz man!'

'Yes, that's right,' I said. 'How'd you go today?'

'What?'

'Did you win?'

She shook her head. 'What do you mean?'

'The footy!'

'There is no footy. The fucking season hasn't started yet. I'm here to meet someone.'

'Look,' I said, eager to get the thing over and done with. 'I'd like to apologise.'

'Apologise?'

'Yes. I don't know if you remember, but the last time we spoke . . . well, I was rude to you.'

'Were you?'

I could see Gavin waiting at the bar for Gary to serve him.

'Yes,' I said, 'I spoke to you very rudely—after a game of pool actually.'

'Did you?'

The knowing smile on Wendy's face left me in no doubt that she was well aware of what I was talking about.

'Yes I did and, well, I'm sorry.'

She stopped smiling and stared at me, her expression earnest and captivating. I waited for a response. The distant warbling of a poker machine was momentarily masked by the gush from a soda gun.

'Take them off!'

My hope that a heartfelt apology would suffice had been unrealistic. I stood contemplating the ramifications of her command.

'Can we do this in the beer garden?' I asked. I reasoned that, because the pool game had been played there, the removal of my pants should take place there as well. I was also counting on the beer garden being less crowded than the interior of the pub.

'Very well,' she said.

I got up from the table and led the way.

*

There were more people than I had expected. Both pool tables were occupied with doubles' matches and there were about fifteen or so other people enjoying the drab atmosphere of the outdoor entertainment area.

Wendy seated herself with her back resting against a table. I stood before her, my hands nervously toying with the now loose ends of my belt buckle.

I took a deep breath.

'Ok then,' I said.

I unzipped my fly and between the thumbs and forefingers of both hands I clasped the waistbands of my jeans and underpants. Quickly, I dragged them downwards, to my ankles. I felt the chill of the evening wind on my exposed flesh as I stood upright once more.

A gasp came from someone nearby. A pool player let out an ironic wolf whistle. I heard a woman say 'Oh my god!' Instantly a half dozen or so smart phones were whipped out of pockets and held in front of faces; large, electronic tablets obscured the entire heads of several people.

Wendy examined me, tilting her head to the side—an expert physician confronted with an interesting case.

'Turn around,' she said.

I obeyed.

At first it sounded artificial—her laughter—as if she needed to get it up and running before she could actually enjoy it. When she did finally relax into it however, there was no mistaking her satisfaction in what, to her, was a comedic tour de force.

'Wiggle a bit.'

I acquiesced.

The macabre sound of her chuckling was now punctuated by the clapping of her hands in a quasi-rhythmic fashion, an involuntary response to the excess of mirth she could no longer contain in laughter alone. Metres away, a pool player began applauding conventionally. It was probably the same guy who had earlier wolf-whistled.

Other people in the beer garden started to join in on the revelry with cheering, whooping and clapping.

I heard a woman say: 'this has gone way too far!'

I caught sight of Doc standing, beer in hand, near the glass doors of the beer garden's entrance. He was clearly enjoying the carnival atmosphere. I assumed he'd witnessed similar scenes during his brief stint in the armed forces.

All I needed now was for Laird to make an appearance and, right on cue, my needs were met. He was actually running when he pushed open the door.

'Working as a lap dancer now are you?' he yelled, before succumbing to uncontrollable sniggering at his own comedic brilliance.

'What in fuck's name is going on here?' said Gary who, having heard the commotion, had followed Laird outside. With his arrival, the beer garden fell silent. I hitched up my trousers and began buckling my belt.

'This gentleman just exposed himself to me,' said Wendy.

'I lost a game of pool without sinking any balls,' I said. 'And so I had to do this.' I pointed with both hands at my trousers.

Gary stood for a moment, taking in what I'd just told him.

'You're out of control, mate,' he said.

Acknowledgements

I would like to thank Ed Wright for his generous encouragement, expert advice and patience throughout the entirety of the project. Also, Lindsay Barrett, Jim Denley, Tom Stitt and Anthony Pateras for their helpful suggestions concerning the various drafts along the way. I also thank Anne Cooper for her incredible insights and support.

www.ingramcontent.com/pod-product-compliance
Lightning Source LLC
Chambersburg PA
CBHW032241010726
47494CB00002B/579